For Jools.

For the push.

1

AN INTRODUCTION

At the height of the Cold War, the Central Intelligence Agency of the United States of America was secretly experimenting with a phenomenon known as *remote viewing*. The theory was that carefully selected 'psychic spies' could, during a sleeping state, leave their physical bodies and float beyond their enemy's lines to gather information. In some cases, these spirit projections were even being used to attempt to assassinate a chosen target. Any record of actual success in remote viewing is sketchy at best, buried in an avalanche of internet hearsay and clouded by a fog of unsubstantiated conspiracy theories. The special remote viewing research facility, based at Menlo Park in California and run under the supervision of Agent Dan Banks, was closed down in the late 1970s, citing a lack of private and government funding. Despite his firm belief in remote viewing, Agent Banks was subsequently discredited by his superiors and many colleagues, before being reassigned to more mundane national security duties. But the truth is, he and his specialist CIA unit, were on to something. They just hadn't figured out the reality behind the idea. If only they had known that bogus fairground clairvoyants were not the key and that the real ability lay in children – specifically gifted children. If only they had understood that when people left their bodies they were no longer in the same physical world, but somewhere far more wonderful.

And considerably more terrifying.

PROLOGUE

The small ginger-haired boy in the oxygen tent had never met the half-Persian urchin girl. But they *had* seen each other – fleetingly, in dreams. In their waking states, they had no recollection of each other. Their faces were just lodged in some deep subconscious location. But at night, as they slept, they were acquaintances who had never quite been introduced. They were friends in waiting.

Through his plastic shroud, and out of his small hospital window, the fifteen-year-old boy, who, in his sickly state, looked at least several years younger, could see blue sky, but not the mighty Gibraltan landmark rock just to the right, and not the sea below.

The girl, a year older, had arrived in a strange and bustling north African port, accompanied by the six-year old child she 'adopted' on her long nomadic journey. Both were ravenous, having had no meaningful meal in days. They had relied either on the kindness of strangers or the gullibility of street vendors to get what sustenance they could – often just a tangerine or a few figs. She stood with him, on a beach, regarding the sea with a sense of wonder and trepidation. And, although neither her nor the hospitalised boy had any inkling of it, it was just this narrow piece of busy seaway, connecting the Atlantic Ocean to the Mediterranean, that separated them by less than ten miles.

They were soon to get that introduction.

Taking off his light grey wool knit beanie and reflectively stroking his dark goatee beard, Aleck Branko wondered whether all the English took their tea like this - loose leaf, bone china, tea strainer. It seemed such a wonderful palaver. In all his ten years in the US Marine Corps he had just been grateful to get something hot, brown and sweet. And here he was, just a day before he turned thirty-one, in London for the first time, pondering the eccentricity of a national habit and the strange and unexpected nature of life. *His* life. A throwaway comment to a friend and a quick email and suddenly he was three and a half thousand miles from his home in New Jersey, sipping Darjeeling in the *Tea and Tattle* on Great Russell Street.

"Surprise me," he'd said cheerily to his waitress when she'd returned for the third time to ascertain his tea choice.

"Certainly, sir," came the patient response of a woman who was obviously used to tourists, particularly American ones, taking their time over the list of unpronounceable blends.

But Aleck was no tourist. Certainly, he wanted to see the sights whilst he was here, particularly Buckingham Palace. He was fascinated by the notion of the Queen's Guards who stood motionless and impassive in their sentry boxes outside the gates. Maybe it was a soldier's professional respect for their art.

No, Aleck was here for a very specific appointment. An appointment he was characteristically early for. The English Professor of Literary Antiquities had told him 8.30am over the phone. It was still only ten past, so he had plenty of time to enjoy his morning tea before strolling the few hundred yards across the road to the British Museum.

Despite his better judgement, he started flicking through the pages of *The Times* that the table's previous occupier had left behind. As Aleck had waited to be seated in the café, the woman had, in one blur of *'dammit-I'm-late-for-work'* movement, checked her watch, scribbled an answer to a crossword clue, stood with a screech of her chair leg and knocked back the remains of her beverage. He'd smiled and nodded gently at her as if to say 'do you mind if I take your place' but she simply dashed for the door, leaving the newspaper.

Aleck didn't enjoy a great relationship with the news. To say it depressed him would be simplistic. It confused him. He was presented with the knowledge of events but not the *why* of them. In the army, the news had been a simple thing. You knew what your Commanding Officer told you:

Here is the enemy.
This is his name.
He's done bad things.
He needs to be stopped.
It's your job to do it.

But once outside the cocoon of this slim, concise and palatable supply of wisdom, Aleck's mind was overloaded. There seemed to be enemies everywhere and all with differing, contradictory agendas. Today's news was no help: a car bomb in Mogadishu, an airliner hit by a shoulder-launched rocket on take-off in Egypt, a high school shooting in Utah, more US soldiers killed by a roadside bomb in Afghanistan. Too much. He desperately sought something else in the dread-soaked pages of the *The Times*. He found the cryptic crossword that the woman had been doing. She'd only completed one clue. Six down, four letters: *'Bad things when you live upside down'*. In neat pencil, she'd filled in the boxes: *EVIL*.

Norm Talbot had endured a restless night. He'd drunk a little too much celebrating the birth of his beautiful baby granddaughter. Norm and his wife Sally didn't usually drink, but the neighbours had brought round a few bottles of cheap Prosecco and it would have been rude not to polish off both bottles with them. And the neighbours, being good neighbours, had allowed the Talbots to take the lion's share of the fizz. As a result, Norm's usual solid eight and half hours of uninterrupted snoring had been fitful to say the least, with more than several visits to the bathroom. And so, as he set off to work driving his London black cab, Norm was feeling a little groggy.

At exactly twenty-seven minutes past eight, as Norm pulled out of Willoughby Street onto Great Russell Street, he spied a Japanese family of five desperately trying to hail a taxi as they wrestled together with an oversized London street map. First fare of the day. But between euphoric thoughts of bouncing baby Billy - eight pounds and six ounces (he took after his side of the family in the heavy baby department) - and his growing hangover and lack of sleep, things went a little awry.

Despite the officious elderly gentleman in the porkpie hat waving for her attention, waitress Libby was staring out of the window of the *Tea and Tattle*. The good looking young American who had taken an age to choose his tea had left with a sweet smile and gentle nod towards his vacated table, where he'd left the largest single tip that Libby had ever received. As she held the ten-pound note wondering whether to keep it or declare it, she watched her benefactor walk down the street and begin to cross towards the museum entrance. She also noticed the black cab accelerate out of the side street and briefly mount the pavement.

Norm had dropped his mobile phone whilst looking at the pictures that he'd snapped the previous afternoon of his daughter Molly and baby Billy resting angelically in their hospital bed. Groping furiously in the dark void beneath the driver's seat, fuzzyheaded and bleary-eyed, Norm tried to remain semi-focused on the waving Asians. But unable to locate the phone blindly he afforded himself a single glance down. That's when he felt the tyres of his London Taxi Company TX4 hit the pavement. And that's when the flurry of desperate steering wheel wrestling began. And half a second later that's when he hit something hard. And that something was a person.

Libby shrieked. She dropped the banknote. She couldn't take in what she'd just seen. The American had been right in the middle of Great Russell Street, about twenty feet from the out-of-control cab, and he'd been completely oblivious. She presumed that it was the noise of rush hour London traffic that had masked the sound of the encroaching taxi. But then someone else appeared. Someone Libby hadn't noticed. There had been no one between the taxi and the big-tipping American, just clear air and the sense of death-by-cabbie. But a tall black man dressed in purple was now stood right in front of the taxi. Right in front. The taxi stopped dead. Had it hit the man? Surely not. If it had struck him the man would be on the floor writhing in pain, or worse - still, silent and lifeless. But he remained standing, calmly and with hands casually tucked into the pockets of his trousers. Libby could see that he was smiling. Smiling pleasantly at the cabbie. And there, with the black cab ground to a complete halt, five grateful tourists from Tokyo clambered aboard.

Both cabbie Norm and waitress Libby spoke of this story for many months to come, neither of them quite sure of what they had experienced that morning, both of them perplexed at the fact that the tall pedestrian in the purple suit seemed to vanish into the crowd as soon as the Japanese family had swarmed the cab. Norm was unable to explain the obvious dents to his bumper, bonnet and radiator grill (much to his annoyance when dealing with the insurance company) and neither of them were able to work out why no other single person on Great Russell Street that morning seemed to see a thing – including, Libby noticed, the generous American.

The gent in the porkpie hat never managed to get Libby's attention that morning. Frustrated, he simply left the café with a dismissive wave and snorted something unintelligible about *the youth of today*". He found another café to serve him his lapsang souchong and never went back to the *Tea and Tattle*.

After making himself known to an attendant at the main reception desk, Aleck stood in front of the old central Reading Room in the Queen Elizabeth II Great Court of the British Museum. For most of the ten minutes that he waited, he had his head tilted back to fully appreciate the spectacular, undulating multi-panelled glass canopy. There, in the largest covered courtyard in Europe, he gazed up at the thousands of unique panes, enjoying the penetrating London sky and how the effect of this bright blue tessellated umbrella contrasted with the cool cream of the stone floor and walls of the massive hall. So, when the museum security guard finally arrived to escort him to Professor Pipkin's office in the basement, Aleck's neck was so stiff he found it hard to look him in the eye, which made Terry, the security guard, think the American rude and aloof.

With a combination of curt nods and outstretched hands, Terry took Aleck to the main lift, down a single floor, and then, as the lift doors opened in the basement, he simply waved Aleck through to a corridor on the left.

"Second door on the right, sir."

"Thanks, er…"

He searched for a name badge. There wasn't one.

"Mr British Museum Security Person."

Terry didn't respond. Not a blink. He just pushed the lift buttons and disappeared behind the sliding doors, leaving Aleck alone, still rubbing his sore neck.

"Don't suppose you used to be one of those Buckingham Palace sentries?" he muttered to himself as he turned to walk down the corridor.

It was a moment of auto-response levity to compensate for the nerves. Sergeant Aleck Branko had rarely felt so out of place. Just what was he doing here? He was a soldier. OK, an ex-soldier. But it had been all he'd known since leaving his parent's home. He'd experienced the sheer hellish numbness of fear in close-quarter fire fights. He'd held dying comrades in his arms. He'd pulled a trigger and watched a man fall dead as a result - numerous times. And now he was in the basement of a museum in London's Bloomsbury, just because some eccentric old lady had paid for the flights and hotel.

"Come," came the shrill command from the other side of the door after Aleck had knocked.

He recognised the voice from his lengthy transatlantic phone conversation. He paused, sighed a final 'what-the-heck' sigh, and entered Professor Venetia Pipkin's office with a summoned smile.

"What a hearty knock! And a fine looking American fellow," gushed the sixty-three-year-old academic, practically standing to attention before punching out a stiff, straight arm for a handshake.

The Professor was a striking looking woman. Her grey hair in an immaculate shoulder-length bob, she wore a broad-collared, crisp white shirt beneath a navy blazer and large blue-grey spectacles that jutted out beyond the sides of her face. Her energy was a little disconcerting and her bright, youthful eyes darted all over Aleck as if she was searching for hidden clues to his character and background. She was slightly surprised by the casual nature of his attire. Although stylish in a surf-chic sort of way, she had pictured him as more of a collar and tie ex-army sort, yet here he was in a loose black t-shirt, a woolly hat that pulled his dark hair back and revealed the blemish-free complexion of his forehead, and sporting a string necklace of small ethnic beads. His light brown eyes nervously scanned the Professor's office and she had to swivel her head from side to side to try and capture his gaze.

"Well, sit down. Take the weight off. You've had a long journey." She spoke in quick, rhythmic salvos.

"How was your trip? Good flight?"

No time for a response.

"Oh, where are my manners? Some tea?"

"No, thank you, m'am, I've just… partaken."

Partaken? Aleck had never said that word in his life. Ten seconds in the presence of a posh English professor and he was trying too hard not to come across as unrefined.

"Very well."

She sounded slightly dejected. But only for a moment. She shuddered slightly as if to brush off the beverage rejection before regaining her momentum and gesturing to Aleck to sit.

"Soooo."

She lingered on the word for an age, lending it added portent. "To the book."

"To the book," confirmed Aleck. "You have it here with you?"

"Of course!"

And she thrust her right index finger upwards and swirled it around as if to say 'yes, it's here somewhere but I'm not saying where just yet'.

"But you *do* want me to see if I can read it?"

"Yes, yes, yes, but let's not run away with ourselves. First thing's first. Tell me again how you knew about the book."

"Well, m'am..."

"Call me Venetia, please."

"It's a lovely name. Italian?"

"Yes, my mother was Italian. My father British, hence Pipkin. Do you know what a *pipkin* is, Mr Branko?"

"Aleck," he beamed, returning the offer of informality.

"It's an earthenware cooking pot. There. Now you know. The British Museum, full of useless information!"

She forced a single high-pitched laugh that sounded more like a squeak.

"Anyway, *Venetia*, as I told you over the telephone last week, I saw the book on the news. CNN to be precise. It was one of those snippets they put at the end of the bulletin. You know, the slightly light hearted ones."

"Yessss." she delivered in another elongated and fascinated hiss. "So you said. But do keep going, keep going."

She whisked the air in front of her face with her index finger.

Aleck adjusted his posture, realising he might be in for the long haul. The Professor obviously wanted to examine his story with the forensic skill of an academic whose professional reputation relied on leaving no stone unturned in the pursuit of truth.

"OK, so the reporter had said that you'd discovered a book here at the museum in England."

She shot up a flat palm to halt his flow.

"Did they say England? Or the UK? Or Great Britain?"

"Er, I'm not sure. Is that important?"

"No, not really. Just curious what you Americans call us Brits."

"Brits, usually."

Another screeched hoot from the Professor.

"They showed a clip of one of your museum colleagues holding up the book to the camera and you could clearly see the front cover," Aleck continued.

"The front cover that is adorned with indecipherable logographic script?"

"Yes, apparently."

"Not *apparently*, Mr Branko," chastised the Professor.

"Aleck, remember?" countered Aleck.

"Not one of the finest minds in the fields of logographics, phonographics, hieroglyphics and literary antiquities has ever seen markings like this before. No one, not one single scholar, professor, lecturer, historian, archaeologist, butcher, baker or candlestick maker has been able to read this book. Not the front cover, nor the inner contents."

She slammed the desk lightly as to make the point before prayerfully pressing both palms together beneath her nose and breathing in deeply.

"But you, Aleck. But you, you say you can read it."

"Yay," he returned with mock celebration and two jovial waving hands.

No professorial laugh this time. Just deadpan.

"Yes, I could read it. It was plain to me. I saw no foreign symbols or weird writing. Well, that's not true. I did see it but I just knew what it said. It was really lucid. Like a voice speaking in my mind so convincingly. Like a literal voice."

"And the voice said…?"

It was right at this moment that Aleck thought what a monumental waste of time this was. This was truly stupid. He could be back in New York now looking for that private security or bodyguard job that he had thought made good sense. He could be going for interviews and registering with all the appropriate agencies. But instead he'd told his old army friend Trent about the CNN report and how he thought he knew what the book cover said. Trent had convinced him to send an email to the British Museum and tell them. He'd said things like 'stranger things have happened' and 'you never know' and 'what've you got to lose'. And besides, Aleck was so sure of the voice he'd heard in his head. It had been audible. A male voice. Low, resonant, relaxing. He'd found the news clip again online and had watched it over and over. Each time the camera had lingered on the book cover he heard the voice. It never changed. It just said the same thing. But right now, sitting in front of this Professor Venetia Pipkin in the bowels of a hallowed English institution, that voice no longer seemed real. All that seemed true was that he was a retired US Marine in need of a job and a little normality after the horrors of war.

"Look I think this is just a mistake," he blurted out. "Clearly you don't believe me. You said it yourself. No one else, all those learned people, they couldn't read it. How can I?"

The Professor slowly leant forward some inches as if inviting Aleck to quietly conspire with her. And she whispered.

"But I *do* believe you, Aleck. Why would I blow such a huge amount of my non-existent budget on your airline tickets, taxis and accommodation? It's because I think you *can* read the book cover. And hopefully the whole book. So, tell me. Tell me again, here and now, face to face, what did the voice say?"

He paused, thumbs to temples and fingers rubbing scalp, staring down at the professor's old oak desk. Finally, looking Venetia in the eye, he said: "*The Sixty-Fourth Book of Dreams*. The voice told me that the cover read *The Sixty-Fourth Book of Dreams.*"

Professor Venetia Pipkin picked up the telephone on her desk and in her most serious voice told the person on the other end to "bring it in now". She and Aleck sat in a sterile silence for several minutes, the Professor simply nodding slowly with a thin smile as if it to say 'just you wait and see this', before a young male intern brought in a tray of tea and placed it on the desk between them.

"There! Now you'll take some tea!" she enthused as she reached for the pot. But as quickly as she'd exploded with joy at the sight of the tea, she suddenly forced her face into pantomime disappointment.

"Simon?" she said slowly and reproachfully. Simon froze on his way out of the door. "You've forgotten the biscuits. The nice ones, mind. What did I tell you about having guests? Always the good biccies."

Simon nodded in compliance and left. Aleck wondered whether the British class system was still alive and well, with lowly interns not allowed to speak to distinguished academics.

"Oh, and Simon," she yelled after the boy, "Bring the book, too!"

No bone china this time. Aleck held his mug up to read the slogan printed on the side: ARCHAEOLOGISTS DIG TEA. He glanced over to Venetia's mug. Although she was cradling it in both hands he could just about make out that it said: HOT SINGLE ENGLISH PROFESSOR.

"Are you?" he teased nodding at her mug.

"What, hot?" Another sharp laugh.

"Single?"

"That would be telling, Aleck."

Aleck was wondering why he'd begun that line of jovial questioning and was more than grateful when Simon re-entered. This time he was carrying a large silver, metallic case and a small plate of shortbread biscuits. He placed them both on the desk in front of his boss and then released the two clasps that held the metal case closed, opening it so that the Professor, but not her visitor, could examine the contents.

"Thank you, Simon," as she waved him away.

"Yeah, cheers, Si," Aleck chipped in, giving the intern a friendly wink.

Simon furrowed his brow in a perfect combination of disapproval and confusion then turned and left the room.

"I've never seen him make that face before," Venetia confessed, almost troubled.

"Me neither, Venetia."

She placed her mug carefully on the desk away from the case. Pulling her chair closer in she slid her arms gingerly around each side of the open case beginning to quietly, rhythmically tap its dimpled metal surface with her fingers.

"And so, the book."

She could have gone for a dramatic tone but said it with an almost throwaway lack of import.

"Yeah, the book." Aleck tried to mock her nonchalance with his own disinterested response.

"Did I tell you how we came to have this book in our possession here at the museum, Aleck?"

"No, no you didn't mention that."

"A little girl brought it in."

"OK." He sounded more interested now.

"Just walked in one day and said she'd found it."

"Found it where?"

"On the bus."

"A bus? An average London bus."

"The number 24 to be precise. Along Tottenham Court Road. One of the oldest, most fascinating and mysterious pieces of literary antiquity was found by a twelve-year-old girl on the upstairs seat of a bus whose route takes it within a few hundred yards of the British Museum, where works the world's leading expert in such objects."

Aleck was silent.

"That's me, by the way. I'm the world's leading....well, you know."

15

"I'd figured that."

"Strange, don't you think? Not from an excavation in Jordan. Not locked away in the hidden vaults of a Nepalese monastery. But on the number 24 bus. Left on the seat like someone's lost shopping. The girl, prompted by her parents or teacher or someone, decided to bring it in here, realising that it looked old and important. The receptionist on duty called me immediately and it was in my hands within minutes."

"And you'd never seen anything like it before?"

"Oh yes, several times."

"You have?"

"But only briefly. Only two volumes like this have ever cropped up before. One in a library in Iran back in 1958 and another located by the Smithsonian Institution in Washington DC. Both had very similar but equally unreadable markings on the front cover. Ostensibly it looked like the same phrase. The phrase that you say reads 'the sixty-fourth Book of Dreams' except for just a few of the markings or letters which are ever so slightly different."

"Different numbers," blurted Aleck, surprising himself.

"I say, what?"

"Well this is volume sixty-four. The others were different numbered volumes. Thirty-one or two thousand and nine."

Venetia nodded sagely.

"Perhaps," he added. 'You're the expert. World's leading expert. And so, these other books, no one was able to translate them either?"

"No, not at all. And they never will."

"Why's that?"

"They've both disappeared. Vanished. Lost. Despite being locked away and with the highest of security, both previous books just went missing one day. Never a sign of a break in. Very embarrassing for both institutions."

"Very. Well then, we better get on with it. Before this one vanishes, too."

Venetia went from looking initially shocked at the suggestion to a nodding approval.

"We better get on with it, Aleck."

With that, she spun the case around toward Aleck so he could view the contents for the first time.

The book was sitting snugly in a foam cavity inside the case. It was fourteen inches square and the colour of sandstone. The markings on the cover were a deep ochre with their edges slightly bleeding into the surface of the almost cotton-like material. It wasn't a neat, ordered type of writing, but more random. No straight lines, as if someone had written it on the move. Not a single recognisable word, letter or image appeared. Not like Egyptian hieroglyphs, where you could make out the occasional image of a bird or sun. Not like Greek or Chinese script in any way. But clearly a kind of writing. And as Aleck saw the real thing for the first time, the voice in his head was clearer than ever; the low, reassuring, kindly voice from before but now filling his head, reverberating to the point where he could feel it in his belly. He was reading and hearing at the same time. He was experiencing the words and he knew that they were real and that what he was taking in was true. Not only true but also important.

"Do you know why I'm so convinced that you are not playing a prank on me, Aleck," asked Venetia, now more warmly than ever before. "Do you know why I funded your visit here to the British Museum? Because I've heard that phrase before. *The Book of Dreams.* It's a legend. A myth. Something spoken of for centuries but only in the closed circles of certain investigative historians. It was suspected that the other two volumes were examples of this fabled book. I believed it. Only a few others did. And then you, a thirty-one-year-old soldier from New Jersey with no education or experience in such things, mentioned those words over the telephone to me. I just had to see if you could read the whole thing, the whole book. Shall we find out, Aleck?"

Fifteen seconds passed before Aleck answered. Fifteen seconds during which time he tried unsuccessfully to summarise everything that had been going on between the moment he first saw that CNN report and this one.

"I guess we should," he said reaching across for the book and lifting it from its housing.

"Wait, Aleck!" She had jumped up and reached across the desk to place her hand down on top of the book. "Before you open that book you've got to be certain that you want to. Because, right now, it looks like you are just about the only person in the whole world that can. And that means something. That means that you are meant to be here. That means that none of this is chance. And it probably means that when you turn that cover over and begin to read the contents of the *Sixty-Fourth Book of Dreams* your life will never be the same again. Are you ready for that, Sergeant Aleck Branko? Are you sure you're ready for that?"

And she took her hand away from the book and sat down.

"Well, I could just get up, walk out of here and go see Buckingham Palace, have some fish and chips, take a turn on the London Eye, enjoy a pint of warm British beer and then fly home. But then what's a trip abroad without a good book to read?"

Aleck opened the book and began to read aloud....

THE SIXTY-FOURTH BOOK OF DREAMS

The FIRST Chapter of the Sixty-Fourth Book of Dreams:

Where a reader reads,
dreamers dream,
and spirits battle.

Firstly, you must understand that this is no book of actual dreams; not in the subconsciously invented sense; not sleep-induced stories or nightmares that take place only in the nocturnal mind. But all of it – every word – is real, literal, true. None of it dreamt. That said, the nightmarish will appear, in the form of almost insufferable evil. However, you will find great good here as well as.

Secondly, most cherished reader, in the understanding of these words, you are blessed with a supernatural insight whilst, at the same time, weighted with an awesome assignment. In other words, you have been chosen. What you have been chosen for will become clear through the exposition of this volume. At that point, you will have a choice, for there is free will here.

We will begin this book as we have begun its sixty-three predecessors, with an introduction to the Battle of the Ages; a battle that has raged since the dawn of creation, in which the armies of all of heaven's realms have warred for the souls of those who live on the earth. In this unseen place - a place whose name is unpronounceable to human lips and so, for the sake of this account, we shall call Somnambula – there are angels and there are demons. In this place war Keepers and Darkangels. For thousands of years, the effects of every battle, skirmish, strike and blow in Somnambula have broken into your earthly realm. When Keepers triumph, then good will break out into a specific environment on the earth. But when Darkangels wreak their wickedness, it means something dreadful will occur in the world of humans. The violent, fantastical events of Somnambula are mirrored on your earth. To you and your kind, your history may seem like a combination of both random happenings and self-determined choices, but it is not – not exclusively; a great deal of it is very much fashioned in heavenly war.

But not all of this war is waged by the angelic and the demonic. There is a place in Somnambula for certain humans. This book is the most recent story of such humans. It is the story of the Sleepwalkers and their Sentries; of how Somnambula is entered through the dreaming mind of children; of gain and of loss; of deception and sacrifice; and ultimately of how this continuing Battle of the Ages will become your story, too.

Well, that is more than enough of an introduction for now. We must get to the story; and the story starts in your world.

In the land you call Italy.

The SECOND Chapter of the Sixty-Fourth Book of Dreams:

Where a journey begins,
an old rivalry is renewed,
and a threat is revealed.

The brief early morning downpour varnishes Piazza San Marco with a bright, glossy sheen that hurts the eyes. Venetians and tourists criss-cross the open square hurriedly, shielding their gaze from the reflected sun and making their way to work, to market, to school to college and to the many tourist attractions. It is a busy, normal Tuesday, chilly and fresh in a brisk Adriatic November breeze.

Murray is not troubled by the glare; he is sitting in the darker recesses of Caffé Florian, admiring the rich crema on the surface of his espresso, readying himself for that first hit.

He specifically likes the blend here; its deep, intense roasted nuttiness greets him at the same time each morning.

The waiters, in their crisp white jackets, recognise Murray from his daily visits and automatically deliver his coffee without him needing to order. It arrives with a simple, warm *"signor"* as Murray takes his usual seat in one of the ornately decorated back rooms of the establishment.

He likes the fact that this is one of the oldest coffeehouses in the world. He likes the fact that he is recognised as a regular. He likes the fact that they know his usual. But he also very much likes the fact that not a single person here, including the cheery waiters, know anything about him. If they did, he wonders often, what would they think then? If they could see what he has seen and know what he knows would his espresso arrive with such a welcoming salutation? Would it arrive at all?

All that any Venetian knows about Murray is that he owns a boat at the Marina La Certosa; one that he does not seem to sail anymore. He just arrives for his morning coffee and then wanders around Venice before strolling along the Riva dei Sette Matiri and through the Parco delle Remembranze, back towards his mooring, where he spends each night. This has been his pattern for several years ever since he first sailed into the lagoon.

A retired sailor, they surmise. One or two of the waiters go a little further, just for the sake of their own entertainment, and imagine a story of a broken heart and of a lost love; a man running from the trauma of heartache and hoping to find solace in this city of ancient, soothing beauty. With his long, chiselled face and wavy, almost-shoulder-length brown hair, and the way he always dresses in a full-length tan coloured wax coat, they think Murray a handsome looking gentleman. His hazel-eyed stare is both piercing and engaging, sad yet friendly, and despite clearly being in his late fifties he carries himself with the athletic poise of a man much, much younger. This all helps fuel the waiters' notions of his lost love being a very beautiful woman. How could she be anything other?

Murray, with elbows resting on table and hands clasped, extends an index finger past his nose as a waiter dashes from the outside tables to the kitchen. He enjoys testing them. The knowledge that just the tiniest of gestures can get their attention pleases him.

Not only is it one of the oldest coffeehouses in the world, it is one of the most efficient. The waiter delivers an almost imperceptible nod to match Murray's signal. Barely sixty seconds later another espresso is gently laid with a theatrical flourish in front of him. A nonchalant "*grazie*" from Murray, a crisp "*prego*" fired back. He regards the crema again, and, as always, reflects on the way this gentle, frothy white mantle disguises the thick, strong pitch-blackness below it. A good espresso is such an enigmatic thing; an instant promise of something light but the subsequent discovery of a much darker world beneath. He takes the little cup's handle, lifts it just several inches and arches his neck and head to meet it halfway, then stops, freezes; not to appreciate the moment and the aroma as Murray often does, but to recognise the presence of someone; the presence of someone familiar.

He carefully repositions the cup on its saucer but his eyes stay fixed on his drink.

"Hello, Sanntu," Murray offers, somewhere between warmth and regret. Then he begins to slowly shake his head from side to side.

"I suppose I knew you would show up at some point. Like a coffee?" He doesn't wait for a response; he knows the answer.

"Of course you don't. You can't."

Now he looks up to see his old friend, Sanntu, sitting directly opposite.

Sanntu is male, tall, slim, has tightly cropped dark hair, a perfectly sculpted moustache and slight beard and wears a purple crushed velvet jacket. Murray notices Sanntu has trousers to match his flamboyant coat.

"New suit? It's nice. Makes you look.....regal."
Sanntu is smiling broadly, enjoying the familiar tone of Murray's humour; lapping up the sarcasm.

"It's good to see you, Murray." Sanntu's voice seems impossibly deep and resonant.

"You know I'm enjoying my retirement, right?" Murray says suspiciously.

Sanntu peruses the room, craning around at the other tables and customers, taking in the scene, concocting a response. Then it comes.

"Firstly, you don't look like you are enjoying it. And secondly this is not retirement. This is retreating."

"Same thing," spits Murray, hurt. "Yes, I retreated. I needed to retreat. I'd seen enough. I'd done enough." A pause, a deep sigh and forlorn look to the ceiling. "I *lost* enough."

"Yes, you had," is his friend's genuinely compassionate response. "You had, Murray. And you did everything you could, and more. You did your job. You did what you were born to do as a Sentry."

"They died, Sanntu. They both died. I was their Sentry and they both died. Now I'm here, trying to deal with that and trying to somehow forget. Or at least put some distance between that part of my life and now. And I was kind of doing okay. Kind of. And now you're here." Murray looks to his cup.

"And my crema is dissolving."

"You know me, Murray. I'm your friend, and I wouldn't be here unless it were important."

"It's always important, Sanntu. I know that. I know everything you're going to say about a world in peril. About good versus evil. How none of us who have seen behind the veil can ever just go back to being normal, but I just…"

Murray is suddenly aware his voice is raised and he is animated. He can see that the waiter who served him earlier is looking at him from across the room and that several customers are staring in his direction. He realises how ridiculous he must look sat on his own talking to himself, remembering that very few humans can see angels unless the angel specifically wants to be seen. He slumps back on his chair, exasperated.

"I just can't do that life anymore," he continues more calmly. "Besides, Sanntu, I'm a Sentry. I *was* a Sentry. I need Sleepwalkers to guard, and there are no more Sleepwalkers. The very nature of my job description makes me redundant."

He takes a quick, frustrated jolt of coffee and stares deliberately away as if to make his point. He slams his cup down causing another reason for people in Caffé Florian to look.

"And now my damn coffee's cold, Sanntu!"

Sanntu holds his gaze on Murray, lips pursed in readiness of a carefully prepared speech, which never actually comes. Murray eventually reconnects with his friend's eyes and sees something there in the silence; a realisation of why he is here.

"Oh, good grief, Sanntu," he unfurls with slow, cautious but growing awe. "There *are* more Sleepwalkers, aren't there." It isn't a question; it is an epiphany. "There are Sleepwalkers out there and you need me to be a Sentry to them."

Sanntu feels no need to confirm Murray's conclusion.

"Things in Somnambula are...." Sanntu pauses to choose the word, "... catastrophic. Something has to change soon. And, as you know, that means that things here in your world will be equally dangerous. The war is escalating, Murray. Like never before."

"The old Battle of the Ages, eh?" says Murray with as much flippancy as he can muster.

"Yes, the Battle of the Ages," Sanntu throws back with corrective gravitas. "A battle we will win, Murray. But a battle that needs you again. And, yes, needs the Sleepwalkers to dream again."

"So where are they, these new Sleepwalkers?"

"Let's take a stroll, Murray."

They cross the Ponte del' Accademia to the echo of Grand Canal life below them; the gondoliers with their operatic serenades, the low throbbing of the vaporetto ferrying their over-compressed freight of tourists, and the clicking of a thousand camera shutters as the Basilica di Santa Maria della Salute hoves into viewfinder.

A lute player sitting on a crate in the centre of the bridge picks out a bright tune and couples follow tradition and clamp padlocks to the metal railings of the bridge to celebrate their alliances.

Murray and Sanntu walk in silence; Murray, after several years of living unassumingly in this city, looking now with new eyes at the fragile joys around him; remembering how he used to fight for the protection of this peaceful way of life rather than just succumbing to it. Over the bridge, they enter the Galleria dell'Accademia and begin to join the funereal shuffle of bodies around the famous art gallery's rooms. After several minutes, Sanntu signals Murray to sit on one of the viewing benches in the centre of one of the larger exhibition spaces. Still no words shared between them; Murray earnestly processing his sudden change in circumstances, and Sanntu allowing him the space to do so.

Sanntu sits upright, hands on his lap, diligently examining the oil painting hanging on the gallery wall directly before them. He breaks the silence.

"*Abraham and The Three Angels*," he announces with a sense of delight.

"How come I only get one? Heavenly cut backs?"

Sanntu ignores the joke and continues to appreciate the painting.

"Oil on canvas, by Giovanni Domenico Tiepolo. Nice guy, fine painting. But absolutely no clue what an angel actually looks like."

"Yeah, he missed the gaudy purple velvet suits."

A smile now from Sanntu, warming to his earthly friend's humour.

"You remember one of the key roles of an angel, Murray? To announce news. Both good and bad news. They came to tell Abraham that he and his wife Sarah were going to have a baby. That was a good news day. I've had to do that, too. Those are the jobs you look forward to. But today is not one of those days. And although it is good to see you again my old friend, I take no pleasure in delivering this message to you now. But it is no less important."

"Well at least there's some good news," Murray offers.

"What good news?" Sanntu responds confused.

"I'm not pregnant."

Murray laughs and slaps Sanntu on the back, who, in turn, begins to enjoy the joke, and the unlikely pair look again at the painting of the Jewish patriarch and his celestial visitors.

"So, tell me about the Sleepwalkers then," Murray reluctantly prompts.

"There are two."

"There's always two. But who are they? *Where* are they?"

"There's a boy. He's in Gibraltar. But he's....*special*."

"He's a Sleepwalker, of course he's special, Sanntu."

"Well, this boy is *more* special. He suffers from a condition that makes him rather fragile. He'll need extra care from his Sentry."

The gallery is busy and now a large crowd of people with German accents are standing in front of '*Abraham and the Three Angels*', obscuring their view and making them feel hemmed in. Sanntu stands and walks away. Murray remains sitting for a few moments, shakes his head as if to say 'I can't believe I'm going to go along with this' and then shuffles after him. As he catches him up, Sanntu speaks.

"Have you ever seen the archangel Raphael?"

"You're the only archangel I've ever met, Sanntu."

"No, I don't mean met in real life. I mean have you ever seen his statue?"

"Can't say that I have."

"You've been here in Venice *how* many years and you've not been to the Chiesa dell'Angelo San Raffaele?" he chastised.

Outside the gallery, they head for the Dosoduro area of the city.

"And there's a girl, too," says the archangel as the pair sit on the edge of the Rio Angelo Rafaele, the near-midday sun now warming the dank winter air. "A feisty one. You will like her."

"If you say so. And, where is she?"

Sanntu thinks for a moment, unsure of how to respond.

"I don't actually know. She's a wanderer. Nomadic. I have sort of lost track of her. So, we will focus on the boy first. Titus, Titus Bigsby. You must get him first and then you will find the girl."

"And how do I get this Titus Bigsby?"

"You still have your boat. In that, of course."

"*The Dreamweaver*? I can't. It needs a crew. Lasaro and the girls are back in Spain. Plus, it needs some attention. It's not even seaworthy."

Sanntu, despite being angelic, manages an inscrutable smile that Murray spends a few seconds examining with narrowing, suspicious eyes.

"All done," Sanntu announces proudly.

"You haven't? You conniving, sneaky, underhand heavenly being, you," comes the part impressed, part disgusted response.

"*The Dreamweaver* is waiting for you. Your old crew, a few alterations, and ready for Titus's needs. Shall we go inside now and say hello to Raphael?"

"Whatever, man. But first tell me what the plan is. What are we doing it all for this time?"

"Yes, it is time you know everything. It is time for you to know what I know. It is ironic that we do this here in Venice, in a city of bridges."

Murray knows exactly what his friend proposes. He has endured a spirit-bridge before; a process that only Sentries and Sleepwalkers are allowed to experience; a way for humans to share the thoughts of angels, and a way to glimpse something of Somnambula without physically entering it. It is neither enjoyable nor painless and something most definitely not to be done in broad daylight in public. They enter the Chiesa dell'Angelo San Raffaele and see that it is empty, save for an elderly lady in a blue headscarf lighting a candle to the side of the altar. They sit several pews back and wait for her to finish the whispered prayer, genuflect, cross herself and leave. There, in the sombre quiet, beneath the imposing altar centrepiece statue of the archangel Raphael, the archangel Sanntu softly cups Murray's bowed head with both his large hands and then exhales a few near-inaudible words.

"My heavenly thoughts to your human mind."

He repeats it, softer this time, and then again; and once more, but this time the words are no longer perceptible on an earthly level; they are now only echoing in Murray's subconscious and swirling around; an audio kaleidoscope, changing in order and volume and starting to draw in other words and phrases. This is the initial chaos and white noise of the spirit-bridge, where the human senses try to adjust to the enormity and other-worldliness of the data that is flooding in. Like opening your eyes to a bright day after a long sleep and squinting painfully in the sunlight, your brain struggles to stem the influx and re-route the thoughts, hopes, pains, fears, joys and memories that come thick and fast. It takes Murray less than a minute to stop physically wincing. Despite it being many years since the need for a spirit-bridge, his body remembers how to react. The very first time it took the better part of an hour to come to terms with what was happening and for the crazed patchwork of facts and feelings to become a coherent, focused picture.

He sees a large, pulsing blue diamond embedded into a rock formation, at least nine feet in diameter and arching upwards. With every pulse, the diamond seems to grow and around it stand dark shadows. From these shadows, Murray feels the collective power of their hatred and evil and knows that their strength is drawn from the throbbing gem.

He sees an angel army gathered, encamped and ready for a great battle on the edge of a forest that is cloaked in a dim green radiance and knows that Raphael is there at its head. He feels Raphael's trepidation and he is not used to knowing the fear of an angel.

He sees a frail, red-haired boy of fifteen in a bed, surrounded by a transparent plastic tent and feels his sadness and frustration.

He senses the familiar presence of Night Reivers but cannot place them. The initial miasma of images start to coalesce and Murray begins to know more; he begins the process of knowing everything that has happened since his own involvement and tragedy in the *Sixty-Third Book of Dreams*.

The cold, hard reverberation of his waking gasp in the empty church disorientates Murray, confusing him into thinking he is still in the grip of the spirit-bridge, and so he stares at Sanntu's face in disbelief.

"You are back," he reassures him. "You are back, Murray. You are in Venice. In the church. Breathe. Come on, you remember. Now listen to me very carefully, I have something to say that is very important if we are to succeed. Something you need to know right now. Are you listening?"

Sanntu scans him closely for any sign that Murray can hear him clearly. Murray finally nods, sweat running from his forehead.

'What, what is it?"

"It's this. Run!"

"Run?"

"Night Reivers. Here, now. In Venice. I've only just sensed them. They must know about the Sleepwalkers and assumed I would come for you. They want to stop this before it has begun. Run, Murray, run. Get to *The Dreamweaver*. I will do what I can."

A still dazed Murray is helped to his feet by Sanntu, shakes off his delirium and begins to stumble toward the main church door. He stops, composes himself, breathes a deep, deep breath, readjusts his body and then with renewed clarity turns in the opposite direction and runs to the side of the altar and past the imposing Raphael. He glances up to the stone angel.

"Any help from you right now would be good," he snipes before he grapples with a small wooden side door. Sanntu remains standing in the centre of the church. He too looks to the altarpiece.

"He does not mean it, Raphael. It has been a tough day for him. He is only human."

And Sanntu leaves by the main door, emerging into the daylight to hear the slow, rhythmic chug of a cruising motorboat as it turns towards the Chiesa dell'Angelo San Raffaele out of the Rio de San Sebastiano. Aboard the polished wooden-decked boat are three figures, each in crimson berets that bear a gold badge and each in black leather waistcoats with an embroidered name writ large on the back; in a Gothic font, it reads *NIGHT REIVERS*. The broad, thuggish-looking gang members vigilantly scan the buildings, canal side and passageways as the boat nears the church, each enacting a sinister, robotic swivel-headed sweep of the scene. They all see Sanntu standing calmly at the church door. The Night Reiver who steers the boat puts it into neutral as they gently glide to the side of the canal.

"Don't bother with the sinless," he barks to the other two in a voice that is both well-spoken and pained. "We can't touch him. It's the Sentry scum we need."

Despite their bulk, they each leap from the boat with ridiculous ease and surround Sanntu. With spitting malevolence, the chief Night Reiver goes nose-to-nose with the angel.

"Where is he, sinless? Where's your Sentry friend? Is he still mourning his loss?"

There is a sense of glee to this last question.

"If I were allowed to, Brax, I would kill you right now. Be thankful I am not. But I will do everything in my power to stop you and your demon-possessed gang of bikers. Like keeping you talking like this while Murray escapes into the labyrinthine recesses of this city."

Just a hiss from Brax and a wave of his hand to martial his lieutenants.

"Go in the main door. I'll check the back," Brax orders.

They leave Sanntu but the angel calls after them.

"I didn't know you could drive a boat, Brax. Good for you."

He closes his eyes, bows his head and vanishes.

`

The tiny stepped bridge over the Rio di San Sebastiano is busy from the midday tourist trail. Even in the winter months the city is claustrophobic and hard to navigate in a hurry. Now that his life depends on it Venice seems all the more cramped. Murray takes the first step of the bridge at speed.

"Scusi! Scusi! Scusi!" he fires at the shuffling sightseers. But no one moves; they all gawp in the transfixed pose of mannequins and Murray cannot help but jostle them as he sprints to the other side. If he keeps in a straight line along the Rio Organisstanti, he is thinking to himself, and then takes a quick right he could maybe lose the Night Reivers and catch the vaporetto at the Zattere stop across to Giardini and from there it would be a quick run to his boat. But what if there is no immediate waterbus and he has to wait? That would be too risky. Maybe it would be better to just keep running and go back across the bridge at the Accademia and try to lose his pursuers in the melee of bodies in the busier San Marco region of the city.

He does not make an immediate decision, but what does happen is that Murray realises something; he realises that a small part him is enjoying the thrill of having to make a decision. For the last several years here in Venice, life had been at a snail's pace and the most taxing choices were only ever whether to order another espresso or to go and enjoy a plate of his favourite cicchetti on Campo San Giacomo. Now his heart was pounding fast again, his lungs fully expanded again and his legs moving fast again. More pertinently, his life was in grave danger again. What had been a city of hazy daydreams and aimless wandering, of languid lunches and museum meanderings, is now, in a moment, transformed into a blistering assault course; a louder, faster, adrenalin-fuelled landscape of movement and peril.

He runs faster now, his mind fully free of the spirit-bridge aftershock. He makes his decision and crosses another bridge to his right, choosing it predominantly for its lack of people and ease of travel.

The narrow passageway directly ahead looks clear and quiet, and now his muscles are enjoying the exercise, he feels he can build up some speed. In the shadow of the passageway, where the sun has no say, he feels the immediate chill of the air and the damp, cold crumbling walls on either side. After less than eighty feet his error is apparent. This is not a passageway in the sense that it gives any kind of passage to anywhere, other than to the doorways of the apartments and houses along the way. The route ends abruptly with a wall. The only purpose it serves for Murray is for him to briefly extend an arm to as he bends over to catch his breath. With his head lowered, he has an upside-down view of the passageway entrance behind him and the silhouette of a broad figure. He can just make out the distinctive shape of a beret. Murray stays very still in the hope that the Night Reiver cannot see down the dark passageway and tell that he is there.

"Nowhere to run, Sentry!" comes the rasping, hollow echo along the tiny street.

"Yeah, he can see me," Murray wheezes to himself. He stands erect and launches himself at the nearest doorway. It is locked.

"Of course it's locked," he spits, exasperated, going for the next one. "I'll probably have to try half a dozen of them before one of them actually...." This one opens immediately. Inside, by a steep staircase, is a short, elderly Venetian woman mopping the stone floor. Murray glances back at the passageway to see the single Night Reiver moving with startling agility towards him. He regards the staircase, wonders about the possibility of a rooftop escape and goes inside, slamming the door behind him. The Night Reiver arrives at the door and reaches inside a leather waistcoat pocket to produce a small black walkie-talkie.

"I've got him, Brax. Down a passageway, through a door. I'll go after him on the roof," he growls into the device. He grasps the doorknob, turns it and swings the door open with a sharp kick from his heavy motorcyclist boot. The wet, soapy mop end that strikes him in the face breaks his nose and sends him reeling back into the passageway. The second blow that Murray applies is a full golf swing of the mop, breaking the handle over the Night Reiver's head and leaving him motionless on the ground. Murray straddles him with half a mop handle still in his hand and a bemused Italian cleaner in the doorway. He hands her back the remains of her implement, smiles weakly and runs back up the passageway.

"After nearly three years of doing nothing but walk this city you'd think I'd know where the dead ends were," he chides himself as he emerges back into the warmth of the open canal side.

Back in the passageway, the dazed Night Reiver stirs and radios in the news of the defeat to Brax. He fails to mention the mop handle but says something about a brave struggle and of being eventually overpowered and that he is still in pursuit, even though he is not. Murray emerges on the main waterfront across from Giudecca island and, along the busier walkway, decides to slow to a more respectable, less conspicuous trot.

The floating pontoon vaporetto stop of Zattere is there before him and he pushes his way into the waiting mass of bodies. One minute to the next vaporetto, announces the digital board. He looks westward to see if the waterbus is approaching from the previous stop and instead notices the motorboat with two Night Reivers. Brax sees Murray at the exact same moment and accelerates the boat towards the pontoon.

"Go!" Brax yells to his remaining sidekick, who promptly leaps ashore amongst the dispersing crowd. Murray takes off running again, with the Night Reiver close behind and Brax almost alongside him in the speeding boat.

33

Another chase, another choice: keep running and hope to lose them or do something more drastic? Murray opts for drastic. With every ounce of strength that his long-idle legs can muster he increases his pace and his stride and launches himself across the watery void towards the motorboat that Brax is piloting. He lands awkwardly and painfully on the rear, five-feet square deck, scudding across its shiny teak surface but managing to save himself from overshooting completely by grabbing the wooden frame of the window. He steadies himself and climbs down into the space behind the cabin. Brax is ten feet away through the low, roofed cabin and only just aware of what has happened. One minute he was tailing his prey from the water and the next he was not even there. As he realises what has occurred and that Murray has come to him instead of the opposite way around, he turns to face him, their eyes meeting over the top of the boat's canopy.

"Good one, Murray," says Murray to himself. "You've just leapt aboard a boat containing the leader of a demon-possessed cult dedicated to the painful death of, amongst others, me."

Brax bends low and charges bull-like through the cabin towards the boat's stern and Murray, with the boat still moving fast but un-steered out into the open water of the southern Venetian lagoon. Taking hold of the sliding cabin door handles Murray pulls them quickly shut and Brax's head smashes through the glass panels. Seizing the moment, Murray jumps up onto the cabin roof and, staying crouched to keep his centre of gravity out in the wind-exposed waters, shuffles to the front and jumps down to take the wheel, jerking it left to narrowly avoid careering into the Lido car ferry. Murray makes for land, gives the motorboat full throttle and immediately feels a fat, solid arm around his neck. He can smell the blood from the glass cuts in Brax's face and is not sure which is more unnerving – the iron-scented stench of blood or the iron-like grip that the Night Reiver applies to his throat.

The boat thrashes in a snaking, bouncing run towards Piazza San Marco as Brax tries to wrestle his quarry from the wheel, but Murray continues to grip the controls to avoid the other lagoon traffic. With the way momentarily clear, Murray lets go of the wheel, cups his right fist in his left hand for leverage and stabs his elbow as hard as he can into Brax's belly. It gives him a second's respite and enough time to regain control and take the boat hard right as it ploughs into the flotilla of gondolas tied to their moorings on the edge the square. The sudden wake causes dozens of gondolas to violently undulate and clatter together, and the motorboat comes to a rest between them. The impact knocks Murray and Brax apart and to the floor. Murray is first to seize the opportunity and clambers to the bow of the wobbling boat. He hurdles towards the nearest of the moored gondolas, using them as stepping-stones, skipping across each blue canvas covered stern until he clears four of them before finding a wooden jetty that takes him to land. Brax watches from the motorboat, deliberating whether he can follow such a bravura act. As he does, there is the sudden sound of sirens from Venetian water police approaching from all sides of the lagoon. That is all the incentive he needs and, much to the gesticulations and profanities of the gondoliers gathered on the jetty, he bounds between the elegant craft in a way that is far from elegant. Several of the angry gondoliers take the brunt of his rage and end up in the cold November water. The chase continues on foot into the piazza and Murray instinctively takes a left under the covered arcades of the Procuratie Noeve.

"Back at the coffee shop," he blurts to no one in particular as he races along towards his habitual morning haunt, clawing people from his path and disturbing neatly laid tables.

"Stop, Sentry!" he hears from behind him; much closer than he possibly thought Brax could be. Murray stops, not just because he is told to, but because that is not the only sound he hears; he knows the sound a handgun being cocked and he also knows that in this long, straight arcade he would be an easy target. He is directly outside Caffé Florian and sees his morning waiter standing to attention in the open air, empty tray clasped across his chest in readiness of an order. Murray manages a polite smile and his waiter returns it. A customer on one of the outside tables is holding a copy of the day's *la Repubblica* newspaper and doesn't even seem to notice the hulking Brax slowly walking towards him, his hand holding a gun half exposed from beneath his leather waistcoat. The newspaper remains fully open, raised and crisp.

"Let's go inside and finish it quietly," Brax nods towards the inside of the café.

"I'm good, thanks, Brax. If I had any more coffee I'd be wired for the whole day."

Brax reveals a little more of the gun for threatening effect, aware that he must hurry this up before the police from the lagoon realise where they now are.

"OK, well maybe a decaf then," Murray offers, raising his hands slightly to show he understands Brax's intentions.

Another waiter exits briskly from the café whistling a cheery tune and delivering a tray containing several flamboyant hot chocolate beverages and a large silver pot of tea. His sudden arrival diverts Brax's attention from Murray. It also seems to cause the customer with the newspaper to become less interested in the news. The paper is swiftly lowered and a man in a purple suit pulls it tight in both hands, lifting it hard beneath the waiter's tray of hot drinks and steering it deftly towards Brax's face. The confluence of fresh, open glass cuts, scolding tea and sticky hot chocolate spiced with forty per cent proof triple sec liqueur is all too much for the Night Reiver. He is on the ground holding his face in agony. Sanntu casually picks up his newspaper and gathers Murray under his arm to lead him away from the scene. They walk to the centre of the piazza and lose themselves in the tourist throng; leaving behind them Brax, as he is brought to his feet by two armed policemen, as well as several confused onlookers and a waiter who cannot understand how a tray of drinks just flew out of his hands from the force of a flying newspaper.

"Now go, Murray. To *The Dreamweaver*. You know where to go. You have it all in your head now."

Sanntu physically spins Murray around to face east and the direction of the marina. Murray starts to walk. He makes it a few paces then turns. Sanntu expects something serious, but he should know better.

"You do know that the purple suit looks silly, right? I mean it's so sixteenth century?"

Sanntu smiles as broadly as he has ever smiled and stretches out his arms, closing his eyes and lifting his face to the sky as if basking in glorious sunshine.

"Perfect, then. After all, this *is* Venice."

A pianist starts to play on a raised platform at Café Lavena and the archangel Sanntu, in his ecstatic pose, begins a slow, measured pirouette to the music. Murray looks on and enjoys the moment, watching his friend dance to Sonata in F Minor by Domenico Scarlatti in the centre of Piazza San Marco. And then he turns and runs.

The Dreamweaver is ninety-eight and a half feet of breathtaking, varnished pine sailing yacht; a twin-mast, eight cabin Turkish gulet, built in the coastal city of Bodrum, and it sits in its expensive lagoon moorings of the Marina la Certosa.

Three people are aboard; newly arrived although completely familiar with the vessel, and still wondering why they are there.

Lasaro Zambrano is sixty-four; a short, tough Spaniard who looks every inch the classic sea dog, complete with jaunty naval white cap with a black peak. He has the tanned, rugged skin of someone who lives his life on the deck of a yacht.

Marissa and Marina Zambrano are his nineteen-year-old twin daughters; both with shoulder-length blond bobs and clear, bright, smiling faces. Marissa, known to her friends and family as just Rissa, has a button nose that points upwards slightly, while her sister, Rina, has a more rounded face, with a chin that dimples when she grins. But, to most of the world, the two sisters are physically indistinguishable.

Father and daughters stand admiring *The Dreamweaver*, stroking its rails, breathing in its freshly oiled wood with a look that could be described as nostalgia. The moment is broken as Murray, breathless and animated, appears, climbing the ladder to the aft deck.

"Buenos dias, amigos," he announces. "Reunion pleasantries later! We've got to get out of here fast! Cast off and set sail. We're off to Gibraltar."

Murray heartily pats Lasaro twice on the shoulder as he pushes past him towards *The Dreamweaver*'s deck saloon and disappears below to inspect the cabins.

Rissa and Rina notice the look of deep satisfaction on their father's face, and then they all dart, with well-drilled efficiency, to their relative yacht crewing stations so that *The Dreamweaver* can sail again.

The THIRD Chapter of the Sixty-Fourth Book of Dreams:

Where a sick boy breaks out,
two strays turn up,
and dreams become real.

"I dreamed you," Titus delivers through his plastic cocoon. The fifteen-year old redhead is unfazed by the presence of a stranger in his hospital room and fixes Murray with a cool stare.

"Yes. Yes, you probably did," responds Murray with a voice that is meant to convey calm but sounds more like pity.

Titus Bigsby furrows his brow, cocking his round, tufty-haired head to one side, confused why the intruder is not surprised by his comment.

"I dream a fair bit. Something to do with being permanently in a bed," he continues cheekily.

"I know, Titus. It's why I'm here. My name is Murray."

Titus concentrates, face screwed-up in pained, forced recollection.

"You're here because…." he struggles.

The reason eludes him and he exhales in mental exhaustion.

Murray steps closer to the bedside, his nose almost touching the transparent sheath that is draped fully around Titus.

"I'm here to help you dream more, Titus. To dream much, much more and to do things that you wouldn't believe if I told you here and now. But we haven't got time. The thing is, I have to take you somewhere else. You can't stay here. It's not safe now. Because I now know who you are, there will be others who know about you, too. And they, trust me, are not good people. So we have to move. And I know that somewhere deep inside your mind you know what I'm saying to you right now is true because you've probably glimpsed it. Seen it in one of your dreams."

"I don't know whether you've noticed all the blinking and bleeping machines and this rather fetching plastic sheet but I can't really leave."

Titus turns his head to the banks of medical paraphernalia that are stacked up to his left and he waves a thin arm in an arc to emphasise his encasement.

"It's alright, Titus, I know all about you. I know about your mastocytosis and your reactions to being exposed to the world for too long, but I've got everything prepared for you. You'll be fine."

"On a sailing yacht!"

Titus triumphantly discovers the memory.

"I've seen it. I've seen me sleeping in a cabin on a rather cool boat."

"Yes, it's a boat, Titus. And it has your own room. And you'll get to see some amazing places and escape from this hospital."

"And see some scary stuff, too, I think."

Murray pauses, not knowing quite how to answer, and he chooses not to.

"But first we have to get you out of the bed and over to that boat. Is that ok, Titus? Do you understand? Can you trust me?" Murray realises just how ridiculous his last question sounds having only walked into the boy's life a few minutes ago, but he banks on the fact that Titus subconsciously half-knows his destiny.

"I've only ever known this hospital, Mr Murray. I've been here since they found me as a baby on the church steps of St. Peter's in the centre of Gibraltar. So, sailing away into an adventure sounds like just what I need. I'll get my hat."

"You need a *hat*?"

"No, I just thought I'd say that. Not got a hat, no."

Murray delivers no verbal response, just bounds to the far side of Titus's room and briskly brings a wheelchair to his bedside. He unzips a canvas bag he had at his feet and reveals a rubber mask connected to a large metal canister.

"Oxygen," he informs the boy as he invades the plastic veil and begins to lift him to the wheelchair. He is much lighter and frailer than any teenage

40

boy should be; all bone and sinew from his life of hospitalised inactivity; and he gasps fearfully as his protective bubble is broken and he feels the rush of cool, unsanitised air in his lungs and on his pale, freckle-strewn skin.

"Put this on and breathe normally, Titus. You'll be fine for the time it takes to get you to my boat," Murray tells him, fitting the mask around his face after placing him as carefully but as quickly as he can in the wheelchair.

"Good?" he asks with a vigorous nod.

He doesn't wait for an answer.

"Good," Murray says for him with another nod. "Then let's go."

The journey down three storeys in the lift to the ground floor and out of the hospital's main entrance goes without a hitch, Murray, trying to look as casual and as natural as possible, but also wary that he has to be quick. He is thinking about Night Reivers and whether they were aware yet of the emergence of the new Sleepwalker, and he is thinking about the medical and security staff of the hospital and just when one of them will realise that a total stranger is stealing away with their longest serving patient. But he is also thinking about Titus and how his body is warring against just about everything the world has to offer; how his immune system sets off painful alarms when confronted by contact with air, water, everyday chemicals, human touch and more.

He had told Titus that he understood his condition but he only knows what Sanntu had revealed during the spirit-bridge and it was certainly not enough to turn him into his doctor.

In the wheelchair, Titus stays frozen with a heady cocktail of fear and wonder. When he woke from his dreams this morning, it was just another day in his bubble; another day of trading pleasantries with Sascha, his kindly nurse; perhaps another day of asking the hospital chaplain to read again the story of the humble shepherd boy who defeated the giant with just a slingshot and pebble before becoming a nation's king – he liked that one. But now he was out in the open air and could see, for the first time, the huge, imposing Rock of Gibraltar that loomed over the hospital. He had heard it mentioned so many

41

times that it began to sound like a legend and not a real geological feature. Yet, there it was – the looming limestone monolith, and one of the mythical Pillars of Hercules, silently guarding this southwest tip of Iberian Peninsula.

"Great view, eh?" Murray shouts down to Titus without actually looking at the view. He is intent on steering the wheelchair through the sliding doors and out across the main road that separates them from the harbour.

"But that's nothing to what you're going to see."

Marissa Zambrano is waving at them from the harbour side and Murray spots her, steering Titus towards his gesticulating crewmate.

"Nearly there, Titus."

"Rapido! Rapido!" cries Rissa, becoming aware of the gaggle of white-jacketed hospital staff gathering outside the building's entrance, some of them pointing towards Murray and Titus.

"Fire her up, Rissa!"

Rissa clambers down the harbour wall ladder to the rubber dinghy with outboard motor. It is *The Dreamweaver*'s tender, *The Sweet Dreams*. She yanks the starter and the engine responds with an immediate snarl. Murray pulls Titus from the wheelchair and glances across to the hospital. Several doctors are now beginning to jog towards them. Two burly security staff burst from a side entrance. They take a moment to assess the scene and orientate themselves.

"Over there!" informs a distressed nurse, pointing to the harbour and Murray, who now has the feeble boy across his shoulders and starting to disappear over the edge of the wall.

By the time the hospital guards and medical staff have reached the ladder *The Sweet Dreams* is skipping across the harbour water, taking Titus out of their care forever. As they stare in disbelief there is the purr of motorbike engines as six flame-red Harley Davidson '48 Panheads come to rest. The rider at the front of the tight formation asks them what is happening. They try to explain the events to the bikers in the crimson berets.

The Rock of Gibraltar grows small as *The Dreamweaver* motorsails swiftly out of Gibraltan waters, aided by its twin diesel engines and heading southwest across the notoriously windy Straits.

"Tangier," says Murray to Lasaro, who is at the wheel. "We'll get supplies there. And then quickly on from there to…"

A pause as he remembers something with a fondness diluted by distant regret.

"…well, you know where, my friend. I better go and check on our important new guest."

Murray goes below deck. Through the kitchen and dining area, he enters the largest of the eight sleeping cabins.

"Like a home from home," he offers cheerily to Titus who is lying in his berth, once again surrounded by a sealed plastic curtain. Titus is breathing more shallowly now after the hyperventilating excitement of his hospital breakout, and he lies stiffly in his new bed, not sure of whether to be relieved or scared.

"Look, I know you must have a thousand questions, Titus." reassures Murray as he pulls up a wooden stool. "Like, how the heck did all this medical equipment suddenly arrive on my ship?" he asks mainly to himself.

But Titus just rolls his head towards his captor, expressionless.

"You're shocked. I understand. But for now, I'll just say this. We're on our way somewhere where we can rest and I can explain all this. We have to get to a safe place. First we're going to stock up with supplies in North Africa and then off to our final destination where we can moor for a while."

There is still no response from Titus.

"Right, ok, I'll, er…leave you for a bit. This is a lot to take in. But….you're safe."

Murray stands up and makes for the door. He pauses and turns.

"You're with friends, Titus. My job is to look after you. That's literally my job. It's what I was born to do. To look after you."

He opens the door but Titus suddenly speaks, weakly but clearly.

"Are you good at your job, Mr Murray?"

Murray is caught off guard and is unsure how to answer. He does not turn around to face his questioner but stares ahead at the still-closed door, his hand gripping the handle.

"I will do everything in my power to keep you safe. Everything."

He tries to hide any note of remorse in not being able to give his young charge a more affirmative answer. With that he leaves quickly.

"Ah, Tangier," Murray says with delight as he jumps down onto the jetty.

Already the sights, sounds and smells of the Moroccan port fight for his attention, stirring memories of adventure and triggering powerful nostalgia. He stands erect, inhaling deeply, face to the sky.

"It's been a while, Lasaro. Good times, eh?"

Lasaro is still securing the boat's ropes.

"Good times? If that is your special nautical code for near-death experiences, close shaves and last minute escapes, then yes, good times, Captain, all good times," chastises Lasaro cheerily in his sing-songy Andalusian accent, before laughing.

"Papi, you love it. Don't let him tease you, Captain," shouts Rina as she lowers a large plastic fender to protect the boat's hull from the jetty.

"Yes, papi, you were so bored just fishing all day back home in Cadiz," Rissa now joins in, appearing from below deck with a tray of tea.

"When we got the message to join you in Venice…" continues Rina.

"…he was so giddy with excitement," completes her twin.

"Well, I missed *The Dreamweaver*," Lasaro unconvincingly lies.

"Well you can miss her some more, Lasaro. You can go and get all of the supplies we need in the medina while I stay and look after Titus and do a few jobs around the boat," Murray orders, enjoying the strange feeling of having someone to command again.

"Fishing in Cadiz is suddenly looking good again," sighs Murray's first mate, followed by something vaguely impolite in Spanish slang.

"You never caught a thing," mocks Rina.

"Rina and I always bought the fish in the market," says Rissa, running with the joke.

"I'm going, I'm going."

Lasaro waves a hand to dismiss their derogatory jibes and ambles along the jetty towards the city.

He brushes past a dark-haired teenage girl holding hands with a small six-year old boy, but does not register them.

The two of them look dirty and ragged, weary and slightly lost as they walk slowly towards *The Dreamweaver* and stop.

Murray and the twins are all on the main deck sipping hot, sweet tea and still enjoying the camaraderie of mocking the easily riled Lasaro. They are oblivious to the two figures quietly surveying them.

The girl turns and crouches to face the boy. She motherly places her hands on his shoulders.

"I think we are here, little Almas," she says to him with a broad, brilliant grin. The boy manages a feeble smile in return and faints into her arms.

"Help me, please," she cries up to Murray, Rina and Rissa. "The boy. He needs food and water."

Murray is down the ladder, on the jetty, in seconds and carrying the boy up onto the deck. He lays him carefully down on the impeccably mopped floor. The girl climbs aboard, too.

"We've travelled a long way to find you," she announces after clearing her throat. She delivers this in the slow, pronounced way of someone who has practiced it many times for maximum effect.

Murray is giving the boy all his attention yet registers the girl's news with a momentary turn of his head.

"Rina, Rissa, get some food and more tea quickly," he barks. "I'll take him below and get him comfortable."

The twins scurry into action and Murray picks the boy up again and carries him down into a bed below deck.

"He's fine now," Murray assures the girl as he joins her at the galley table.

She is enjoying a tuna sandwich and a cup of tea and, despite her obvious hunger and urchin-like appearance, she conducts her eating and drinking in a refined way.

Murray is instantly aware that this is no normal street girl and certainly not Moroccan. Her looks are more Middle Eastern, with hair as black as wet tar and wide eyes of bright, almost lurid blue below strong, slanted eyebrows. She wears a scarlet silk headscarf that wraps over her head and neck, draping over her left shoulder, effectively framing her olive-skinned face in a red oval halo. There is a serenity about her, but a sense of deep grief, too. She finishes a mouthful of her sandwich, licking her lips and savouring it before steadily preparing her next words.

"My name is Bina Nash. I am, what I like to call half-Persian. My father was a British doctor working for an aid agency in Afghanistan. He met my mother there, who was originally from Iran, and they married. Three years ago they died in a car accident in Kandahar. Since then I have been homeless, nomadic. But I had a goal, a vision."

Bina pauses to take another sip of tea. She wants to devour the rest of the delicious sandwich but knows that her story is too important to interrupt.

"Go on, Bina. What was your vision?"

"It was a boat."

"*The Dreamweaver*?"

"Yes, *The Dreamweaver*. Every time I dreamt, I dreamt this word. At first I didn't know what it was and then slowly, like a telescope being focused a little at a time, I began to see this name written on the side of a boat. I knew that I had to travel west."

"What about the boy?"

"Almas."

"Yes, Almas. What about him?"

"An orphan, too, like me. I met him living off the streets in Tehran. All he could say when I found him was *Almas.* Over and over he said this word, so that is what I called him - Almas. I just knew I had to look after him. He seemed such a bright, beautiful little thing. I've been his mother ever since and we just kept travelling, begging, borrowing and stealing our way, always searching for *The Dreamweaver.* I would get little clues as I slept and we would carry on. Eventually we came across Iraq, Jordan and North Africa before arriving here in Morocco. We've been in Tangier for two weeks and I just knew we were close. Then I heard some sailors outside a café this morning as I was begging for coins, and they were talking about this boat that had just sailed in to the port. They said it was one of the most beautiful boats they had ever seen and they said its name – *The Dreamweaver.* After three long years I've found you."

With her story out, she breaks her calm and sobs.

"No, Bina, I think it's the other way around. It's me that's found you."

"What do you mean?" she just about manages between tearful sniffs.

"You knew about *The Dreamweaver,* but I knew about you. I was told to find you."

"Who? Who told you?"

"A friend."

"In a dream?"

"No, not a dream. I was fully awake."

"None of this makes any sense."

"And you don't know the half of yet, Bina. You think *this* doesn't make sense, wait for the rest of it. Wait until I tell you why I had to find you."

"So, why did you?"

Murray puffs out his cheeks and exhales slowly, shaking his head and thinking about how he always finds this the hardest part. He does not mind so much all the running and the fighting and the protecting; it is the counselling and the explaining that causes him more discomfort and pain. He hates telling young innocent minds what they were born to do and how they have a singular, unique ability to enter a whole unknown spiritual realm to do battle with the greatest levels of evil that they will ever experience. He wishes that someone else would do this bit.

"It will be best, Bina, if we do this all together."

"Together?"

"With your other Sleepwalker. That's what you are. A Sleepwalker. And there are two of you. Two of you right here and right now on *The Dreamweaver*. The gang is all here. And once we sail out of Tangier I will explain it all to the both of you. Now, finish your sandwich. I think I've got some ice cream in the freezer."

"Ahoy, Captain," shouts Lasaro from the jetty. He is accompanied by two stout Moroccan gentlemen pushing handcarts loaded with food and sundry supplies. He signals to them to take everything aboard. They do not move. Sighing he pulls out a wallet from his back pocket and unfolds several bank notes. The two porters immediately begin to convey the goods aboard, scurrying past Lasaro and snatching the notes from his hand without a word.

"Well done, Lasaro, good job," Murray shouts back.

"Once we're loaded up, let's make haste and set sail."

"I'll do the shopping, tip the porters, untie the ropes, sail the boat," the Spaniard grumbles, picking up a stack of lavatory paper rolls. He looks at the rolls. "Maybe you think I should wipe your…"

"Lasaro, hurry up, we've got to get going."

Lasaro climbs the ladder to the main deck to see Bina sat there by the wheel, deliriously scooping ice-cream straight from its carton with a long spoon. He stops and shields his right hand with his left, making repeated tiny pointing gestures in the girl's direction.

"Did I miss something, Captain?" he says, confused.

Murray spreads his arms out wide and beams.

"We've got a full set!"

"She's a......?"

Lasaro deliberately stops himself from saying the word.

"Yep, she's a..."

Murray mimics his pause.

"But."

"I know. Stroke of luck, eh? Or not. Anyway, we're good to go. Once you've loaded those loo rolls, my friend. Oh, and be careful when you go into cabin three. There's a small boy in there sleeping."

Lasaro tuts dramatically and disappears below deck to reluctantly do his captain's bidding.

"I don't know, you leave for a few hours and the story suddenly has two new characters," he mumbles to himself.

The two porters continue to carry all the supplies onto *The Dreamweaver*, stacking it in neat piles in the galley, whilst Rina and Rissa make all the necessary preparations to cast off and begin their departure from the Moroccan port.

Murray sits again at the galley table and begins to pour over nautical charts, smiling a self-satisfied smile and humming an imperceptible tune.

Influenced by the prevailing winds, the surface currents flow eastwards in the Alboran Sea and *The Dreamweaver* is carried emphatically on them towards the Mediterranean and its next destination – the island of Patmos.

Its two main sails and forward, overlapping headsail, are all fully unfurled and catching the wind, and the yacht enjoys a good turn of speed thanks to the length of its sleek waterline.

Lasaro is on the aft deck, just behind the spacious deck saloon, taking the external wheel and steering a course, with Rissa helping in a midship position, continually adjusting the fast-fluttering sails.

Below, Rina is entertaining young Almas, who is now fully fed and rested. She sits at the galley table with him playing 'snap' with a deck of cards. Almas, now clean and fresh-faced, is transformed from the exhausted, malnourished waif who had stood earlier on the jetty. He is laughing and snorting with delight as Rina pretends to be too slow to recognise the matched pairs of cards, allowing the jubilant boy to shout *'snaps'* in his heavy Arabic accent. His old dirty, frayed clothes now in the trash, Almas wears on oversized black t-shirt with a Gibson guitar logo emblazoned across it that Rina had liberated from Murray's cabin.

"You're so good at this game, Almas," she raves. "But maybe you're cheating."

She gives him a very serious scowl of mock disapproval, holds it for a few seconds and then launches two hands at him to tickle his ribs. Almas explodes with more giggling.

Murray holds on to the handle of Titus' cabin door and pauses deliberately, fixing Bina with a stern gaze.

"Are you ready?"

"I don't know," responds the girl blankly.

He opens the door wide and allows Bina to take in the sight of Titus sitting up in the oxygen tent that surrounds his single bunk. Although blurred through the plastic veil, Bina can make out his scruffy, short ginger hair, freckles and near-circular face, and a deep recollection stirs in her.

Titus shuffles himself further upright in his bed as he sees Bina, his head shaking from side to side with both nervousness and confusion. He tries to speak but just ends up making a series of truncated monosyllabic huffing and puffing sounds.

"Hello, Titus. I'm Bina," says the girl warmly, taking several slow, measured steps towards Titus.

"I believe we've met," Bina adds with a reassuring smile.

Still shifting uncomfortably, Titus looks down for a moment as if seeking inspiration from his floral-pattern bed sheets. Looking up suddenly, he speaks with sadness.

"Such a long journey."

Bina looks shocked.

"Yes. Yes, it was, Titus. A very long journey. But I'm here now."

Murray, who is still standing in the doorway, steps forward to join Bina.

"I've got so much to tell you both," he says.

"I'm remembering so much," declares Titus, almost pained. "I have seen your face so many times. And have known your name. Bina. Bina."

Titus has never said the word out loud before but has heard it countless times somewhere deep in his sleeping subconscious. There, in *The Dreamweaver* cabin, he mumbles it over and over, thinking hard and glimpsing a dense, intricate medley of encounters with Bina; the girl who he has never met in the flesh. A bewildering barrage of sorrow, loss, distress and disappointment surges through his mind and spirit. There are moments of laughter and joy, too. He sees Bina's loving parents and happy family occasions as if he is remembering actually being there; being present at birthday parties and Christmas mornings. He stands by a graveside and sees two shiny coffins being lowered into the ground on a frosty, bleak day and identifies with the indescribable loneliness of the sobbing, dark-haired girl. Although, as an orphaned baby, he has no recollection of his own parents and no idea of what it feels like to be genuinely mothered or fathered, he is now seared with the tragic, sensations of deep parental love and the unfathomable ache of loss at the very same moment.

Likewise, Bina senses all the quiet, still, forlorn bed-ridden years of confinement that Titus has only ever known. She can see his hospital room as if she had sat there herself for hours on end, and she can hear the cheerful morning greeting of Nurse Sascha when she comes to check on him.

Both of them know moments shared together in strange, unearthly places, hazy projections of the highlights of lost fantastical dreams, accompanied by the disorienting realisation that these are not just things imagined, but genuinely experienced in some alternative reality. It all crowds and churns sickeningly around in their minds until Murray interrupts.

"Okay, I know this is all too much. Bina, you need to sit down. I'm going to try and explain everything that's going on here. But it isn't easy and I need you both to just listen. That's all, just listen to the whole thing."

Bina slowly takes a seat; a simple wooden chair to Titus' right, and Murray pulls up a small stool so that he too can sit, and then begin the story.

He tells them that he was chosen a long time ago to be a Sentry, someone sworn to take care of a special breed of young people known as Sleepwalkers. He tells them that they are both living examples of these Sleepwalkers, children endowed with an ability to ascend during periods of sleep to a very real heavenly place, known as Somnambula. A place inhabited by warring angels and demons – the Keepers and Darkangels.

He tells them of the Night Reivers, an earthly gang of Hell's Angels who have been possessed by certain Darkangels in order to track down Sentries and Sleepwalkers, to prevent them from entering Somnambula.

He tells them that everything that they and the other heavenly spirits do in Somnambula is reflected in various ways here on earth and that Somnambula itself is a dream-like expression of much of the 'real' world.

He also tells them that pretty much everything that human beings dream is not merely nonsensical subconscious delusion, but real spiritual encounters in the heavens, but that it is only true Sleepwalkers who can enter the higher levels of Somnambula.

For two hours below deck, on *The Dreamweaver*, Titus Bigsby and Bina Nash are speechless as they learn of the reason for their existence and of their destiny to help save the world by fighting the forces of evil in their sleep; and because they have already glimpsed fragments and splinters of this in their dreaming minds as they have grown up, it begins to make sense. Not for a second do they doubt any of it. For both of them there is a very real sense that they have finally come home.

"And so," Murray offers with a final flourish. "What I'm doing here, right now, with you two young people, gives a whole new meaning to the word 'kidnap'."

He means it as a joke. Neither Titus nor Bina laugh.

"*Kid* and *nap*, you see…"

His explanation trails off dismally.

The FOURTH Chapter of the Sixty-Fourth Book of Dreams:

Where Sleepwalkers rise,
three strangers deceive,
and a Keeper is angered.

"They're coming. The Sleepwalkers are coming," Jibarial announces, as he briskly enters the ornate tent of the Archangel, throwing aside its garlanded entrance drapes. The interior of the tent is plush but makeshift. There are plump cushions in rich colours, deep rugs layered and criss-crossed, a large bed of silks and fine wool blankets, a few simple wooden chairs and a table covered with ancient charts.

Raphael is stood at the table, his tall, slender frame is bowed over, eyes scrutinising the outspread maps. Like all Keepers, he is ageless; at first glance somewhere in his mid-thirties but with longer and closer examination the suggestion of millennia appears in his eyes – the fatigue of long-held wisdom and the weight of unending battle. His gaze turns sideways for a second to take in his Lieutenant's arrival and declaration.

"Then it starts," Raphael unfurls in a slow rumble.

He keeps his stooped poise for a few moments, considering now what the future holds, then snaps upright, spinning to confront Jibarial and opening his arms wide. "Better prepare a warm welcome for them, Jibarial. You know what it is like for first-timers."

"I do, sir," agrees Jibarial. "And it will be done. We will make them feel at home."

He turns to leave but stops abruptly and, over his shoulder, delivers a further report.

"Oh, and sir, I nearly forgot, the two spies we sent forward have returned. They reached the edge of the rainforest and saw only wasteland, a scorched savannah, but they could see the glow of something beyond that. Something just beyond the horizon. They camped there a few days and could see the glow increasing, pulsing larger. Do you think....." Jibarial hesitates. "Do you think, sir, that it could be it?"

"You can say its name, my friend. It is permitted. We don't do superstition here," Raphael reassures with fatherly warmth. "And yes, it could be *it*. It could be the Hell Diamond."

The sharpest of nods from Jibarial and he is gone.

Titus lies back in his plastic-enveloped bed on *The Dreamweaver*. A few feet to his left Bina is laying down on an unfolded sofa bed. Murray is sat and pulls his chair closer to them both, positioning himself in between.

"OK, we've been over this enough times now. You know what to do. But Titus, remember, things for you will be very different up there. You'll be able to do things that you've only ever..."

"Dreamed of?" Titus interrupts with some glee.

Murray smiles and nods.

"Yes, all the stuff you've dreamed of being able to do. To run and jump, to touch and feel the world. But it's a different world so don't get too carried away."

"We're ready, Murray. Titus is ready," Bina delivers as a mild rebuke.

"Alright then. Close your eyes. Time for your first ascent. Your first ascent to Somnambula."

Murray's tone is lower, calmer and his delivery slower now.

"Turn off this world.

You're no longer on *The Dreamweaver*.

You're entering sleep.

Not dreaming.

Not dreaming.

Not dreaming.

Your thoughts are real.

The place you see is real.

The things you feel are real.

Somnambula waits.

The heavenlies wait.

The Keepers of truth and peace wait.

Go higher.

Much higher.

Break through.

Keep ascending.

Keep ascending.

Keep ascending.

Through clouds.

Through visions.

Through chaos.

To a higher level.

It's Somnambula.

It's Somnambula...."

Neither Titus nor Bina hear Murray say anything else; and, from experience, Murray knows he can stop. He knows they have taken flight. He now just has two sleeping children to watch over as *The Dreamweaver* lies anchored in the serene waters of a tiny bay off the western shores of Patmos.

Jibarial wakes suddenly. He is, like the hundred other Keepers in his company, lying by a campfire in the almost perfectly circular clearing in the Forest of Green Light.

Half the clearing is bordered by a sheer rock face, eighty metres high and intersected with a waterfall that feeds the impossibly still pool in the centre of the camp. On the other half are tall trees covered with dense vines, and beyond them mile after mile of dank, dangerous forest.

The whole area is dimly lit in a cool neon-like emerald that seems to emanate from the cascading water. He regards the scene with suspicion and then concern.

Everyone else still sleeps. But Jibarial, who is gifted with a special sensitivity when it comes to Sleepwalkers, is aware of a problem.

'They are here," he whispers to himself. 'But yet they are not *here*."

He leaps to his feet, his hand instinctively reaching for his belt and sword and he swiftly, nimbly negotiates the sleeping bodies whilst securing his weapon to his waist, all the time heading for a break in the tree line. He plunges into the forest alone.

Titus and Bina are standing in dense undergrowth. Towering, slim black trees that drip with blood-red oily resin surround them on all sides. They open their eyes and only a hint of distant green light allows them any ability to work out where they are. Bina looks straight to Titus.

"We're here," she reassures quietly.

Titus breathes in deeply. Although the air is sickeningly damp and cold it fills his lungs without pain for the first time he can remember.

"Somnambula," he exhales slowly.

He rubs the palms of his hands together roughly, gripping his fingers, wringing his hands, enjoying the new sensation of touch. He looks down to his feet and then upwards through the soaring trees, rolling his head, scrunching his shoulders, stretching and testing his muscles in every way.

"I'm...I'm...*taller*," he says and Bina cannot quite tell whether it is with joy for the now or sorrow for his past.

"I don't want this to be a dream, Bina. I need this to be real."

"Titus, it is real. It's happening. This is you."

She is nodding insistently to show him she means it.

"So, what now?" Titus asks, intently running his finger up and down the sticky surface of the nearest tree.

"You asking the tree, or me?" responds Bina.

"Both. I'm currently sleeping on a yacht in the Mediterranean but I'm also in a dark Somnambulan forest waiting to meet angels. Why shouldn't the tree talk?"

He gives a look of disgust as he rubs his fingers together, trying to remove the gooey substance.

Bina tilts her head and scrunches her mouth as if to say 'you've got a point' and they both stand silent for a few seconds.

"No, tree's not talking," she blurts, grabbing Titus' hand from the tree and leading him off at a march into the forest undergrowth.

"So where are we going?"

"Don't know. Somewhere. Towards the light," she offers efficiently, jabbing a finger at the far-off green-ish glow.

"Towards the light? Never walk towards the light, Bina. Have you not heard that? Have you not seen that movie?"

"Which movie?"

She is still dragging him, eyes fixed forward, flicking the forest's brittle, sticky branches and wet fronds from her face.

"I don't know. Lots of them. Walking towards the light is always a bad thing. In a ..." Titus adopts a shrill, distressed pantomime tone. "....don't walk towards the light, Bina, or you will die..." And returns to his normal voice. "...kind of way."

"We're in a very, very dark forest. We are meant to be meeting Keepers. I think in this particular movie the *walking towards the light* thing might just be a *good* thing."

"That's a theory," Titus concedes meekly.

He pulls from Bina's grip and pushes past her, taking up the lead and the branch-avoidance duties.

After ten minutes of brisk marching, the distant light remains as distant as it did. The two pause for breath.

"So, it *is* possible to get tired here then." Titus announces with some disappointment.

They both regard the scene, hoping to see something different to the dense mass of identical towering trees. Titus suddenly does.

"There. A light."

"Where?"

Titus just nods to indicate the direction. Bina focuses. It takes her a few seconds to find the pinprick of light. It seems to hang star-like in the air but hovering just above the ground, piercing the arboreal gloom.

"Follow the light," Titus says triumphantly.

Bina responds with just a hint of suspicion.

"Why *that* light?"

"Oh, *now* there's bad light?"

"I'm just saying..."

"Look, it seems nearer. More pure, warmer. Come on."

With renewed energy Titus heads in the alternative direction, towards the whiter light. Bina sighs deeply and plunges after him.

This time the light source grows stronger with every step they take. Their arms are tired from continually holding back the encroaching foliage and the more they press ahead the more each springing forest extremity stings or slaps them around their faces and necks. But the enlarging glow energises them.

"It looks like a fire," Bina says wincing as another branch lashes out at her but yet still managing to notice the now yellow tint to the light.

"A campfire," offers Titus, half guess, half hope.

With more haste in their movement they even begin to feel the warmth of the nearing light. Their exhilaration is almost indistinguishable from their fear now. They both just want to get somewhere, anywhere. Their feet pound the hard, knotty forest floor that twists and folds beneath them. Their arms are no longer outstretched for protection, just flapping tired at their sides. With backs bowed and heads tucked in they bowl awkwardly and gasp for breath, their ungainly flight now just a frantic last surge until they explode together in a rolling mess of arms and legs onto the floor of a small clearing.

Facedown, both Titus and Bina can feel the welcome heat of a fire and hear the lively crackle and fizzing of burning wood.

They hear a male voice that delivers similar comfort.

"Welcome, travellers."

The voice is rich, ancient.

Then another voice.

"Pick yourselves up, come to the fire. There's room."

This one is younger, higher-pitched, female.

And a third.

"You look lost. Rest with us. We have food."

There is a stern quality to this one.

Cautiously lifting their gaze to the campfire, Titus and Bina see a trio of figures through the dancing orange flames. They are sitting side by side on a single log, gazing into the furnace. Sparkling embers rise and twist into the clear dark air above the forest clearing, creating a canopy of reddish starlight. As each ember burns and fades it is replaced by another from the fire. The explosive popping of the fire-licked wood is loud, with an almost percussive pattern. It is a compelling and soothing scene for the teenagers. They get to their feet and walk towards the seated figures, their heartbeats steadying, their lungs breathing shallower and their minds now less restless.

"As I say, rest with us, sit," says the stern-voiced one, making it sound more like a command.

He is the only one that looks up to them. The others remain focused on the fire's glow. He is round-faced, whiskery and plump with dark, hessian-like clothing and a baggy hood that is down around his neck.

The woman, sitting in the middle of the three, now gently raises her face to them. She smiles a warm, broad smile and with the flat of her outstretched palm indicates space on the log for them to be seated. She is dressed in the same dark, rough material but her hood is up over her head. Her features are hard to distinguish other than a worried expression and furrowed brow. Titus and Bina both sit so that they are all lined up together on the timber bench, eyes fixed forward, engrossed in the forest bonfire.

After several minutes the final stranger speaks. His voice fills the night air, rich and velvety, deep and rolling.

"You are very brave to be here. So young. So courageous." It has hint enough of a question that a response only seems polite. Bina obliges.

"I don't feel brave, sir. And if I were I am not sure what I should be feeling brave for." Her tone is respectful and trepidatious.

"We're just a little lost, I think," adds Titus. "We were expecting to meet……er…. people."

"And you have," says the stern one. "You've met us."

"And lucky for you that you did," the woman reassures.

"The forest is not a place for night-time rambles," the old one warns.

He is by far the tallest of the three, his long angular face looks a hundred years old but there is a much younger glint to his bright eyes and a quick, nibble manner to the way he picks up a nearby log and tosses it on the fire. The flames briefly cry louder as they hungrily devour their new fuel. Titus notices the look of pleasure on the old man's face.

"My name is Bina and this is Titus," Bina offers as cheerily as possible, attempting to break the tension.

"Yes, Titus. What do you call yourselves?" Titus continues the foray into joviality.

The three exchange slow, thoughtful glances with each other as if conversing without words and searching for a response.

"Call ourselves?" the stern one muses.

"We don't really call ourselves anything," reveals the woman sounding almost confused.

"Why should we call ourselves something?" The stern one seems to address this to the woman beside him.

"Indeed," she agrees.

The old one looks up to the sky.

"Names, names, names," he pours out enigmatically, rubbing his throat as if to see how these alien words feel. "You see, *we* know who we are. We know what we represent. We don't need a label to talk to each other. We just……talk."

"But how…" Titus is interrupted.

"But if you need names then we shall give you names, young Titus," continues the old one. "You can call me…" He pauses and searches for it, leaning forward towards the flames as if looking for his name in its blazing centre. "Hero. There. That's a good name. Hero."

"And you can call *me* Faith," says the woman.

"And I shall be Pure," the final stranger announces with his now characteristic flintiness.

Titus leans forward, tilting his head to view the row of seated figures. He points to the far end and to each person in turn.

"Hero, Faith, Pure, Bina…" He jabs at his own chest finally. "…Titus."

There, we all know each other now," Bina smiles.

Pure disagrees.

"We know a name. We don't know the person."

"But a name helps," she counters.

"I am glad," Pure says not sounding at all glad.

"Food!" shouts Hero suddenly standing. "We promised you food and no one should ever accuse Hero, Faith and Pure of being false."

Faith stands, too, scurrying over to some black pans nearby.

"Yes, we have a root vegetable broth. It is delicious and we can quickly warm it on the fire. Bread as well. And fruit. From the forest."

"And then we will talk more." Hero claps and clasps his hands, shaking them in a merry gesture of hospitality. "But first, eat."

The five of them perch on the log, noisily sipping thin, brown broth from knobbly pot bowls, occasionally dipping wedges of crusty bread into the liquid. Hero, Faith and Pure nod enthusiastically to themselves with every slurped mouthful. Titus and Bina keep catching each other's gaze, unsure of what to do and say. They have no idea of their next move and no way of knowing whether these are the angels they are supposed to meet. After many minutes of feasting, Pure wipes his mouth on his sleeve with a flamboyant wave of his arm and seizes Titus and Bina's bowls from them before collecting up the empties from his two companions. He takes them to where the pots lie and throws them into a large bowl of water.

"Washing-up's done," he says somewhat petulantly, spinning sharply and returning to his seat. The meal is suddenly over, although Bina is left with a chunk of bread in her hand and does not quite know what to do with it. She passes it from one hand to another, nervously picking the odd crumb and discreetly placing it to her lips.

Titus silently regards his shoes, his mind drifting back to his sterile plastic oxygen tent, and he does his best to force himself to enjoy the stimuli of this moment – the heat and sound of the campfire, the lingering taste of real food, even the tension and nervousness of the unknown. Life in his waking state in his Gibraltan hospital room was full of certainty and sequence, of routine and just a limited number of familiar faces. This is new, and new should be good he thinks to himself.

Behind their tree trunk perch, Hero arranges two stumps of wood and beckons his guests to be seated on them with an indiscreet cough and a precise nod of the head. Titus and Bina oblige slowly. Both Faith and Pure reverse their positions, putting their backs to the fire. Hero remains standing but draws closer to the teenagers. If it had not been clear to this moment, it is obvious now that he is in charge.

"Interrogation?" whispers Bina out of the side of her mouth to Titus.

"Recruitment?" he responds in the same manner.

Almas is swinging his legs over the side of The Dreamweaver, bashing a gentle beat on the hull with his bare heels and enjoying both the starlit tranquillity and the joy a full stomach. In his six and a half years of life he had never had a Spanish omelette and he had eaten a lot. Rissa had made it to what her father Lasaro had assured him was a special family recipe.

"It's all to do with adding the right kind of chorizo," he had beamed as he demonstrated to a still bemused Almas that it was safe to eat, making a grand, exaggerated gesture of consumption. Almas had no idea what chorizo was but had responded with a chuckle and immediately began to devour portion after portion of the omelette. They ate together in the large deck saloon of the yacht as Titus and Bina slept below before everyone retired for the night.

"I simply can't sleep because someone is playing drums on my boat," teases Murray as he appears on the deck to join the young boy.

Almas looks guiltily to his feet. "I am sorry," he says, saddened and in slightly broken English. Murray eases himself down beside him.

"It's alright. I'm just joking, Almas. I couldn't sleep anyway. Besides you're a good drummer." He mimes playing a full drum kit and finishes with an affectionate, gentle elbow nudge to Almas's ribs.

"It's a beautiful night."

"Yes, it is beautiful. Where are we?"

"Greece. Patmos. It's an island."

"An island of dreams."

"Yes, that's right. What makes you say that? How did…"

"It's thin here."

"What's thin, Almas?"

"The space between the land and the heaven, I think."

Murray is taken aback by the boy's understanding.

"It is, Almas. That's just what it is. Who told you that?"

"No one."

"Okay, okay."

Murray ponders pressing him further but decides against it for fear of making him more scared and uncomfortable than he already is. But Almas continues.

"Is Bina in heaven now?"

"Oh no, no, no," reassures Murray urgently. "No, she's fine. She's very much alive."

"I know she's alive. I mean is she alive in heaven now, while she sleeps."

"Er, yes, she is. She is *dreaming*."

"Not dreaming, I think. In danger, perhaps."

"She'll be fine. They will both be fine. I'm here to look after them. And look after you, too, Almas. You know that you're safe now?"

"Yes, this is where I am to be, I think."

"Yes, good. It is. And plenty more omelettes to be had."

They sit in silence for a while, both with arms behind them and hands on the deck, angling themselves up to the sky to absorb more of the infinite, twinkling, shimmering galaxies above them.

"How do you like your t-shirt?" Murray asks.

Almas touches his chin to his chest and pinches the fabric at his bellybutton, pulling it out to read it more clearly.

"The Ramones?"

"Yeah, the Ramones," breathes Murray with excitement. "Now there was a band. You're very privileged, you know. I mean I don't lend my 70s punk band t-shirts to just anyone. And if you're very lucky I might let you have my Clash tour t-shirt tomorrow. Just try not to spill omelette over it like you did with my Gibson t-shirt."

"Punk?"

"Music. Drums, you know."

Murray mock-drums again.

"Never mind. It's okay. I'll play you some tomorrow."

"I dream, too, Murray."

"We all dream, Almas. We *all* dream."

"Oh."

Almas starts up another beat with his heels.

"So, what do you dream, Almas?"

"Devils."

Murray pulls himself upright and turns to face the boy.

"Almas, how did you meet Bina?"

He is more serious now although he tries not to sound it.

"She finds me. She *found* me. I was lost. No mother or father. I can't remember them. I looked for food and places to sleep. But always dreaming of the devils. *Sometimes* an angel. Then Bina finds me. She is an angel, I think. She finds food and fed me. She walks with me and we go different places, always walking and getting rides, begging for money, getting on trains, running from angry people. Bina says she is looking for somewhere good and safe. She dreams of this place. This."

Almas pats a rhythmic flourish with his hands on the deck to emphasise exactly where he means.

"I am good at drums, no?" And he grins the broadest smile.

"You are *very* good at drums. Just wait until you hear The Ramones."

"It's like this, children, you should go back now. I cannot say it any less plainly. Go home. This world is dangerous." Hero's voice, although warm, resonates in their chests like a deep bass rumble.

"And you are so young." Faith continues with pity.

"A liability to those who are to look after you," mocks Pure.

"So, you aren't the ones that we are supposed to meet?" asks Bina.

"Or is this just a test?" from Titus.

"A test?" Hero sounds perplexed.

"To see if we're up for it. Ready for the challenge."

"No test. There is no challenge. No one should send you here. No one should do this to you."

Hero pauses now and thinks hard, biting his lip and shaking his head.

"We each of us have something to tell you. We want you to listen hard. Just listen. No interruptions. Hear our arguments, I implore you and trust us that we have your best interests at heart. Are you ready, Faith?"

Hero's splayed hand entreats her to stand as he sits. Faith rises to her feet and begins her speech.

"You are clearly both spirited, confident and brave children."

"Teenagers," interrupts Titus.

"Please, I said no interruptions," Hero chides. "Continue, Faith."

"Brave teenagers, yes. But you've seen this forest and experienced its darkness. But here is just one tiny element of this domain. Have you had time to think what is here and whether you are equipped to cope with it? No, you haven't. Have you had time to ponder what special skills you possess? Do you have any special skills? Think about it. Are you especially strong or fast or clever? Maybe you are. I do not know. But shouldn't you have time to think about it? Are you braver than all others around you? There will be times here when you will be lost, cornered and in danger. Are you the clear-headed, quick-witted kind? Will you take what you have at hand – which could be next to nothing – and find a way out? Fight your way out? Maybe you have all these things. Maybe I shouldn't doubt it. That is up to you to decide."

Faith nods to Hero and sits.

"Thank you, Faith. Pure. It is your turn."

Pure seems reluctant to stand. It seems to pain him to do so. Slowly he does, and he speaks.

"The two of you come here together. Just a pair. And as such you rely completely on one another. Your safety is in the hands of the other. You are responsible for the other. How would you feel if something were to happen to your friend? And something will happen sooner or later. Regret is a pain that never leaves you. When you die, you feel nothing. When someone who relies on you dies you feel everything. And what about those who you love back at home, wherever your home is? If something were to happen to you here how will they feel? What will you have done to them? Be responsible. Be wise. Don't suffer the everlasting agony of a scarred conscience. This trip you are now on, don't make it one of guilt. End it."

Pure exhales noisily as if to say 'there, done it' and collapses heavily to his seat.

"And my turn," from Hero as he stands again and quietly walks around and behind Titus and Bina.

He reaches out with both arms towards the fire, his fingers delicately undulating. As they do, the fire seems to take on a new life. It roars louder and its flames reach higher into the night sky. The tiny, glowing, rising embers multiply and grow, twisting more vigorously in the air. The heat from the fire strikes their faces with a violent gust and they both recoil. Hero is encouraging and manipulating the blaze. His face is expressionless as he takes his turn for his monologue.

"As Faith has already said, you seem like brave young people. Bravery is a noble attribute. But bravery is relative and can only be measured personally by what you have already experienced in life that causes you to be afraid. What have you both experienced so far in your young lives that has caused you to be afraid?"

Titus can listen meekly no longer.

"Apart from living my life under the threat of death from an incurable, debilitating disease, wondering what next unseen bacteria or unwitting touch will kill me. And apart from being abandoned by parents scared of who I am. *And* apart from Bina here having her mother and father snatched away from her and having to scavenge for her survival through the worst warzones known to man. Apart from that, you mean?"

Hero nods in faint approval and understanding as he turns his hands downwards to calm the fire.

"Yes, you both have suffered and yet survived. Courage indeed. I can see that. These are circumstances you have slowly borne and become accustomed to and it does you great credit. But here, in this place, there are things way beyond personal loss and pain. Things that surpass disease and sadness. Faith, Pure and I live here. We know this realm. We have seen the many sources of its fear. And we choose now to live here as peacefully as possible in the forest, as far from it all as we can be. The evil here is of a kind you cannot begin to dream."

"But we are dreaming... sort of," Bina interjects pointedly.

There is quiet for a few seconds.

"Yes, I see. We have heard of your kind. Sleepwalkers they call you, yes?" Hero acknowledges. "Many have come here apparently, and many have never left. More sacrifices in an unwinnable conflict. More young people whose lives are cut short. Why are wars always about taking the young? I think in your world, too, no? Your many pointless wars have cut swathes of misery through the younger generations. No eye has seen the horrors and no ear has heard the kind of screams that have been prepared here for those sent to try and make a difference. *We* have seen and heard them. And even we hide from them. Never before have we met a Sleepwalker, so never before have we had the chance to warn one. Grant us that privilege now. Allow us that honour. Just one brief moment in the presence of the mildest of horrors here and your young hearts will be frozen so solid you will fear that it can never beat again as it once did."

Hero sits. Faith and Pure applaud him warmly and they, all three, bow their heads as if finally resting their case.

Titus and Bina stare at each other, mouths opened in readiness of a comment but nothing comes. Every word they have heard from their three advisors tumbles around their restless minds. They each revisit everything that

69

Murray had told them while on *The Dreamweaver* and contrast it with all they have heard in this Somnambulan midnight forest clearing. Physically agitated, they both stand, pace up and down in front of the fire, stopping occasionally to glance at each other and their audience of three.

After almost two minutes of this, Bina confronts Titus, taking firm hold of both his shoulders.

"What do you think, Titus," she demands.

"I'm just….I'm only a…. kid. A sick kid, Bina," Titus implores.

"Murray didn't tell us enough," Bina sighs, saddened.

"This is real, Bina. This is real stuff here."

"Are you *frightened*?" she asks pointedly.

"Well, er….yes."

"Me, too."

"I suppose the question is, can we make a difference? Just us two?"

"I don't see how, Titus."

"Yeah, I mean if this is, like, you know…heaven or something, then just two teenagers coming here are surely not going to tip the balance in any way."

"It's too immense, yes."

"And I don't want to be responsible for you, Bina. I live with enough pain already every day in my bed. I can't live with more. Right now, that hospital is looking like a very safe place."

Hero, Faith and Pure do not even look at the Sleepwalkers as they debate between themselves; they just continue to sit, still, with prayerfully bowed heads.

"So, what then, Bina? What do we do?" Titus huffs, stroppily pulling away from her grip.

"There's nothing we can do *here*, Titus," she responds sadly.

"There's not a lot I can do *there*," he answers, referring to his home.

"You can live," she suggests weakly.

"Not much."

"Maybe they will cure you soon, Titus. There's always breakthroughs. You're still young. You could have a whole life ahead of you."

Titus's shoulders just rise and fall heavily with a large exasperated sigh.

"And I could take Almas somewhere and find a home. Maybe someone to take care of us. Maybe we could visit you in your hospital. We could all be friends there."

Bina desperately injects as much hope and optimism into her tone as she can manage.

There is silence between them before Titus turns lethargically back to face his friend, his mouth smiling thinly but his eyes betraying the despondency.

They nod to each other in sullen agreement, wordlessly acknowledging their decision and both turning to address Hero, who is still, like his associates, frozen in reverent neutrality.

"Tell us, how do we go home?" asks Bina, miserably.

In perfect, practiced unison, Hero, Faith and Pure slowly lift their heads, a faint look of gratification on their faces.

Hero looks ready to deliver an answer, his countenance building to a delighted grin, but then his head and body jerk awkwardly as if suddenly irritated by something. He grits his teeth angrily and hisses, sensing an unexpected arrival.

From across the clearing there is a long, booming, angry cry and a dazzling, white-light flash that shoots from a break in the trees and through the air, like low-level lightning and its accompanying thunder roll. The lightning has form and it is the form of a person. The person leaps through the fire's harshest flames from the opposite side through to where the group are sitting. It screams an unintelligible battle cry and lands with the force of an earthquake, a single knee knelt and with arms front and hands clenched together gripping an enormous white-hot broadsword that is plunged down into the reverberating earth. Jibarial lets out another single, elongated cry.

"Liars!"

Another destructive sound wave emanates from his wrath and the roaring fire at the centre of the clearing is instantly extinguished. He pulls the sword up out of the ground and throwing it towards the sky it spins full circle and lands back with its hilt in his right hand, pointing directly at Pure.

"Your name is Guilt, and you have no right here," he commands.

Pure combusts into a single fizzing ember that screeches into the dark forest. Jibarial trains his blade on Faith.

"And you are Doubt. I know you and I call you out. You have no authority. None!"

Faith's human form, like Pure's before her, is reduced to a flickering red piece of fiery debris before shrieking for the shelter of the trees.

The point of Jibarial's sword swings to Hero.

"And you. Your name is Ancient Fear. I really do not like you.

"It doesn't matter what you like or do not like, warrior angel. You'll never be rid of me. Even *you* know my voice," Hero mocks defiantly.

"Yes, I recognise your voice. And that's your mistake. Fear, I cast you out to where you came from, to the darker recesses of the Forest of Green Light. You have no authority over me or these Sleepwalkers. Go!"

Hero remains intact, a smug look now on his once benign face.

Titus, who, like Bina, has been hitherto transfixed by the angel's arrival strides towards Hero.

"You know," he declares as nonchalantly as he can muster, "you were never that convincing with the whole 'fear' speech. Trust me, I've watched a lot of movies. I mean *a lot*. And I can spot a good performance when I see one. That was a bit hammy, TBH. So why don't you just do like the angel dude here says and get the hell out of here."

He gives Jibarial a cheeky sideways glance.

"Do your flashy, swordy thing again, lightning guy."

Jibarial, with a momentary look of disapproval aimed at Titus, forces his broadsword down into the ground again with a loud exclamation.

"Fear, out!"

Hero struggles with an inner pain, doubling up, crumpling to the ground and writhing, clearly fighting the effects of Jibarial's command. His shrivelling body glows bright red and ignites into a giant flame. Jibarial flings his sword towards him and it lands in the middle of the crumpled pyre, reducing it to a single hot coal. The coal shoots several feet into the air, hissing and smoking and bullets towards Titus. Jerking his body to one side, he avoids the imminent collision but the fiery projectile grazes a bloody scorch mark across his cheek before darting out of sight into the lightless undergrowth. Titus falls to his knees with a yelp, holding his hand to his injured face.

"Okay, so that was a *little* scary," he yelps.

"Titus! Are you alright?"

Bina rushes to him, falling to her knees and embracing him. She looks up to Jibarial imploringly.

"What does this mean? Will he be alright?"

There is a deep, genuine warmth to the angel's large smile that reassures them both that they are now in the presence of the right party.

"He will be fine. It just means that Fear has left his mark. That's no bad thing."

"Who are you?" asks Bina staring deeply for the first time into the face of their rescuer.

Jibarial's initial lightning glow is fading, revealing a more recognisably human form. He is handsome, nearly seven feet tall, no more than eighteen years old by earthly standards and clad in a dark brown suede leather-like jacket with what looks like sheepskin lining around the collar. His trousers look leather, too and his black ankle length boots have deep, rugged soles. He collects his sword and returns it to its black leather sheath that hangs from a wide black belt around his waist.

"My name is Jibarial," he says straight to Bina with an intensity that makes her nervous, although she does not know why.

"Well, thanks, Jib," groans Titus standing up and throwing out a hand to the angel.

Jibarial shakes it and laughs.

"Oh, and don't say it," warns Titus.

"Say what?" Jibarial is puzzled.

"Aren't you a little short to be a Sleepwalker?"

"I wasn't going to say that."

"No, it's a joke, you know.... Stormtrooper, Sleepwalker, Leia, Luke."

Jibarial looks to Bina questioningly. Bina just shrugs.

"Lead balloon. Moving on," sighs Titus still wincing in pain and rubbing his cheek with the flat of his palm.

"Yes, we need to move on. You were supposed to arrive at our camp but sometimes on the first ascent to Somnambula, it is not always easy to get it just right. And sadly, you ended up in this forest. And with the territorial spirits."

"Territorial spirits?" asks Bina.

"They hold sway over this place and so, in turn, have an effect on certain geographical places in your world. You met Guilt, Doubt and Fear. It's their job to speak into the atmosphere here, spreading their lies. Most of what they speak will work its way into the minds and hearts of humans on earth. Their voices just sound like people's own consciences. They are usually subtle and believable but they rarely meet any actual human souls here in Somnambula, so they thankfully weren't that damaging. Anyway, come, we need to get you to our camp. Our division of Keepers is leaving in the morning. And you need to leave with us."

"Where are we going?" asks Bina.

"Raphael, one of the archangels, will explain all. It is best you hear it from him."

Almas grows chilly in the midnight air and finally tires. Murray takes him below deck to a cabin next to the sleeping Titus and Bina. On the way, he opens their door to show the boy how safe and peaceful his friend looks. Almas looks content at the sight of Bina, eyes closed and breathing deeply on her makeshift bed alongside Titus's oxygen tent.

"Time for *you* to sleep," affirms Murray softly.

"And for you?"

"Maybe later."

Murray sees the boy to bed and heads for the kitchen where he places the kettle on the hob for a cup of tea.

These are the night hours of his Sentry duty, where he watches over his young charges, ensuring nothing or no one interrupts their nocturnal missions. He has not been in this position for twenty years, but he had never enjoyed a full night's sleep in all that time and had often found himself awake for hours, making tea or reading a book. The habit of a natural born Sentry does not fade easily, and neither do the pain and regret of loss.

He stops the kettle just short of its shrill whistle and drowns a teabag in the not-quite boiling water. He watches the liquid in his mug turn brown and listens to the friendly, gentle creaking of *The Dreamweaver* and the lapping of water outside against its hull. And then another familiar sound. It is the voice of Sanntu who has appeared and is sitting at the kitchen table.

"That stuff will keep you awake."

Murray is not surprised. He expected a visit at some stage during Titus and Bina's first ascent.

"I'm counting on it."

"They're doing ok, Murray."

"Thank God."

"A bit of a problem at first but it's all fine."

"Nothing ever goes to plan first time, eh?"

Murray eases himself down on a stool to face Sanntu.

"But you seem a little ill at ease," the angel prompts with concern.

"Well...." The response is long and thoughtful.

"Well what?"

75

"Well, you know, it's been a long time."

"It's more than that, Murray. You're a Sentry. This is what you do. What you were made to do. There's something else on your mind."

"It's just that there's another element this time."

"The young child."

"Yes, Almas."

"What about him?"

"I don't know. I'm just wondering why he's here. I'm used to Sleepwalkers. Just Sleepwalkers and my crew. But this young boy...." Murray trails off, staring down into his tea.

There is silence for a minute. Murray finds his train of thought.

"He dreams, too, Sanntu."

"Of?"

"Devils, he says."

"Scary for a six-year-old."

"Yeah, but he knows stuff, too. Like it's inside of him."

"You think....?"

"What? That he's a Sleepwalker, too? No, Sanntu, he's no Sleepwalker."

"How do you know for sure?"

"I'm a Sentry. I commune with angels in purple suits. I can read the Book of Dreams. I guard Sleepwalkers. And I have a killer collection of late 1970s punk and new wave vinyl. One of those things doesn't matter, but what does matter is that I know Sleepwalkers and Almas isn't one."

"Okay, alright then. Which raises a more perplexing question."

'Maybe. But he's just a kid, Sanntu. Just a kid.'

"I'll give it some thought, Murray. I'll, you know, take some advice."

Murray gives his often-inscrutable friend a furrowed brow look that is halfway between puzzlement and accusation and that says *I don't know what that means and I don't really want to know what that means*.

It is a look he has given him many times.

Jibarial leads them into the camp. All around them Keepers dressed in the same leather military attire are readying themselves – gathering backpacks, fastening belts, cleaning swords. One by one they notice Titus and Bina as Jibarial marches them through the throng, stopping whatever they are doing and standing almost to attention, many giving a faint, respectful nod of the head.

"Hi, how you doing?" greets Titus to them as he tries to keep up with the pace. He is turning his head and spinning on his heels to take it all in.

The all-pervading emerald glow from the waterfall in the centre of the mighty crag casts everything in a surreal neon hew. Some of the Keepers are washing by the side of the still, circular pool. Others are swimming in it. It feels like morning but there is no sunrise, not even the hint of a dawn, just the bustle and energy of a new day. There is no chatter, clammering or boisterous camaraderie, just the tranquil efficiency of an army with one mind and one unquestionable cause.

The Sleepwalkers notice that the gathered militia is made up of both male and female warriors; tall, slender yet muscular angel soldiers of every race and colour.

"We're moving out in an hour," Jibarial barks over his shoulder to the teenagers.

"To?" Bina ventures.

"I told you, all will be revealed."

"By Rufus." Titus shouts from the rear.

"Raphael," corrects the angel.

Around the high rim of the encircling crag the silhouettes of large, powerful figures become visible in the misty green glow. Jibarial notices Bina looking up at them with concern. He halts his march, turns and places a reassuring hand on both of her shoulders.

"It is alright, Bina, they are with us. They are our lookouts. While we sleep. Like your Sentry. They protect us."

"I was wondering, too, Jib," Titus chips in.

"I was talking to you, too."

"Didn't look like it."

Jibarial ignores the jibe and examines Bina's face to see if she understands. A long blink tells him she does.

"Over there, that tent.'

Jibarial points.

"It is Raphael. He is looking forward to meeting you. Now if you will excuse me I need to get my equipment together and board the riverboat. At least I think it is a riverboat. That is what it appeared to be earlier, but then that bit, like so much else here in Somnambula, is completely up to you."

The FIFTH Chapter of the Sixty-Fourth Book of Dreams:

Where fortresses loom,
an island beckons,
and a weapon awaits.

The enormous red paddlewheel at the stern of the ornate steamboat effervesces the river water, churning the glowing algae and materialising rainbows of a dozen green shades as the waterfall's glow hits the wet mist. Around the craft's six pristine white decks stand Keepers in battle-readiness; all in rough, long brown leather jackets with heavy-set sheepskin collars, khaki trousers, black gloves and adorned with swords and leather backpacks; each gazing vigilantly outwards to the riverbanks as the steamboat pulls powerfully away from its berth and into the middle of the wide river.

Titus and Bina stand with Raphael on the third deck, above the paddlewheel. Titus can't control his excitement.

"It was a Western," he shouts above the noise of the two thousand horsepowered rotor. "A movie. About people playing poker on a Mississippi riverboat. I just loved the look of the boat. And now…"

"And now it is here," completes Raphael, smiling a paternal smile. "You brought your powerful memory into this world."

He has the tone of a proud parent regarding a young child's first painting.

"It's what you can do. It's what you can both do. You have the ability to furnish this world with certain specifics. This one was inadvertent and subconscious but you will both learn to do this more knowingly. It is one of the ways in which Sleepwalkers are special here."

"*One* of the ways?" Bina queries.

"Just one," the archangel confirms.

"What other ways are there, Raphael?" she pushes.

Raphael leans over the deck's filigree balustrade and further into the moist, sparkling air, closing his eyes and enjoying the sensation of cold on his face.

"*Technically*, you cannot die here," he announces to the river.

The Sleepwalkers look at each blankly, unable to process what this means. Titus registers a thought.

"But *un*technically?"

Raphael opens his eyes, readjusts himself and spins around, and in doing so stretches out both long arms, scooping Titus and Bina into an affectionate huddle.

"There is so much to tell. But it has to unfold a bit at a time. This is an infinite world and there are infinite possibilities. You have skills that we angels do not have. Sleepwalkers have finally returned to Somnambula and there is much to do. We have to get you ready for your first mission and I cannot encumber you both with facts that will confuse. Your first test is just a day away."

"But we only have a night." Bina sounds apologetic. "Murray told us we have to do everything during our sleep, one night at a time."

"That's true. But a night on earth is a lot, lot longer here in Somnambula. While you sleep on earth you could achieve a week of activity here, so do not worry, you have time."

Titus puts on his bravest and most assertive voice to impress Raphael: "So what's the first mission?"

Another warm, fatherly smile of pride from Raphael.

"Come, my brave Sleepwalkers, let's go to my stateroom and I will explain everything. I think it is this way. But then again, Titus, you would know. It's your boat."

He laughs to himself as he ushers them along the deck and inside.

In the quiet of his elegant stateroom, Raphael tells his seated human friends of what is to come. He tells them that it is their ultimate mission to help destroy the Hell Diamond; the power that is growing daily somewhere towards the south. He tells them that, like all evil and demonic power in Somnambula, the Hell Diamond represents something terrible on earth; something that could trigger catastrophe. Although, he admits, no one quite knows how this power is reflected in the land of humans. It could be a person, a government, a corporation or an event. But whatever it is, it must be prevented from reaching its potential through the total destruction of the Hell Diamond.

There, in Raphael's dimly-lit riverboat stateroom, he tells them the story of the The Spear that sits guarded at the top of the central peak of the island of Kerberos; a weapon created eons ago and, with its angelic glass tip and cedar wood shaft, is the only way to disable the Hell Diamond. Plunged into the heart of the demonic jewel, The Spear will help the Keepers triumph in this one battle. But only a Sleepwalker can approach the Hell Diamond; no angel can withstand for long the sheer demonic radiation that it emanates. Raphael explains that Titus and Bina have to steal The Spear from Kerberos and then escape the island with the weapon. But, he concedes, there is even more to it than that. Centuries ago angel forces tried to capture The Spear but failed, and, in doing so, many Keepers were imprisoned in soul-cages by the Darkangels. They have been there on Kerberos ever since, languishing in an inescapable coma-like existence behind bars of living serpents. Once in possession of The Spear, the Sleepwalkers must use it to pierce the serpent bodies and free the Keepers.

"And with one hundred re-awakened angel troops, you will escape the island and get back to us here on the boat. From there we will head towards the Hell Diamond," Raphael concludes as he sits.

He folds his hands together making a steeple with both index fingers and then points to Titus and Bina in turn, and, with slow, meticulous care says: "But first you need to get *on* the island."

"You fly us in!" Titus suggests exuberantly.

"Angels don't fly, Titus. No wings. Well, most of us don't."

"What? Next you'll be telling us you don't play harps."

Raphael ignores the joke.

"So, how *do* we get onto Kerberos, Raphael," says Bina.

"We cannot simply get you past the outer island fortresses. There are too many and they are too heavily occupied to guarantee we could get you through. No, it is up to you to get onto the island alone using a very different method. A way that only Sleepwalkers can manage. You *drift*."

"Drift?" they say together.

"As Sleepwalkers, together, as a pair, you have the ability to visualise a location, dematerialise and then rematerialise in that location a moment later. It's called *drifting*. But you can only do it as a pair, with your combined power, never alone, and only across relatively short distances. We will sail the riverboat as close to Kerberos as possible and start to engage the outer fortresses. That will draw the Darkangels' attention and hopefully divert them from the fact there are Sleepwalkers drifting onto the island. You will then drift close to The Spear, take it and then free the Keepers imprisoned there. Together, you will escape the island by sea, and then..."

"Whoa there, Raff. Stop you there," Titus interjects. "None of the escaping by sea malarkey. Bina and I will just drift back with The Spear. Drift in, drift out."

"Sadly, you cannot, Titus. "You and Bina do not have the same physical bodies in Somnambula as we angels do. Your appearance is an astral projection of your earthly souls. It seems real, it looks and feels real, but it is not. That's why you can drift in this way, and why we cannot. But The Spear *is* real. If you try and drift back The Spear will simply be left behind. You will have to leave Kerberos with the freed Keepers. They will help you. They are good warriors."

"Er, except that they got caught in the first place," quips Bina.

Raphael fires her a suspicious, accusatory frown, from which Bina feels the force.

"I was just saying it before he did," she says apologetically and pointing at Titus.

"It was a fierce battle and many died. Many Darkangels and many Keepers. A lot of friends fell that day. We made a mistake in thinking that The Spear would not be protected so strongly. But now we know and are ready. While we draw their fire from the front, you will escape from behind them."

"I'm sorry, Raphael." Bina nodded repentantly.

"It's alright, child, for they will soon be free. I know it. I have faith in you, our two new Sleepwalkers. But first you must rest and then Jibarial will tell you more about Kerberos, The Spear and how together you are to drift, whilst we plan our distraction tactics with whatever defences they now have around the island."

"You don't know?" Titus inquires with faint accusation.

"No, and I'm not sure even they know. Now you are both here there is a lot about Somnambula that is uncertain. But you will soon learn how to give it certainty. The island's fortifications are just...."

Raphael is interrupted as Bina recoils violently in her seat; crying out and shaking her shoulders as if trying to dispel a nightmare.

"The fortresses!" she cries out. "I've seen them."

Raphael is up from his seat and at Bina's side, reassuring hands on her shoulders and looking intently into her eyes.

"What do you see, Bina? What is it? Your mind is bringing something to our reality? It's so soon. Describe it. Picture it again, Bina."

"Yeah, what can you see, Bina?" adds Titus.

"I saw them all. Hundreds of them, planted into the sea, standing off the coast of the island, all facing out......like, like...."

She searches for something in the recesses of her mind, knowing that it is there to be found; a memory of something that matches the momentary vision; and then an epiphany. Bina gasps suddenly and with it her eyes open wide and seem to stare into the distance, past Raphael's visage and into infinity.

"I've seen them before, in a book. My father had a book he used to show me to tell me about his homeland. He was so proud to be British and showed me pictures every night from this book. Pictures taken from the air of places all around the British Isles. But there was one picture that fascinated more than all the others. You know when something frightens you but yet you cannot stop looking at it? It was The Sea Forts of Redsands."

What Bina describes to an intent Raphael and Titus is from her recollections of a book entitled 'Britain From The Air' produced by London's Royal Geographical Society. She carefully recalls all she knows, telling them of the eerie appearance of giant, orange, rusting iron and steel oblong boxes thrusting upwards from the waves on four splayed tubular legs, with small windows, gun turrets, ladders and antennae all about the structures. Bina describes just how unworldly these corroded, robotic sea forts seemed to her as a young child.

"My father said they were built to protect Britain during the Second World War and placed out in the Thames Estuary where they could fire on German planes. But after the war they were just left there, rusting and rotting, steadily looking more imposing and frightening. I think that's what is around Kerberos. Many of them, in a protective ring all around the island."

Bina breaks her distant gaze with another fevered shake of her body and shoots a distressed look at Raphael before bowing her head as if exhausted.

"Bina, listen to me," reassures a tender Raphael. "You brought this memory into Somnambula and, if you are right, and if these sea forts of Redsands are really what the Darkangels are using to protect Kerberos, then you have done us a favour. We now know what we are fighting. If you describe them in all the detail you can, we can face them with more confidence, target their weaknesses, understand their advantages. This is good, Bina. This is a good thing."

He rubs her shoulders to console her.

"But I'm the one that has seen them. I'm the one that knows how terrifying they are. And it's not a good thing at all."

The low resonant blast of the steamboat's horn rouses Titus from his brief rest in the small, sparsely furnished cabin and he slowly becomes aware of the sounds of activity about him; the pounding of boots on the timber decks and of almost indecipherable barked instructions and their obediently shot-back responses. He also senses that the pace of the giant paddlewheel and steam engines that power it is slowing.

He gets up, goes out onto the deck where the sounds of activity explode more violently in his ears, and knocks on the door of the next cabin where Bina is sleeping.

"Wake up, Bina. I think something is happening."

Bina is at the door in seconds, clearly already awake herself and joins Titus out on the deck, wrapping her crimson scarf around her head and shoulders. They look out together on what is now open sea in a hazy dawn light. It looks at first like a normal seascape but as they regard it, with every passing moment, they are increasingly aware that it looks very different. The sea itself has a backlit chartreuse glow to it and seems too serene, almost flat calm. In the morning sky, although still fairly dim, there are no stars, no moon, just an aurora of coruscating streams of reddish light, flowing and folding their way from horizon to horizon. The two stand hypnotised at the softly pulsing aerial display.

"Don't you think it's funny," Titus begins slowly, still looking upward in the sky's thrall, "that our bodies are currently asleep on a boat on earth whilst we've been sleeping again on a boat here in Somnambula. I mean that's a lot of sleep."

"Jibarial says that we need to rest here in the same way as we do down on earth."

Bina doesn't break her fixed stare on the sky either.

"Oh, you've been talking to Jibarial, have you?"

"Yes, after he showed us both how to drift he walked me to my cabin."

"Nice of him."

"I guess so."

Another blast of the steamer's horn shakes them from their skyward reverie and two Keepers in full battle dress appear from behind and whisk them along the deck towards the bow.

"Come, Raphael and others need you on the bridge," says one of them firmly.

"I think we have found your sea forts, Bina," announces Jibarial as the Sleepwalkers are ushered onto the steamer's bridge. He nods towards Raphael who is holding large brass binoculars to his eyes.

"Take a look," Raphael invites, handing the glasses to Bina. "See if they are the same ones as your father showed you. There."

He crouches so his eye line is the same as Bina's and stretches out his long arm to point her gaze out across the sea. She follows the outstretched finger and looks through the glasses, taking a few seconds to adjust the focus and lock on to her subject matter. Suddenly she winces and lowers the binoculars, takes a breath and raises them again.

"Yes, those are the sea forts of Redsands. The ones from the book. The same ones."

"And just beyond them, Kerberos," adds the archangel gently.

"It's nearly time," says Jibarial with as reassuringly a wide smile as he can manage; first to Titus but then to Bina, holding it longer there and adding a few deliberate nods.

"The only slight difference with *these* sea forts," chips in Titus with an over-forced sarcasm, "is that they are full demonic, fire-propelling hell monsters intent on destroying Keepers, growing a diabolical diamond and taking over the earth."

He grins.

"Yes," agrees Raphael, going gamely with the joke. "But we've got the secret weapon."

"What?"

"You."

The angelic paddle steamer's engines are cut as it comes to within six hundred feet of the line of sea forts. It is close enough for all aboard to see flickering red glows through the small windows of the hulking rectangular structures; fiery light that darts in and out of view as each one passes the open portals, creating a sense of hurried activity within. The seabed-planted fortresses glisten in the morning light with countless shades of rust, like colossal mechanical beasts frozen in a state of ancient menace. It is now apparent that the entire island of Kerberos is encircled by the sea forts; each a hundred and fifty feet from the next, and connected via wire walkways from roof to roof. Their four angled concrete legs connect at the top to a solid slab that supports the iron fort structure, and plunge down into the sea to form a wider base. Crustaceans and green algae cling to the visible lower reaches of the legs adding to their sense of inert, timeless foreboding.

Standing alone on the lowest bow deck Titus is not looking at the iron forts; his focus is on the island beyond and his concerns are with his and Bina's mission to drift there and then escape back to steamer with The Spear and the captured Keepers. Now that the engines are no longer pounding and the large paddlewheel has stopped thrashing the water and each angel is stilled in hushed regard of the enemy, the only soundtrack to his thoughts is the slow creaking of the timber craft and the gentle flutter of the bunting that adorns its balustrades and poles. It is this peace that amplifies his fear and he starts to ponder what Raphael meant about not being able to die and why he used the word *technically*.

Kerberos rises up from the sea like a jagged, craggy grey spike, flecked with a series of tiny verdant plateaus that cut into its steep slopes. From this distance, it is impossible for Titus to tell just how high its summit is, but he can make out the highest of the grassy platforms that he would choose to drift to with Bina; the one that would give them the shortest access to the pinnacle where The Spear apparently sits. From there it would be a case of locating the island's long-standing prisoners; and then freeing them.

An unexpected voice from behind him interrupts his mental plans. It is guttural and rough, less precise and well-spoken as the other Keepers he has met so far. It is Axyl, another of Raphael's generals.

Axyl is as equally ageless as Raphael but has a ruddier glow about him and a softer, rounder countenance. His battledress jacket is bulkier and longer with more pockets that seem to bulge with unseen contents, and is not the brown leather of the other troops but a pale olive. The hefty sheepskin collar does not lie flat but surrounds the back of his head like a furry halo and runs down to the hems of his open jacket.

"It's all about equilibrium, human."

Axyl is brusque but not unfriendly.

"What's that?" Titus responds, turning to face the angel general.

"They've probably not told you that bit yet."

"Equilibrium?"

"You and the girl being here creates symmetry. And that makes things…"

Axyl searches for the perfect word and cannot find one.

"…better," he chooses, audibly disappointed with it.

"I'm sorry, I….."

"Axyl. I am Axyl. I came here to look at Kerberos, like you, I suspect. The island and I have….."

He seeks the word again.

"History?" Titus ventures.

"Yes, *history* is the perfect word. Well done. I'm not good with words."

"What kind of history?"

"The in-the-past kind."

"Funny."

"Oh, it wasn't meant to be. But I see what you mean now."

"So, what *are* you good at?"

"Eh?"

"Well, you're not good with words. Anything you are good with?"

"Ah, yes."

Axyl twice taps the hilt of the sword that hangs off his belt.

"Killing. I am good at killing."

"Good to know. So, tell me about Kerberos."

Axyl takes a few steps towards the deck railings and grabs them firmly with both hands, steadying himself in a stoic pose and breathing in deeply, recalling something old and wounding.

"The others that are there, the imprisoned Keepers," he begins, "I was one of them. I helped lead the raid to find The Spear. We were outnumbered and overrun. The Darkangels could have killed us all…"

"You can die?" asks Titus, genuinely shocked.

"Yes, we can die. We just cease to exist. Oblivion. But that's not what an angel fears the most. The worst kind of punishment is the soul-cage. An eternal prison of conscious stillness. Not able to move or act, just think and….."

Axyl hesitates again, chasing after the language.

Titus tries to supply the word again.

"Hope?"

"Fear."

"That would have been my second guess."

"They rounded up the entire raiding party and put them in soul-cages on those grassy areas on the mountain. But I slipped away in the confusion, managed to climb down the mountain and away in one of our small boats."

"You got past the sea forts?"

"Well they didn't look like that then. That is your memory creating the equilibrium."

"Bina's actually," corrects Titus.

"But most of the Darkangels were on Kerberos waiting for us."

A chilling thought enters Titus' mind.

"Could there be Darkangels there now, waiting for me and Bina?"

"There could. But it seems that all the sea forts are busy with demonic activity and we haven't had any reports of extra forces being sent to this region, so there's a good chance that there is very little presence on the island. We don't think the Darkangels know anything about the Sleepwalkers' ability to drift. So, to them, these sea forts would seem tactically sufficient to protect The Spear."

"Mmmm," ponders Titus, "not at all comforting."

"Reliving the past, Axyl," barks Jibarial from out of nowhere.

"Just filling in the blanks, Jibarial. The boy was scared."

"*Was*?!" exclaims the boy.

"Good job, Axyl."

Titus seizes the opportunity to tease Jibarial.

"Hey, Jib, was that a little sarcasm?"

"Definitely not," is the deadpan response.

"I was telling the boy…"

"Titus," both Jibarial and Titus say at the same time and then give each other a mutual glance of approval.

"I was just trying to tell *Titus* about Somnambulan and earthly equilibrium."

"Another time, Axyl. Raphael just needs them to focus on retrieving The Spear. We can tell them both more as time goes on. And we tell them together. Bina deserves to know everything at the same time as Titus."

"Yes, you are right, Jibarial. I just came out to look at the island and the boy…er, Titus, was here."

"I understand, my friend. Kerberos is painful for you and I know you are thinking of your troops. And I know that our Sleepwalkers here will help you see them all again soon."

Jibarial means it as a confident assertion of his hope in them. Titus takes it as a challenge.

"No pressure there then."

Murray cradles another cup of the coffee that helps him through his night watches and leans forward in his chair to look closer at the faces of the sleeping Titus and Bina. He does not always stay this close to his charges during their nocturnal missions but moments earlier he was passing their cabin door and heard a faint yelp from inside. It was not unusual for a Sleepwalker to react in his or her slumber to the events they were experiencing in the heavenly realm.

The Sentry places his hand on the plastic membrane that separates him from Titus; feeling it moving softly, but fitfully in and out with his now irregular breathing. It connects him to Titus and, in some small way, lets him know that he is there for him. Bina still sleeps calmly in the other bed; her expression impassive and untroubled. Murray knows all too well that Titus is scared right now but cannot do a thing to help, just continue to stay with them, watching over them.

Behind him the door squeaks open but Murray stays fixed on Titus.

"That you, Lasaro?"

There is a moment's pause before a still, small, timid voice responds.

"No, it is me," says Almas.

The Sentry looks to his left shoulder to reveal his profile to the boy.

"Oh. You okay? Still can't sleep?"

"I heard a cry. Is he alright?"

"Yes, Almas, he is fine. Just...you know, dreaming."

Almas takes the few steps to stand at Murray's side, looking in on Titus. Murray extends a comforting hand to Almas' back.

"He is scared," says Almas forlornly.

"A bit like you, Almas, being on this big old strange boat, eh?"

Murray tries to inject some joviality as a distraction tactic. "Why don't we go and make you a hot chocolate? I bet you've never had a hot chocolate like the ones I make."

"I've never had any kind of hot chocolate."

"No, I don't suppose you have."

"They're making him do something he doesn't want to do," Almas offers, placing his hand on the oxygen tent wall just like he had seen Murray do.

Murray is silent.

"Something dangerous, but I don't know what. I wish I did. We could help him. Maybe wake him up?"

"No!"

Murray stands quickly and pulls Almas' arm away from the plastic sheet, startling Almas who steps back sharply.

'I am sorry, Mr Murray," as if about to cry.

"No, I'm sorry, Almas. I didn't mean to…."

He drops to his knees to go face to face with the frightened child, smiling broadly and nodding.

"… it's just that you can never wake them. They must wake up for themselves. When the time is right."

"Bina used to wake *me* up. Whenever I slept somewhere she would wake me up and say 'Almas, it is time to leave'. We were always leaving quickly and going somewhere new. Always we would run. Always a new place. Always waking me up."

"Bina was looking after you, Almas. She wanted to get you somewhere safe. And she did that. You're here. This is the safe place she was always looking for."

Murray pats the cabin floor to show where he means.

"But why cannot we make them awake? What would happen?"

All Murray does is shake his head and frown, not knowing how to explain in simple English to a timorous six-year-old boy about the mental trauma that a Sleepwalker would experience if shocked out of their Somnambulan flight and how they would probably never recover. Instead he changes the subject.

"Let's get that hot chocolate, eh?"

"You have both fixed the place in your mind?" Raphael cautions the Sleepwalkers, a hand on Titus' right shoulder, a hand on Bina's left.

They both nod once, although Titus's comes accompanied with an audible gulp.

"Then you are ready."

"Remember," adds Jibarial, stepping forward out of the darker shadows of Raphael's stateroom, "that as soon as you drift we will launch the attack on the sea forts to keep their attention on us."

"My troops will help you clear the island once you've .... er..." says Axyl, searching for the right word again.

"Liberated them?" offers Bina.

"Yes. Liberated. Good word."

"Time to go," Raphael directs, clapping gloved hands together.

"Be safe," adds Jibarial directly to Bina.

"I'll try and be safe, too, Jib. Thanks," mocks Titus.

The Sleepwalkers turn to face each other, clasping hands.

"You okay, Bina?"

"*You* okay, Titus?"

"Can you see it?"

"Yes, I can see it."

"What do you see, Bina?"

"I see the uppermost grass plane."

"On the side of the mountain."

"The island of Kerberos."

"Beyond the sea forts."

"Where The Spear lies."

"And the Keepers are imprisoned."

They close their eyes and within seconds their bodies shake and convulse, but not in pain, not through an internal compulsion, but as if through a peripheral force that buffets and stretches them. Between their two shuddering bodies, a rough sphere of bright white light grows and, as it touches their chests, its radiance casts a mantle, at first around their torsos, but then spreading; legs and feet and then shoulders and arms; finally covering their necks and heads. They both arch backwards as if trying to resist the last consuming grasp of the glowing shroud. With a sickening, sucking whoosh, the light implodes into a pinprick, pulling both Titus and Bina's Somnambulan forms into it like a folding star, and the dot of light blinks out.

"Battle stations," commands Raphael, already on his way to the door.

On a mountain shelf, barely twelve feet square, standing ankle deep in thick spiky grass, Titus and Bina regard each other for signs that they are all right. Still holding hands and still shaking, their skin persists with a ghostly white afterglow.

"You know that recurring dream when you're falling?" says Bina stammering.

"Uh-hu," is all that Titus can manage.

"That is what just happened. It felt like I was falling and falling and I could see this grass below me. Just hurtling towards it, wanting to fly, wanting to scream out, but not able to."

"I know," Titus forces out. "It was like we were going to hit the ground at a thousand miles per hour and just as we were about to we were here, standing upright."

"Our first drift."

"Really? Your first? Oh, I've done loads. Piece of cake."

Titus lets go of Bina's hands and turns around confidently. Not immediately aware of just how nauseous and dizzy he is, he collapses in a heap in the sharp grass.

"And yes, that *always* happens," he says with his face in the damp ground. Bina frowns disapprovingly at her friend's humour but is actually grateful for his light relief and his ability to take the edge off her nerves.

"The Spear should be just a few feet straight up, Titus. We need to hurry. We don't know whether there are Darkangels here or not."

"Gotcha. And, according to Axyl the soul-cages should be on the larger plateaus below. Three of them."

"Time to climb."

A cataclysmic crack of thunder shakes the mountain, making the two steady themselves against the rock face. It is accompanied with a near instantaneous fork of lightening that splits the sky open and strikes the crag above them.

"Move!" cries Titus, pushing Bina clear of the rock.

A hail of granite missiles caused by the lightning's impact strafe the ground where the two had stood.

"Thank you," gushes Bina.

"Well, apparently, that wouldn't have killed us. Remember we can't be killed here. *Technically*."

"But we could probably be knocked unconscious and carried off to soul-cages."

"Good point."

Rain like the two has never seen, or any human for that matter, begins to fall on the mountain. It pounds their bodies and weighs them down as they stumble their way back to the rock.

"Looks like someone doesn't want us to climb this mountain, Titus."

"Let's just hope that someone isn't here in person."

That someone was.

The SIXTH Chapter of the Sixty-Fourth Book of Dreams:

Where a fire-fight rages,
an escape is needed,
and a rescue begins.

The diversionary assault on the sea forts of Kerberos starts with a dispassionate nod from Raphael as he stands on the steamer's front deck. One hundred and fifty coracles stretch out around the protective circle of forts. Each half-walnut shaped boat is nine feet in diameter and holds four Keepers; the larger, more powerful looking one with a broad-bladed paddle, and the other three crouched, with crossbows loaded, and eyes fixed forward.

Raphael's nod is translated to a loudly whispered "*forward*" from the paddle-bearer of the coracle closest to the steamer and transmitted to the next in line and then the next, the command to advance rippling its way to the final boat.

A thick blue-grey mist has plumed up around the island and consumed the sea forts and the sea in front of them.

"Do you think they still haven't seen us, Raphael," asks an angel called Tresk.

"No, it is just as planned. The morning mist has rolled in as usual and should have completely masked our preparations. They know we are here but they can't know what we are planning."

Tresk is a military advisor; somewhat shorter than many of the other Keepers and dressed in less bulky battle clothing. He has a calm, thoughtful air of someone who you would want beside you in a crisis.

"All the coracles are slowly advancing now," he states.

The paddle-bearers are leaning out from the willow-rod woven and tarred calico coated hulls of their boats and carving figures-of-eight in the water to propel them onwards and into the dense mist.

Raphael and Tresk watch the curved line of coracles melt into the miasma; six hundred warriors drifting into an unwinnable battle to protect two children on the island beyond.

Jibarial and Axyl, down on their haunches, hold their crossbows at shoulder height in readiness. Portiel, a female warrior angel and bow-woman, and Amanthragan, the pilot, complete the coracle's crew. Amanthragan continually swivels his head from side to side to keep the line and check his pace. His huge arms power deep sweeping movements in the sea, his wrists twisting the paddle, balancing power with caution and causing as little disruption to the water as possible.

"Cannot be far now, Amanthragan," Portiel murmurs close to her friend's ear.

"You sound excited, old friend," he returns, low but soft.

"Less talk," Jibarial instructs, but so inaudibly that it is really to himself.

Amanthragan's paddle is suddenly out of the water and held aloft. His left hand, freed from its grip, makes a flat-palmed mid-air gesture to his passengers. All the coracles within their view have stopped, each taking their cue from the next.

Every angel on every coracle stares more intently ahead, trying to burrow deeper into the mist with their vision; attempting to locate the horizon and find their targets. But their targets do not appear on the horizon. In the haze, high above them and only a dozen feet away, their shapes form; blurry rust-red boxes hanging in the vaporous air. One by one the warriors adjust their posture, lifting their heads to crane upwards at the hulking structures towering over them in the murky sky.

There are cold, steely glances exchanged between warriors, curt bows of acknowledgment that it is time, and crossbows are raised to chin level in preparation.

"Not yet, not yet," says Jibarial, again, more to himself than anyone around him.

High above Jibarial's coracle an enormous iron bulkhead on the top of the nearest sea fort slams shut and then each sea fort follows suit, setting off a cacophonous symphony of arrhythmic, reverberant clanking that shatters the calm of the misty morning and lets the Keepers know that they no longer have any element of surprise.

"RELEASE!" cries Jibarial to his left and then again: "RELEASE!" to his right.

Four hundred and fifty demon-piercing crossbow bolts are let loose and whistle steeply upwards though the air towards every open orifice the sea forts offer up as targets; some harmlessly striking the forts' metal carcasses and glancing upwards, and others flying straight through the tiny windows to do what they are designed to do; to ricochet from wall-to-wall, floor-to-ceiling and find their mark. Crossbows are swiftly reloaded and another wave of bolts fills the air, followed by another and another.

The Darkangels of the Kerberos sea forts are like all others of their kind: vaguely visible dark human-like forms engulfed in a halo of flames; grotesque bodies that appear to be tarred and lit; moving, living infernos of evil intent that powerfully rip through the air with a roaring whoosh.

Inside the forts, they do not speak to each other; some man the small portals with thick, black longbows while others pass arrows that have been held close to their chests so that are engulfed with demonic flames.

As angel crossbow bolts penetrate the forts and rebound around the internal metallic surfaces, the Darkangels perform a fleet, fiery dance to avoid their trajectories. Most are agile enough to stay clear of the bows until, after a dozen ricochets, the missiles' power dwindles and they drop lifeless to the floor.

The few that cannot avoid the bows are instantaneously extinguished and vanish with a fierce crackle and a fizz, like water poured on a bonfire, and just the briefest sound of an agonising yelp. Not one death is acknowledged by a fellow Darkangel, not even a glance in the direction of a vanquished, vaporized brother; each demon wordlessly continues in his protective duty.

The first onslaught of flaming arrows fired from Darkangel longbows rains down on the coracles, but with the mist still disguising the boats in the water, most arrows sizzle harmlessly into the surrounding sea.

"FORWARD!" commands Jibarial, and there is a fury of paddle action as the boats move closer to the forts; the angel pilots digging deeper and harder into the sea, trying to manoeuvre them and their crew beneath the forts and out of the path of the arrows.

"We have to climb. We have to climb now," encourages Bina over the noise of the pounding rain.

Titus looks down at his soaked form and thinks of his weak, earthly body and of his inability to do even the simplest daily tasks; of his panicked breathlessness when faced with the outside world, and his listless years in his hospital bed; and he has to remind himself that none of that matters here. He lifts his palms and face to feel the rain, luxuriating in its sweet sting and allowing it to invigorate him.

"Let's climb, then, Bina. Let's go and find a spear."

The rock face is shiny-wet and slippery but affords enough generous footholds and protrusions to grip onto for the pair to make a start on their ascent.

Bina is quicker and less hesitant; her life of surviving on the streets for so long imbuing her with a bravery beyond her sixteen years. She is reaching higher than the shorter Titus and pulling herself up the treacherous cliff in more athletic movements. Titus is all short, jerky thrusts and grunts, still getting used to what his Somnambulan self can achieve as his doubtful mind wars with his newly able body.

The freezing downpour continues, making their hands ache with cold and almost numb to the flinty sharpness of the rock, but Bina feels the wet grass of a ledge with her fingertips and swings her other arm over to pull herself up.

She flops with exhaustion onto the sodden plateau at the summit of Kerberos, lying on her back for a moment, her red headscarf opened out and drenched in mud. She takes a breath and sits up, crouching and securing herself to lean over the edge and offer a hand to Titus. Titus grabs it gratefully and pedals his legs furiously to scuttle up the last section of rock and join Bina in a muddy pile at the top.

"Look at you, you're climbing mountains," says Bina brightly as they both stare up into the rain-dark sky.

"Yeah, I'm just ticking off firsts today."

"And for our next trick, we steal a mystical weapon."

"Ah, you had to go and spoil the moment."

"Come on, Titus."

Bina gets to her feet, offering Titus her hand again.

"S'alright," he says with a tired but dismissive wave, "I've got this."

He staggers to his feet unaided.

Positioned back to back, they survey the scene, scanning for any sign of The Spear. The deluge causes them to narrow their eyes and it blurs their vision. Each fierce raindrop explodes on the waterlogged surface on the murky mountaintop, creating a low-level haze.

"There," Bina shouts, pointing into the grey heart of the plateau.

Titus screws up his face and concentrates on the spot.

A dark, fat, stubby tree-trunk emerges as they focus. They see its serrated, splintered edges; not formed by an axe or saw but from something more rough and violent. And there, barely visible, protruding from its centre is a long, thin shaft.

"The Spear?" Bina suggests.

"Has to be."

They run as fast as the mud, the rain and their fatigue will allow them.

The stump is six feet in diameter; a cedar tree once struck by lightning and fractured and with no sign of the majestic tree and branches that would have completed it; and thrust down into its gnarly remains is the long shaft of The Spear.

Titus and Bina can see it penetrating the tree-trunk. It is not just a single spear point, but more of a rough, flat, cutlass-shaped glass blade, flat and broad and ending in a sharp point that is embedded in the tree. The tan coloured shaft has a light grain running along its length and is criss-crossed with leather bands that secure the glass blade to it; as tall as any angel and as thick as the grasp of any human, it stands rigid as if it had been there for centuries.

"We just grab it right? Then go?" Titus questions agitatedly.

Beyond The Spear, in the gloom, a vague, shadowy bear-like form rears up; it has no definable edges and seems to bleed out into the dark air around it.

"You can try!" it rasps in a voice like an avalanche of crunching rock.

As the sinister exclamation booms across the mountaintop there is another fork of lightening and another ear-splitting thunderclap. The scene is fully illuminated for a fraction of a moment and the monstrous, indistinct figure suddenly detonates into a towering torch of blistering flame that makes Titus and Bina recoil with a furnace-blast of hot air.

"Do the sinless think the Darkangels would leave The Spear unprotected?" it roars again, but this time with something of a sneer, almost a guttural laugh.

The distorted, shadowy figure of the demon is still visible amidst the flames that now seem to consume it from head to foot; flames that spit at and venomously lick the morning mountain air.

"You shall be imprisoned with the others, doomed to languish there until the final battle is won and never to return to your pathetic mortal bodies." The threat is delivered in a lower, slower, more measured tone but with a rise in volume towards the end that comes with blast of increased heat from the demon's incandescent hulk.

The Sleepwalkers are transfixed by the temperature, with backs arched and hands shielding faces.

"There's no way off here, Titus!" Bina yells.

"And we need The Spear," replies Titus.

"You need a miracle, Sleepwalkers," menaces the Darkangel. "And no miracle is coming."

Another wave of scorching air emanates from the apparition and Titus and Bina gasp as it jolts their bodies.

"We need to go," Titus manages to emit weakly, gulping. "We need to get off here now."

"The heat….it's making me faint…..it's….I can't take the heat, Titus."

Bina is almost on the ground.

"If we black out, Bina, then……."

"We'll…we'll… wake up in a….. in a soul-cage."

Titus realises something and turns sharply to Bina with a renewed sense of energy and purpose.

"There's a way, Bina."

"There is no way," bellows the Darkangel releasing another fiery surge.

Titus leans his face to Bina's right ear and whispers.

"Start thinking of the low plateau where the soul-cages are. Where the Keepers are. Start thinking, Bina. Think now and don't stop."

"What? But….what do you…?"

Bina stops and realises just what her friend is suggesting.

'But The Spear?"

"Don't worry, I've got it covered. Now step back."

Bina slowly backs away from the cedar stump where The Spear protrudes and from the Darkangel just beyond. But Titus stands firm.

"All the way back to the edge, Bina! All the way!" he shouts with a wave of his hand.

Titus closes his eyes, takes a deep breath and lunges towards The Spear. His hands grip its shaft and he twists it, pulling it out from its cedar wood bed but feeling the hellish intensity of the Darkangel's full force. The Spear pulls free with ease and Titus swings it around to aim its glassy point at the demon.

"Foolish child," it chides. "The Spear has no effect on us."

'Worth a try, hot stuff. But that wasn't my main plan."

Titus turns from the demon and runs, weapon in hand, towards Bina, who is now standing at the very edge of the sheer drop. He sprints with all the strength he can muster, channelling the frustration of fifteen inert, bed-ridden years into a mad sixty-foot dash.

"Get ready, Bina. Visualise!"

"But The Spear? We can't drift with The Spear," cries Bina.

"Don't need to!"

Still running hard, Titus lifts the shaft over his head, pulling back his arm, releasing The Spear through the air and out over the cliff's edge.

"Now, Bina! Now!"

Titus hurtles towards Bina, who extends both hands for Titus to take hold of; his weight and momentum taking them both flying out into the open Kerberos sky, away from the pursuing Darkangel.

For a second, they hurtle out and down in the rainy morning air, spinning with their hands clasped together. Between them the glow of light appears and then covers them and they are no longer falling.

Before their bodies vanish into the drift vortex, Bina glances up and sees the Darkangel peering down at them from the edge of the cliff. She sees his fiery visage dim and become just a dark shadow again.

They open their eyes as they both rematerialize with a wet thud on the lowest grassy plain at the base of the mountain. Shaking off the brief nausea caused by their unplanned drift, they examine their surroundings and enjoy the cool relief of the wind and rain after the heat of their encounter.

The Spear is upright in the muddy ground within the grasp of Titus. He reaches out, takes it, pulls it sharply to his side and fires a cocky grin towards Bina.

"And now, we rescue some Keepers."

He spins around confidently before feeling a second irresistible wave of post-drift queasiness and faints to the floor with a facedown splash.

The onslaught of demon fire-arrows from the sea forts is intense, raining down on the angel coracles below; the pilots paddling furiously to achieve shelter directly beneath the rectangular structures. The morning mist that protected them from initial detection is now dispersed and replaced by the stark, clear light of day, revealing the sight of a dozen angel bodies bobbing lifelessly on the surface of the water.

"We're being picked off!" cries Amanthragan, grunting with effort as he gives a final pull of his paddle to berth his coracle on the safe side of one of the sea fort's thick stone legs.

Above them a large iron bulkhead swings open with a rusty shriek and a snarl of flame as a Darkangel appears, bow in flaming hands.

Jibarial's reaction is beyond swift; his crossbow swings up from his side with one smooth arch and its bolt released. The Darkangel above them is pierced and is reduced to a harmless hail of sparks that disintegrate before they reach the sea.

"Keep aiming at the open bulkhead," he calls to Axyl and Portiel. Before he finishes the command, they are both releasing quick-fire bolt after bolt into the fort's interior. The repeated flash and fizz, followed by stillness gives them hope that the fort is now vacant of menace.

"We need to get up inside and secure it. We can protect the others better from up there," urges Jibarial, lowering his crossbow, pulling off his jacket and picking up a thick rope and grappling hook.

The crossbars that connect the four splayed stone legs of the fort are just twenty feet above and easy for Jibarial to target with the rope and hook.

Amanthragan steadies the coracle, both arms hugging the base of the fort's leg while Axel and Portiel train their bows on the opening above just in case not every demon has been extinguished.

As Jibarial shins athletically up the rope he hears more of the unmistakable sounds of arrows thudding into angel battledress and the splashes of bodies hitting the water. Not every coracle has made it to the relative safety of the forts' undersides and many remain open targets for Darkangels.

"Well, we always knew this was something of a suicide mission," sighs Portiel without taking her eye of her aerial target.

"Let us hope that the Sleepwalkers are able to get The Spear, or...." responds Axel.

"..or this is all for nothing," Portiel completes.

"Alright, Axyl, you next!" Jibarial shouts as he pulls himself up on the crossbeam. "Keep your bow trained on the opening, Portiel. Then your turn."

The whole crew are up on the crossbeam in minutes; Jibarial frees the rope and swings it upwards again, further this time, and in through the open bulkhead; the hook just getting enough purchase on the rusty shell.

"Let's take ownership of a Kerberos sea fort," offers Jibarial with just a tinge of doubt and a half-hearted test tug on the rope.

"After you, Jibarial," concedes Axyl with theatrical grace.

"Let's leave the fainting incident out of any post-mission debrief, eh, Bina?" Titus suggests as they gather themselves and begin their search for the soul-cages.

"Won't say a word," Bina responds unconvincingly.

From where they now stand, on the low plain that stretches up from the beach and at the base of the mountain, they can make out the shapes of the sea forts out at sea; and through the still-pounding rain can see the red deadly trails painted in the sky by the arrows of the defending demons.

"That doesn't look good, Titus."

"Yeah, not good at all."

"Let's go, come on."

It is hard to tear themselves away from the terrifying, mesmeric display.

"Axyl said they were just a few hundred yards beyond that large cave," Titus recalls from their earlier briefing aboard the paddle steamer. He points at a cavernous opening in the rock face that seems to spew an enormous white dune that rolls down to the beach.

They both run towards the sandy slope; Bina taking her turn to carry The Spear.

In the soft, deep sand their feet sink and legs tire but they force their way up towards the cave, panting and wheezing; numb now to the freezing, hard rain that has soaked them through.

At the mouth of the cave they cut right across the rocky terrain following the edge of the crag that now runs wet with a river of rainfall. After a few hundred yards of hopping and scrambling between the treacherous moraine, they round a fold in the rock and stop.

There are sixteen soul-cages in front of them, laid out in four rows of four; each one with around ten Keepers standing erect, heads bowed and contemplatively still. The cages are cubic and, through the heavy rain, the thick bars that make up each side and the ceiling seem to glisten and writhe, unlike any iron or steel bar.

Titus and Bina approach the cages tentatively, still catching their breath, and still trying to determine what they are now seeing before them. They remember what they had been told back on the paddle steamer about bars of living serpents that they had not fully comprehended what that meant.

Bina, still carrying The Spear, lowers it instinctively, pointing it forward as they edge closer to the neat matrix of cages.

"What are they?" she whispers out of one corner of her mouth.

"It's just like Raphael said. They're..." Titus is answering before he knows how to answer. So, he wipes the rain from his face and squints; then the answer comes. "They're.....snakes."

As soon as Titus says the word Bina realises it is true.

"It's *all* the bars, Titus. They are *all* snakes."

Each soul-cage is made up of a series of dark, immense pythons, fluidly moving and hissing in the form of a perfectly square jail. Where one snake's tail ends another snake's tongue-darting mouth begins, as they follow each other around to create a serpentine imprisonment that holds the Keepers in a state of unconsciousness. When each snake reaches the ground its body glides along it for just a short space before turning up at ninety degrees to form the next bar, flowing agilely upwards and over the top and down again to the ground on the opposite side; and then beginning again.

"There're no bars or lock or roof. *Just* snakes," notes Titus with sheer disbelief.

"How are we supposed to free them?"

"The Spear, remember. But we mustn't get too near. Raphael says that we can be trapped in there, too."

"And if we do?"

"We never get out. And we can't get back to our bodies."

"And our bodies die?"

Titus just nods.

"So, I just stab at the snakes with The Spear?" cries Bina.

She doesn't wait for an answer, just puts her hands as far down the weapon's shaft as possible to give herself the maximum reach towards the closest soul-cage. As the glass blade nears the writhing snakes that make the soul-cage's corner post, it takes on a cerulean, pulsing glow, causing the pythons to lose their smooth, gliding composure; hissing louder in a sickening reptilian chorus, fat bodies juddering and with their wide mouths convulsing.

Bina senses The Spears power and plunges it forward to the body of the nearest snake, turning her head and closing her eyes tightly for fear of its reaction.

The serpent hisses become shrill demonic screams and Bina begins to wave The Spear from side to side, striking as many of the creatures as possible. As the blade cuts into them, they flop with a loud splash into the wet ground and slither venomously away, still screeching in pain and disappearing into the rocks and crevices.

"The next one, Bina! Strike the next one!" Titus yells.

The first soul-cage is gone, leaving a group of ten Keepers, still standing shoulder to shoulder, faces tilted downwards to the ground and hands clasped low in front of them. Gradually they blink and, with a regal serenity, lift their heads and regard the scene around them.

Bina is frantically waving The Spear through the air at waist height, skipping sideways as she does, moving from soul-cage to soul-cage. The ground is heaving with the fat bodies of black snakes that dart noisily but harmlessly away from the flashing spearhead. Titus follows her, encouraging and pointing.

More Keepers awaken, but none move from their spot until there is a whole company of military angels in perfect columns and rows and every soul-cage is overcome.

A Keeper at the middle of the front row takes a precisely measured brisk step forward, gives a long, respectful bow towards Titus and Bina.

"Sleepwalkers," he acknowledges gently, thankfully.

He draws his long sword suddenly, thrusting it down into the ground and resting both hands on the end of its hilt.

"And now, we must get you both and The Spear off this island."

With the rattle of over one hundred and fifty swiftly unsheathed swords, the Keepers have their weapons, like their commander, point-down in the soaked earth.

"Well then," Titus attempts nonchalantly' "Let's get ourselves off Kerberos and..." He stops himself mid-flow and becomes concerned. "Er...how?!"

The lead angel steps forward again and places a firm, muscular hand on Titus's shoulder and signals out to sea with a curt nod.

"The battle has started. The enemy is engaged. We have boats, hidden. We leave now."

"Good plan. Good plan," affirms Titus as the angel marches in the direction of the cave with his troops behind him.

At the rear of the huge cave that the Sleepwalkers passed by earlier lie scores of stacked, upturned coracles and a pile of paddles.

"It is how we got here in the first place," explains the first angel.

"My name is Bina," says Bina, thinking it high time that things be made less formal. "And this is Titus."

"Hi," beams Titus with a little circular wave.

"I am Klune," says the angel, now with a smile. "Apologies, we have been trapped here for a long time. And we are grateful to you, we are, but our first priority is to escape before any Darkangels stop us. We do not know how many there are."

"Well, we met *one*," Bina answers.

"There will be many more."

"Define 'many'," challenges Titus.

"Many," he repeats plainly.

Klune turns to his men.

"Grab your vessels, Keepers. Let's go," he barks.

The dank, cavernous space echoes with the clattering sound of coracles and paddles knocking together as the Keepers, in well-drilled quartets, lift their long-stored boats above their heads, moving out of the cave and back into the open to stand at the top of the steep, wet dune.

"Coracles down!" shouts Klune through the rain.

With synchronised obedience, the Keepers lower the boats they are carrying onto the sandy, waterlogged surface, and, in their fours, clamber aboard the stationary vessels.

Titus and Bina are each pulled swiftly into separate coracles and placed securely between two rear Keepers. Each pilot thrusts his oar into the sand, heaving his coracle towards the lip of the dune.

Over three dozen coracles ride the river of rain that pours down the wide, mighty Kerberos sand dune to the flat beach below. The smooth, curved hulls of the willow boats zip rapidly on the quarter-mile flume. Keepers stay steely-eyed and front-focused in the disorienting mixture of spray and rain but both Sleepwalkers let out adrenalin-induced screeches and shrieks, trying to steady themselves against the bodies of their adjacent angels or by reaching for the edge of their boats. The velocity is intense, the sting of water on the face painful, and the swerving, jockeying motion of the coracles, as pilots use their paddles to manoeuvre out of each other's path, is nauseating.

For one instant, Titus's and Bina's coracles appear almost side by side before they are skilfully navigated apart to avoid collision. In the moment, Titus wants to give Bina a broad grin as if to say *isn't this exciting*, but his fear-rigid gawp will not yield and all he manages is a series of little punched exhalations that are half laughter, half panic. Bina would not have seen the look anyway; she has her eyes closed and her head low, wanting the ride to be over.

In less than thirty seconds, it is; the coracles coming to a scudding, spattering halt in a pool of water at the base of the vast dune and Keepers leap out together into the ankle-deep water to drag the boats on to the flat, firmer sand. They heave their coracles aloft again, fanning out and marching toward the lapping waves in preparation of launching out to sea.

The battle action of the sea fort raid is now slightly clearer; the dark silhouettes of the metal garrisons just visible in the gloom and the flaming trajectories of the Darkangel arrows illuminating the sky with a thousand red streaks. But there are other shapes in the half-light; just a hundred yards out to sea, in the shallow incoming tide, hover many dozens of indistinct dark ghostly forms, rolling slowly towards the gathered Keepers on the shore. Each shadowy figure's outline seems to fluctuate and alter as if there is no physical nature to it, just spectral inkblots absorbed into the surrounding atmosphere.

Half walking, half floating, the figures move closer and closer.

"*That* many," says Klune coolly to Titus, who stands by his side transfixed by the encroaching horde.

"OK," he replies weakly.

The Keepers gently lower their coracles to the sand and draw their swords in silence.

With a deep, explosive rush, the seaborne shadows erupt into flames; a hundred towering torches blocking the Keepers' way to the sea.

"You and you!" Klune points to two Keepers with his sword. "Take the Sleepwalkers. Get them out to sea."

Without hesitation, the two gather Titus and Bina, drawing them backwards through the ranks as the others make a V-shaped attacking formation and begin to charge the Darkangels.

On Kerberos's rain-lashed beach, it is good versus evil in hand-to-hand combat; angelic steel blades clashing and fizzing with fire-consumed maces.

Klune is at the sharp end of the formation, leading the line, his gyrating sword slashing at fire as the demons close in around the fanned-out Keepers.

"They're carving a way to the sea for us," cries Bina.

Their duo of guardians picks up a coracle and paddle and venture through the middle of the battle; as they do, the two banks of Keepers drive out wider to form a clear passage.

"When I say, push out to sea, paddle and do not look back," orders Klune over his shoulder as he continues to take on his Darkangel foe.

The coracle is lowered into the shallow, lapping water behind Klune and Titus, Bina and the two Keepers steady it, backs arched and ready to leap aboard.

Klune, sensing the moment, summons a wave of energy, releases a giant battle roar and plunges his sword into the Darkangel before him. The Darkangel's falling particle remains fizz into the sea and the path is clear.

"Now! Go now, children."

Three are aboard the coracle but Bina hesitates, looking imploringly to Klune.

"What about you, Klune? There are too many of them."

Klune smiles and lifts his sword to the sky, resting the hilt just before his nose in salute.

"You freed us from oblivion, young Sleepwalker. You freed us to do battle against evil. That is our mission. That is our goal. Thank you for that. Now go. We will fight to the last angel and stop them from following."

Bina makes to say something more, but Klune swings around, raises his sword and rushes towards another Darkangel. She tosses The Spear into the coracle and climbs inside, helped by one angel, while the other paddles them furiously out into deeper water.

Both Titus and Bina regard the frantic beach battle mournfully as they pull away; watching as angel after angel falls, overpowered by their enemy; the two angel protectors staring intently forward as if with no regard for what is behind them.

"They fall with honour, Sleepwalkers," says the paddler without even looking at them.

'And we will mourn them," says the other, similarly focused on some specific point on the horizon.

"We need to get you past these......"

"Sea forts. My idea," announces Bina. "Sorry," she adds.

"Sea forts. Very well."

Titus and Bina tear themselves from the battle they are leaving to consider the battle they are joining; adjusting their bodies in the coracle and giving the Keepers their full attention.

They all now see the other coracles taking desperate shelter beneath the metal structures; the many bodies floating on the surface of the water, arrows embedded and still smoking; beyond that, the vague but obvious shape of the paddle steamer, now with flames rising from several of its decks.

"They've got the boat," cries Titus.

"The boat?" inquires their pilot.

"That one was *my* idea," Titus says forlornly.

"Head for that fort," blurts Bina, pointing at a specific sea fort several hundred yards away.

"Why that one, Bina?" inquires Titus.

"It's...it's..."

Something is in her head; an erratic butterfly of a notion that she cannot grasp. She chases it, screwing up her eyes and blocking out the chaos around them. She finds it.

"It's Jibarial!"

"What?!" Titus is confused.

"In that fort. That one." She points again, this time leaning on the shoulder of the angel with the paddle and jabbing her finger repeatedly for clarity.

"Your Sleepwalker friend is sensitive to him," explains the other angel.

"Yeah, I'd noticed."

"Jibarial is a Sleepwalker angel. He can sense their presence. *Your* presence. Looks like Bina can sense his."

The coracle changes course and the pilot digs deeper with his paddle.

"I think, perhaps, Jibarial has captured that one."

"Yes, yes," agrees Bina. "That's right. He is in there."

Jibarial's empty coracle at the base of the fort becomes visible and confirms their deduction.

"He's there! Look!" bellows Titus.

Jibarial is inching out on one of the wire bridges that connect the chain of sea forts, firing his crossbow at the next structure; Axyl doing the same on the opposite side. Amanthragan and Portiel are both up on the roof providing covering fire over the top of their comrades and towards the neighbouring forts.

"If they can keep that up, we have a clear passage through and out to the main boat," grunts their paddler, giving it every ounce of his strength.

"What's left of it," adds Titus pessimistically.

"Did you have to imagine a *timber* one?" teases the other angel.

113

"Get down low! We are going to go through!"

They all crouch as low as they can in the coracle, navigating right beneath the captured fort, clipping the tied-up and empty coracle and out towards the sea beyond.

Only a few flaming arrows come near them; most Darkangels within range occupied by Jibarial and his crew's actions.

"Keep going, keep going," encourages Titus, excitedly patting the pilot on his shoulder.

There is a faint whistling sound behind them that grows louder into a whoosh and the angel that is crouched next to Titus and Bina throws himself on top of them, rocking the coracle so that water spills in on either side.

The pair can feel his dead weight on them, pressing their faces down into the seawater that now swills about; and they roll him away to see a still-burning arrow embedded between his shoulder blades.

Their pilot pauses for a moment, sighs a deep sigh and continues to paddle towards the paddle steamer; leaving Titus and Bina speechless and stunned, staring at the dead angel.

In a village harbour of white and black timber-framed structures, the paddle steamer lies anchored, now an inferno lighting up the darkening afternoon sky; the timber decks buckling, crackling and splintering as they are consumed. Battle weary Keepers silently clamber from coracles up onto the high stone harbour wall using fixed iron ladders; gathering together in groups, offering comforting hands on shoulders to one another.

Titus and Bina stand on the long, thin wall that juts out into the still harbour waters, regarding the burning boat, feeling its heat on their faces.

"I think I will be taking that spear now," says a soft voice behind them.

"Jibarial!" cries Bina, running to him and throwing her arms around his waist, pressing her head to his chest.

He awkwardly places his hand on her head, stroking her hair as if it is something he had never done before.

"So much fire." Bina says, and begins to sob.

"You made it, then," congratulates Titus.

"More importantly, *you* made it, Titus."

Raphael appears from behind Jibarial.

"We knew you would," he says. "You are Sleepwalkers after all. It is what you were created to do. You have retrieved The Spear."

Raphael gives Jibarial a faint look of fatherly disapproval, and he immediately lets go of Bina, taking an obedient step back. The archangel beckons the two children to him, cupping his broad hands around the backs of their necks. He smiles sincerely, staring deep into their eyes.

"We lost many today, young Sleepwalkers. Many Keepers. And yes, there was fire. Lots of fire. And there will be more. More fire to fight on more days like this. But right now, it is time for you to return. You have won us this small yet important victory and The Spear is in our hands now. But, as I said, you must leave us and rest. We will meet again all too soon."

Raphael gently brings their bowed foreheads together; Titus, Bina and the archangel standing on a high harbour wall in a strange coastal village in Somnambula; and suddenly they are back on *The Dreamweaver*, stirring from their sleep.

The SEVENTH Chapter of the Sixty-Fourth Book of Dreams:

Where heaven breaks in,
a shot rings out,
and a mystery deepens.

The unfamiliarity of a cool, salty breeze on his face awakens Titus with a jolt and makes him grip his throat in preparation of a gasping, coughing panic. His oxygen tent is wide open and he sees the silhouetted shape of Bina standing in his cabin doorway and then Murray, immediately to his side, pulling wide the clear plastic curtains. He looks imploringly at them both, head swivelling from one to the other in desperation.

"It's alright, Titus," calms Bina. "Murray says that it's ok."

"That's right, mate. You can get up. Come on, there's something I want you to see."

Murray extends his hand.

Titus goes to speak, assuming that he cannot, and that his rasping attempt at coherent words would convince Murray that his actions are killing him. But his words flow easily and comfortably.

"But...I can't....my illness....I mustn't be exposed..."

He trails off, confused by the freeness of his breathing, the lack of biting pain in his throat or the creeping, prickling tenderness of his skin.

Murray grabs him roughly and pulls him up.

"You're fine, Titus. It's Somnambula. When you've been there, that realm breaks in here with you. You were well there, and you'll be well here."

He pauses and then adds solemnly: "For a short while. A day, maybe two."

"Don't you see, Titus," enthuses Bina, "You can do things here you've never been able to do. Here on earth, not just in Somnambula."

116

A stunned Titus is led up onto the deck of *The Dreamweaver* where Lasaro, Marina, Marissa and Almas are waiting, smiling. They offer a ripple of applause and Murray points to the east and the large orange sun that is just half-risen on the Mediterranean horizon.

Titus closes his eyes and tilts his head backwards to feel the sun's first rays and taste the tangy air. Sensations that would have once brought him to a dangerous comatose state now bring him to a serene ecstasy.

"Now put on this," commands Lasaro, stepping forward and placing a red life jacket over his head and securing it with the speed and efficiency of a time-served sailor.

"Why, do I need this?"

"Because," explains the Spaniard, leading him gently to the edge of the deck, "you do not swim."

"No, I can't swim, so why..."

Lasaro pushes him over the edge and into the cool, still morning sea as the others cheer and laugh.

Titus flails wildly, fighting the sea around him in a hail of splashes and desperate, gulping cries for help. It takes nearly half a minute for his thrashing arms to slow and for the realisation that he is not drowning to dawn. His frantic shouts become nervous laughter, as he trusts his buoyancy aid and his hands begin to paddle the water gently.

"That. Was. Not. Cool," he manages between deep, settling breaths.

The crew of *The Dreamweaver* roar with laughter and applaud again.

"But...." Titus searches for more words. He cannot find one, so just lets out a long, shrill yelp of joy as he bobs in the dawn waters of St. Paul's Bay, Patmos.

"You guys coming in?" he calls up to the boat.

"You're kidding," calls back Murray. "Far too cold."

"We're not mad," adds Rina.

"Maybe later when it's warmer," says Rissa.

Lasaro lets out a hearty, seadog laugh.

"Ok, guys, maybe we should get him out now?" suggests Bina, the only one who seems vaguely concerned. "Guys? Anyone?"

"Oh, and that's not all, Titus," hollers Murray. "Hurry up and get out of there, we've got to go shopping. On the island. Chop, chop."

The market stalls of Skala are a riot of colour, sweet aromas and Greek chatter as Murray, Titus, Bina, Almas and the twins meander happily through the morning throng.

"Are you sure it's a good thing to bring the Sleepwalkers here, Murray," asks Rissa quietly, examining some local oranges.

"After what they've just been through, Rissa, they need a little 'normal'. Besides, we're safe here. No one knows we're here. We're as far from danger as we can be."

He winks a cheeky wink.

"I hate that wink," says Rina, helping her sister bag up a dozen of the plump fruit.

Murray casts a protective eye across the market to his Sleepwalkers. They are enjoying their shore leave, laughing, joking, pointing out curious items on the market stalls and trying to put the nightmarish incidents of their first Somnambulan incursion behind them. Bina holds onto Almas' hand, pausing at a stall of fresh nuts. She signals to the portly lady stall keeper that she would like to try some and receives a curt wave of the hand that she takes as a 'yes'. Bending down to Almas she gives him a handful of cashews.

"There, my little Almas. Such a far cry from our days of begging and stealing, eh?"

"Yes, these are good days," responds the boy, chewing joyously on the fresh, crunchy nuts.

"Good days," agrees Bina, pinching his stuffed cheeks.

"But not such good nights," Almas adds with sudden concern.

"Do you mean us?" asks Bina pointing at Titus and herself.

Almas ignores the question, continuing to chew energetically.

"Because we're fine, Almas. Titus and I are fine."

The sound of a bouzouki striking up a Greek tune and some accompanying rhythmic claps hits their ears. Almas is attracted to the tune and its beat and runs into the crowd to seek out the musicians.

"Almas!" chides Bina weakly, never wanting to raise her voice to the child that has been through so much; but the boy melts into the market melee.

"We better go and get him," Titus puffs, not used to having any familial responsibility.

On the edge of the market, sitting in an open-air café, Murray lifts a small glass of thick, resinous coffee to his lips.

"What a lovely scene," announces Santo from a seat just behind Murray.

"What is it about you and coffee shops?" says Murray with some frustration.

His angel friend pulls his chair up to Murray's table.

"What is it with *you* and coffee shops?" he fires back.

"Just enjoying some peace, Sanntu, while the others do a little exploring."

He nods towards Rissa and Rina, who are just yards away, buying fresh loaves and eggs.

"And the Sleepwalkers and child?"

"Safe. Just mingling. No one knows we're here, Sanntu."

"Yes, you should be safe here. You're always safe here."

"So, you're here to give me news?"

"Yes, news. They did well, Murray. You'd be proud of them. They got The Spear and escaped from the island of Kerberos. They are ingenious, Murray."

"Yeah, they're good kids. I knew they'd do well."

119

Murray does not sound convincing as he knocks back his coffee in one gulp.

"No, you didn't. You can never know."

"No, I didn't," he agrees.

"But, despite the success, there are ripples."

"There are always ripples, Sanntu. Always."

"Yes."

"What this time?"

"Have you not been listening to the news?"

"I didn't get chance. I was thinking about the boy. About Almas. And he was awake."

"Yes, the boy."

"Anyway, what's in the news? What's happened?"

"Your Sleepwalkers.."

"They're your Sleepwalkers, too."

"*Our* Sleepwalkers. They needed a lot of support in the battle. An army that could have been fighting elsewhere. It was the only way to get them on and off that island with the weapon that we so desperately need. But it was a sacrifice. A necessary one, but a sacrifice all the same. Some battles that were being fought in the heavenlies had to be abandoned for the protection of Titus and Bina, and that has had consequences here on earth. A wave of evil here on earth, Murray. You know how it works."

"Wars, famine, natural disasters?"

"Yes, there's been a lot. The news is bleak this morning."

"Be needing another coffee, then."

"And it will get worse. They're needed again, Murray. They must go back to Somnambula tonight."

"Tonight?! Not tonight, Sanntu, for pity's sake. Give them a rest. They went through hell, almost literally, last night. They're still reeling from the knowledge of who they are and we threw in them into the fray for the first time last night. And you want them to return straight away?"

"I don't want them to, Murray," Sanntu unfolds with emphasised calm. "I *need* them to. The world needs them to. Somnambula needs them to. You know I wouldn't ask them if it wasn't vital."

"You don't ask them at all, Sanntu. It's me that has to ask them."

Sanntu just nods.

"As for the child, well I have no news. To all intents and purposes, he is just a small, unfortunate stray who has dreams and is caught up in all of this by accident."

"You know there are no accidents, Sanntu."

"But there is free will, Murray."

"Bina chose to befriend him. He chose to join her. And now he is here. If he is someone, if he turns out to be someone....well, time will tell. Meantime, Murray, he is just a boy. Take care of him."

"I'll take care of him, Sanntu."

But Sanntu does not hear Murray's promise; he is gone and the Sentry is alone at his café table, nursing his empty coffee glass.

"And, he's gone again," he sings to himself.

Titus and Bina arrive breathless at Murray's table, pausing to look at each other nervously.

"Er, last time I saw you, there were three of you," he says with suspicion. "You know, a little boy in tow."

"He ran off, Murray," Bina confesses, unable to disguise her worry.

"He heard some music and legged it," Titus adds.

"I couldn't stop him," blurts Bina.

"Okay, okay, don't worry, it's a small island and he's just exploring, like young boys like to do. We'll find him. We need to spread out."

Getting to his feet sharply, Murray throws down a five-euro note on the table to cover his coffee and whistles loudly to the twins, who are bagging up their purchases at the nearby stall.

"We'll spread out and we'll find him. He'll be around here somewhere. There's nothing to worry about."

"Other than the fact that I'm feeling a little weak?" interjects Titus.

"Oh. The effects of Somnambula could be wearing off. We'll need to get you back to *The Dreamweaver* within the next few hours."

"What about Almas?" Bina implores.

"We've got to get Titus back to the boat and safely in his oxygen tent. And you must come, too, Bina. I have to keep you both together. Sleepwalkers have to be a pair. That's how it works."

"No! I can't leave Almas," cries Bina.

"It's fine, Bina. He'll be fine. I'll find him."

Lasaro arrives at the café carrying a heavy cardboard box.

"I have the components for the radio we needed," he announces cheerily, before regarding the group's collective look of anxiety.

"What have I missed now?"

No one has time to explain because a local child in short trousers and dirty t-shirt, runs up to Murray and plants a note on the table. He says nothing, just nods to the note, turns and runs away, his flip-flops echoing against the steep, narrow lane of stone houses that he makes his exit along.

Murray cautiously picks up the note. It is a white paper napkin and there is writing on one side in red ink; all in capital letters and obviously scrawled hurriedly. Murray reads it slowly.

We have your little Sleepwalker, Sentry. If you want him, come and get him. Alone. Cliffs of Neptune. Two o'clock. Brax.

There is a long silence as they take it all in. Bina is the first to speak.

"So...so, they think Almas is a Sleepwalker? And they have him? Who are they? Oh, poor little Almas. I should never have...."

"It's alright, Bina," asserts Murray, "I'll get him back. I know this Brax. It's time we sorted this once and for all."

122

Rissa is comforting Bina, who is now sobbing.

"It's not your fault, Bina," she says, pulling her onto her shoulder and stroking her head.

"How did they know we were here, Murray?" Marina asks.

"I have no idea. They shouldn't have done. There's no way the Night Reivers could have known."

"But they are here," Lasaro offers sternly.

"Yes, yes, somehow they knew we would come to Patmos and then to the market today here in Skala," Murray says slowly, mainly to himself, as he gives himself time to think through his options.

"OK," he barks, "Rissa, Rina, I need you two to get down to *The Sweet Dreams* at the jetty and get her fuelled up and ready to go. Go now. Go!"

The twins obey and are off at a sprint towards the port where they had left the small boat they had all come ashore in.

"Lasaro, you stay here with Bina and Titus. You'll be safe here in public together. Give the girls half an hour to get the tender refuelled then get down to the jetty and all of you to *The Dreamweaver*. You need to get Titus back into his cabin and safe."

"Aye, aye, captain," responds Lasaro.

"But I want to come with you to find Almas," pleads Bina.

"No, young lady," Lasaro says with his best paternal charm, "You stay with Lasaro. Murray will find your little friend. You can trust him."

Lasaro gives Murray a confident smile.

"It's ok, Bina. I'll do this. I'll see you all on *The Dreamweaver*. *With* Almas. I have an idea. *And* I have a friend. A friend who can help."

"Sanntu?" enquires Lasaro.

"No, not Sanntu. Someone more earthly and with a very particular skill."

Murray stuffs Brax's napkin note in his pocket and is gone.

Yanni sits on a rocky outcrop holding a cheap fishing rod. He chews on a short, fat cigar and his attention flits between his line that dangles in the sea and a large, old brown book that lays open by his side. He sports a fine, lustrous black moustache and has tightly cropped, spiky dark hair, topped with a tweed flat cap. Although a little rotund, leathery-skinned and in his late sixties, he has a vibrant, clear-eyed sun-kissed glow about him.

"Whoever you are, you should never interrupt a man as he fishes. *And* reads poetry," he says loudly in a velvety Greek accent, without even turning to the person he has detected behind him.

"Once a Sentry, always a Sentry, eh, Yanni?"

Murray steps closer so his shadow covers Yanni.

"And I see the same must be true for you," he says, still nonchalantly looking to his rod and line.

"But *you* really have retired."

"Until now, perhaps."

"Until now."

Yanni exhales a long weary breath, shakes his head and then gives a single, violently hearty laugh. Getting to his feet, he turns and nearly breaks Murray's back with a high-spirited bear hug.

"Good to see you, my dear old comrade."

"Good to see you, Yanni. It's been a while."

Yanni lets Murray go and they stand looking each other up and down, discovering what the years have done to them.

"You were easy to find, Yanni. I just described you at the bar in the market and they pointed me here."

"Yes, here is where you will find me most days. Just fishing, reading..."

"Forgetting."

"How can we forget? The things we know, Murray. They cannot be put away in some box to collect dust. They live with us forever."

Murray just tries to smile.

"I need your help, Yanni. You still shoot?"

"Shoot? Shoot what?"

"Night Reivers."

"Night Reivers? Here on my island?"

"Here on your island, Yanni. I'm sorry, I think I brought them here. And they have one of mine."

"A Sleepwalker?"

"No, not a Sleepwalker. A boy, a young innocent boy. But Brax must think he is a Sleepwalker."

"Brax? The Chief Night Reiver you've told me about? That Brax? You brought Brax here?"

Murray nods meekly.

'The Brax that...?"

"Yes."

"Then we must send Brax away."

Yanni tucks his book of poetry under his arm and reels in his fishing line. He slaps Murray confidently on the back.

"Shoot, you say? I might be an old man but I still have a keen eye. You question whether the Greek army's finest ever sniper can still shoot? Ha!"

"Is that a yes?" Murray responds suspiciously.

Yanni holds out a flat, palm-down hand in the air and scrutinizes it intently for several seconds. It shakes slightly.

"Should be fine," he concludes, neither convinced nor convincing.

Titus starts to feel a prickling irritation on his skin and a shortness of breath as Lasaro carefully herds him and Bina down between the last few houses before the tiny Skala harbour.

"Nearly there, hold on," Lasaro encourages, eyes scanning left and right for danger.

"Wait, I need to rest," splutters the boy.

"Come on, Titus, we need to get you to *The Dreamweaver*. You can do it," enthuses Bina.

Titus takes a brief moment, leans against the warm stone wall, pulls himself together and continues his brisk trot to the seafront.

They cross the open promenade, busy with tourists disembarking the ferries.

"This jetty, here, quick. My girls will have our tender ready."

Lasaro puts an arm around Titus's back, half supporting him, half ushering onwards.

"There, boy, you've made it."

Their feet make a hollow clatter on the wooden slats of the jetty, although Titus is now shuffling rather than running or walking, energy draining from him by the second.

Lasaro desperately inspects the length and sides of the jetty to locate *The Sweet Dreams* and his twin girls.

A deep, scratchy, snarling voice breaks his concentration.

"And here's the female Sleepwalker. And another male."

The towering, muscular figure wears a heavy, black leather waistcoat over his bare torso, leather pants and hefty black biker boots. His arms are a maze of sinister tattoos and a thick silver chain encircles his broad neck. It is the signature crimson beret, tilted to one side that Lasaro recognises most.

Spreading his arms out wide to prevent Titus and Bina moving forward, Lasaro lets out a whispered Spanish profanity.

"Who is *that*?" Titus wheezes.

"Night Reiver," hisses Lasaro.

"Have they not told you about *us*, boy?"

Bina steps forward confidently.

"Yes, we've been told about you. And you have my friend, you demonic thug."

"Ooh, a feisty one."

The Reiver's bassy voice mixes with a rumbling chuckle that seems to rattle the jetty planks.

"Yes, we have your little friend. And soon, your Sentry. But, more importantly I now have you."

He takes two slow, threatening steps closer to the trio, planting himself just a yard away. There is a sharp click as a long flick-knife blade shoots out from his right hand, glinting in the bright morning sunshine and causing them to blink and recoil.

"You can't just kill us here in public," presumes Titus shakily.

"He doesn't care, Titus," answers Lasaro through clenched teeth, "He is a demon-possessed assassin with no thought for himself. He'll murder us here in cold blood and broad daylight. Isn't that right, Reiver?"

Their assailant just laughs again.

"Oh, and while we're chatting, why don't you share your name with us, Reiver. Or shall we just call you Reiver? Mr Reiver?"

"My name?"

"Yes, you do have a name, don't you? It's always good to know who has killed you."

"My name is Terrell," he confesses, now amused.

"Terrell. Is that your real name, or do they give you a new demon name when they possess you? I'm just curious, Terrell?"

Lasaro is on a roll now, his tone becoming increasingly defiant and condescending. Titus and Bina exchange glances, confused and worried by their Spanish guardian's flippancy.

"It's just Terrell. But why should you care?"

Terrell raises his blade menacingly, toying with the sunlight's refraction on their faces.

"To be honest with you, Terrell, mi amigo, I could not care a....." He searches for the right word. "A fig? Is that right? I don't care a *fig*? The English language is so strange. I was merely making conversation in order to distract you from my beautiful eldest twin who is about to strike your head with a large and very heavy oar from behind."

Rissa does just that; swinging the oar she had procured from a nearby rowboat, and striking Terrell with its flat blade, full force on the back of his skull. The Reiver hits the wooden jetty with a resounding thud.

Marina, who is untying *The Sweet Dreams* from the jetty and preparing to fire up its outboard motor, clears her throat as an obvious cue to her father.

"Ah, yes, and while my equally beautiful and very, very slightly younger twin helps us make our getaway."

They carefully step over the lifeless Reiver and clamber aboard the tender as its motor is brought to life with a sharp pull of its cord.

"We should have....you know, finished him off," splutters Titus, looking back at the Reiver on the jetty as *The Sweet Dreams* skips across the harbour and out to *The Dreamweaver*."

"*They* are murderers, Titus. *We* are not," Lasaro shouts triumphantly over the engine's high-pitched whine.

"Good work, girls. I taught you well."

The twins smile proudly at each other.

"Now let's get you back to your cabin, Titus."

Just a mile south of Skala, the Cliffs of Neptune jut sharply up from the frothing, rock-strewn Aegean Sea. An oblong of dry, dusty terrain sits at its top, climbing slightly and stretching to a rugged, rocky outcrop that shields the road from the cliffs.

Brax stands brazenly with Almas, just feet from the edge of the Cliffs of Neptune. Murray, his hands raised high and behind his head as an overt show of meek surrender, steps out from the boulders, edging nearer to Brax. Brax pulls Almas closer, gripping him tightly around the neck with his right arm, whilst digging a pistol, held in his left hand, into the frightened boy's side.

"It's alright, Almas, stay calm," offers Murray, inching forward.

"Nice to see you again, Murray. How have you been since Venice?" rasps Brax.

"Oh, you know, plain sailing. Until now."

"Do you know how difficult it was getting away from the Italian police?"

"Er, *very*?"

"No, actually. It was easy, but then I'm talented that way."

"You say talented, I say unhinged."

"Well I have your male Sleepwalker now. What do you say about that?"

"I say that he isn't a Sleepwalker, and that you just have an innocent young boy there."

"That is exactly what I would expect you to say."

"It's true, Brax. His name is Almas. He means nothing to you."

"But clearly he means something to you."

Murray takes another step forward.

"No closer, Sentry!"

Brax raises the pistol in the air to show his intent.

"Now, Yanni, now," Murray whispers to himself, "Take the shot."

A gunshot rings out from the rocky outcrop and Brax grabs his left hand in pain as his pistol is propelled over the cliff.

"Ah ha!" cries Yanni, lying on his belly, hidden in the rocks above and reloading his rifle, "Question my shooting abilities, would you, Murray?"

"Again, Yanni! Hit him again!" cries Murray, now running towards Almas, who has wriggled free from Brax's grip. But Brax, ignoring his pained, bloody hand, lunges forward to tackle Almas round the legs.

Yanni releases a second shot, which whistles harmlessly into the earth just an inch from Brax's ear as he brings Almas down with a thud.

"Itsa ma bad!" comes the unorthodox Greek apology.

"Murray!" yells Almas in distress.

Brax scoops Almas up easily and shuffles quickly backwards to the very edge of the cliff, halting Murray in his tracks only feet away from him.

"Now Brax, come on. Let's sort this out," pleads Murray.

"Tell your sniper friend up there if he fires again I'm taking the boy over the edge."

"Okay, okay, just take it easy," he cautions, raising a flat-palmed hand in the air as a signal to Yanni to ceasefire.

"Done. Now let's talk."

"On second thoughts, I think I'll just jump anyway."

Brax tightens his grip on Almas and leans backwards, disappearing silently over the edge, taking the young boy with him.

"Nooooo!!!" Murray howls.

Edging to the sheer drop, Murray looks to the frothing sea and rocks more than fifty yards below. He searches for bodies anywhere in the tumult, but finds nothing. He sits down, legs dangling over the edge, head bowed and dejected until Yanni joins him.

"Maybe he swam to safety," he offers unconvincingly.

Murray shakes his head.

"I don't think anyone ever taught him. He was just a six-year-old stray."

"Come, my friend, I need to get you to your boat."

"He was a good drummer, Yanni."

"I'm sorry."

"I've lost another. What kind of Sentry am I, Yanni?"

"A good one, brother. But not perfect. There is no such thing. We are soldiers in a war. And wars have..."

Yanni pauses, realising the insensitivity of his thought process.

"Casualties?"

"Yes, people suffer. They will always suffer. But we know why we do this, Murray. It is for something bigger."

"You sound like, Sanntu."

"Because Sanntu is right. Now, let us go. You have Sleepwalkers to guard."

Murray stands wearily and the pair return to Skala.

Yanni's small yellow dinghy butts up against the hull of *The Dreamweaver* as the daylight is starting to fade and the pair wearily ascend the yacht's ladder.

Up on the deck, everyone is gathered, other than Titus, who lies safely in his oxygen tent; they each stare at Murray intently. He regards their faces in turn but finds no sign of anticipation or expectation. There is something different in their expressions. He sees amazement.

"Are you ready for this?" Lasaro asks.

The group part, revealing a seated figure, wrapped in a brown blanket. It is a teenage boy, around fourteen or fifteen years old, dark hair and wearing trousers that seem comically short. He is shivering and exhausted, but slowly looks up.

"Hello, Murray," he says.

Murray knows instantly that it is Almas; the same features, the same colouring but at least eight years older and with a deeper voice.

"It's true," says Bina, "It's my Almas. But how?"

"I've no idea," Murray declares, shaking his head in stunned awe. "I have no idea at all."

****

"Excuse me, Professor, I'm so sorry to interrupt..." said Simon after a single cursory knock on the door.

"Not now, Simon," Venetia Pipkin barked at her assistant.

"There's a young girl upstairs at the museum reception desk."

"A young girl? You've barged in on...."

She waved her arms frantically around at the Book of Dreams, at Aleck Branko, at herself and at the walls of her office, "....at this, because of a young girl?"

Aleck sat back, ignoring the Professor and Simon, quietly reeling from all that he had read in the book; his mind still not able to take it in, still refusing to believe that he was seated opposite a leading academic in one of the world's finest museums, reading from a previously indecipherable ancient manuscript, and that he was being immersed in a terrifying world of angels and devils.

"Well, it's *about* the book, Professor."

"What do you mean 'it's about the book'?"

"It's the same girl who handed it in in the first place. She's returned. She says she has a message."

Now Simon had Aleck's attention and he snapped out of his reverie.

"What?!" cried the Professor, standing to an abrupt attention.

Aleck: "You better lead on, Venetia."

"You know, I do like the way you say my first name," she said, a little too giddily, flinging back the door and pushing past Simon.

"This is Margot," the museum receptionist said to Professor Pipkin as she marched in her efficient public persona way to the front desk.

"Well, hello, Margot," she over enthused, revealing to Aleck that she clearly wasn't used to speaking with ten year olds.

Margot was in the navy blue and charcoal grey uniform of St. Catherine's Church of England Primary School, located just a few hundred yards away from the British Museum. She stood there in the cavernous, white Queen Elizabeth II Great Court, politely smiling.

"Hello," Margot replied with a compelling, sweet confidence.

Aleck stood a few yards behind the Professor, not wanting to crowd the little girl, but Margot leant over sideways to look beyond her and peak at him.

"Hello," she said again, identically to the first, but this time just to Aleck.

"Hi there."

Aleck produced a silly, childish wave.

"You're the American," said Margot.

"Er, I am."

"What do you mean *you're* the American, Margot," enquired Professor Pipkin, "Did you know that there would *be* an American?"

"Yes, the man told me."

"The man?" they said together.

"The same man who showed me the book."

"So, you were the one who brought the book here in the first place?" asked the Professor.

"Yes, that was me. And I saw the man again on the same bus and he just wanted to check that you got it ok. And that it was safe."

Margot screwed up her face, trying to remember another part of the message and then remembered.

"Oh, and that the American could read it okay."

Professor, slowly: "So, this man, Margot, he gave you the book on the bus?"

"Well, he didn't give it to me. It was on the seat next to him and he just smiled at me as he got up to get off at his stop and then he just nodded towards the book as he got off. I thought he was giving it to me but when I realised it was, like, really, really old and I couldn't read it, I thought I should bring it here. Well, Mrs Radcliffe, my form teacher, told me to, anyway."

"And you saw him again? When? Today?"

"Yes, this morning on my way to school again."

"And he spoke to you again?"

"Yes, he did. He asked me did I like the book and I said I thought it was very lovely but that Mrs Radcliffe had told me to take it to the museum. And he said that he thought that Mrs Radcliffe was very wise and clever."

"She is, Margot. Very," interjected Aleck, over the Professor's shoulder, which made Margot giggle.

"And?" encouraged the Professor.

"Ooh, and...."

Margot thinks hard again.

"Actually, no, I think that's it. That's all. He just wanted me to come in and check that you had the book and that the American..."

"Aleck," said Aleck, a bit miffed at being solely identified by his nationality.

"Well, he didn't say a name, so it might *not* be you."

"Yes, yes, yes," ushered the Professor impatiently, "So who was this man. Did *he* have a name?"

"No, he didn't say."

"What did he look like?"

"Sort of African, I think?"

"You mean black?"

"Yes, black. And wearing a nice suit."

"Nice, how?" pressed the Professor.

"Nice colour."

"Nice colour?"

"Yes, it was purple. All purple."

Aleck and Venetia just stared at each other, neither able to quite process the amount of questions, slow realisations and confusion that was flowing through their minds. Margot simply stood, looking from one to the other, hoping one of them would say something. She wasn't sure if they were pleased with her or somehow angry with her and she wished Mrs Radcliffe were there to help her and tell her what to do and say to these strange museum people. And then she remembered something else that the purple-suited man had told her.

"Oh, oh yes, just before he got off the bus again, he said goodbye and that he had to leave because he needed to go and help his friend on a boat because - and this is the funny bit - the *boy* had suddenly *grown up*. I didn't know what he meant. Is it a riddle?"

"It's happening now! Aleck, it's happening now!"

Venetia grabbed Aleck at both shoulders.

"What do you mean, Venetia?"

"The book. You're reading it but it's happening as you read it. It's in real time. Even the way it's written. It's in the present continuous tense. Like it's not an account of something that once *happened*, but somethings that are now *happening*."

"You're kidding?"

"No, don't you see, it's whatshisname, in the purple suit and he is going to see thingamajig on the boat about the strange boy. He told Margot here that he was going just this morning, and we've only just read about it."

The Professor got slightly hysterical and Margot got slightly scared and started to back away.

"Okay, I'm going back to school now. Lunch break is nearly over and Mrs Radcliffe will want to know I'm safely back."

"Yes, goodbye, child."

The Professor waved dismissively, without taking her eyes off Aleck.

"We're going to have to carry on reading the book, Aleck. Right now. We must carry on. Judging by the pages you've read we must be more than halfway through. We must crack on, eh? And you know what this means, Aleck? Do you?"

Aleck just stood in stunned silence, trying to take in the events of the day that had started so innocently with a nice cup of tea in a quaint English café and then had quickly escalated to a real-time story of demons and angels and Sleepwalkers and Sentries, and of Night Reivers and a Hell Diamond and.....Well, he didn't know what the other 'and' was, but he was certain there was one. Maybe lots of them.

"What it *means*?" repeated the Professor impatiently.

"Er, not sure," is all he finally managed.

"We're going to need tea. Lots of tea. And sandwiches. And cake. Cake, Aleck! Simon! Where's Simon?"

Three and a half minutes later they were back in Professor Venetia Pipkin's basement office and Aleck began to read aloud, from where he left off, from the Sixty-Fourth Book of Dreams……

The EIGHTH Chapter of the Sixty-Fourth Book of Dreams:

Where a city is in ruins,
a trap is set,
and a choice is made.

"If I didn't have to send you back so soon, I wouldn't," Murray confesses to his Sleepwalkers, as he prepares them for another night-time incursion into Somnambula.

"I feel I should stay with Almas," Bina says sadly.

"I know, I know. But I'll be here. I'll look after him. Whatever is happening with Almas, I'll try and get to the bottom of it. But you have a bigger task."

"It'll be ok, Bina," reassures Titus from within his plastic encasement.

He holds up the palm of one hand to touch the plastic sheeting. Bina reaches out with hers to connect with it briefly
and lies down on her makeshift bed.

"Anyway," blusters Murray, thinking of some way to change the subject and distract Bina, "this room is in desperate need of a tidy. I think I'll give it a good going over while you both sleep. It looks like a bombsite."

He starts to pick up t-shirts that Titus had tried on earlier and then left draped over chairs and strewn across the floor.

"Hardly a bombsite," Titus says meekly.

"Maybe not. But I'll blitz it later."

Murray stops, cradling the discarded clothing that he has gathered, takes a deep breath and closes his eyes.

"Time to sleep," he sighs.

Bina, reluctantly: "Time to sleep.

Titus: "Time to kick demonic..."

"Sleep," interrupts Murray sternly.

He clears his throat and begins.

137

"Turn off this world,"

You're no longer on *The Dreamweaver*.

You're entering sleep.

Not dreaming.

Not dreaming.

Not dreaming.

Your thoughts are real.

The place you see is real.

The things you feel are real.

Somnambula waits.

The heavenlies wait.

The Keepers of truth and peace wait.

Go higher.

Much higher.

Break through.

Keep ascending.

Keep ascending.

Keep ascending.

Through clouds.

Through visions.

Through chaos.

To a higher level.

It's Somnambula.

It's Somnambula...."

Jibarial crouches, kneeling on one knee; a hand flat to the earth and the other clutching the hilt of his downward-pointing sword. With eyes closed he is sensing something; discerning a distant promise. His brown leather battle uniform is scuffed and torn and his boots now encased with hardened mud and dust. The ground around him is a small circular field of rough earth with exposed, broken pipes and twisted cables protruding upwards like freakish

138

mechanical plants. Several yards away, the earth rises up steeply all around him.

A faint smile crosses his face and he tilts his head, tuning his senses, focusing on the dim signal.

The very air in front of Jibarial begins to fold in on itself, warping and diffusing the light, blending the reality of his Somnambulan view with echoes of the human world, until the figures of two people begin to materialize.

He gets to his feet and sheaths his sword.

The figures solidify and Titus and Bina stand before Jibarial.

"Well at least you are getting a little more accurate with your arrivals," he greets them warmly.

"Well, you know, Jib," retorts Titus with exaggerated nonchalance.

"Know what?"

Titus did not expect a response.

"Just, *you know*, you know."

"How have you been, Jibarial?" Bina asks.

"I have been fine, Bina. It is good to see you."

"Good to see me, too?" asks Titus matter-of-factly.

"Good to see you, too, Titus."

"You look tired and…and…. like you've been through a lot," Bina offers with deep concern.

Jibarial regards his appearance as if noticing for the first time how battle weary he looks.

"Yes, we have been through much here since you escaped from Kerberos with The Spear."

Titus is curious.

"How long has it been?"

"In your terms, several weeks."

"But we've only been away for a day."

"You should know that time here moves very differently to time on earth, Titus. The single nights that your bodies sleep can represent many, many

Somnambulan days. So, the days that you spend away in your earthly waking state can be just as long. And the battle rages here still. Not just when you are here."

"So, what's been happening?" Bina ventures.

"The power that we seek, the Hell Diamond, is close. We have been fighting our way towards it. We have fought many skirmishes and lost many comrades but we are close now."

Jibarial begins to scrutinise the landscape around him, narrowing his eyes, breathing in the atmosphere.

"And here we are," he says suspiciously, as if not at all sure of where they are.

"Which is?" enquires Bina.

Jibarial pauses, thinking.

"A crater," he finally announces.

"Helpful," Titus responds sarcastically.

"A *bomb* crater."

"Equally helpful."

The angel walks to the steep crater sides and clambers up and out, scrambling through concrete block debris and clay. Titus and Bina exchange a quick glance and then follow.

They emerge from the bowl-shaped void in the ground to swathes of cold mist clouds carried on a stiff breeze. In between each dense grey veil there is a momentary glimpse of a wide river and dark shapes beyond.

"So *that* is where we are," Jibarial says with surprise and just a little delight. "I have never been *there* before. Thank you. Whichever one of you did this."

"Where?" Bina implores.

The breeze stiffens and allows a longer view of the world they now stand in. All around them is the destruction and decay of war; a patchwork of crumbling buildings, still-burning fires, plumes of dark smoke stretching up to the sky. The river in front of them runs black and a few hundred yards across it, on its bank, rises a jagged, broken cityscape.

"London," announces Jibarial.

"London in the Blitz. A bombsite," mumbles Titus.

"Your doing?" Jibarial enquires.

"Yes, I think that would be me," he answers slowly, remembering Murray's final words before they went to sleep aboard *The Dreamweaver*.

"As soon as he mentioned bombsites and blitzing, I couldn't help think about a documentary I'd watched in my hospital room in Gibraltar. It was about the bombings in London during the Second World War. I was fascinated by it. And it just all came back into my head. Just in my head. And now it's here. I've created an entire city."

"You're only just beginning to know what you can do, Titus. All this is still unintentional. But soon you will be able to do this consciously."

"But it's not quite the same. I know that it's London. It *feels* like London but it doesn't quite look right," Titus says, confused.

"But isn't that always the nature of dreams," explains Jibarial enigmatically. "Things are always strangely, eerily distorted. Somnambula is often a dark mirror for your thoughts and memories. Most of what you humans dream is a tentative foray into this heavenly realm. What you dream is very real, but is blurred, enhanced and exaggerated by the forces at war here."

The three stand on the south bank of the heavenly River Thames, staring at a grotesquely skewed vision of a war-torn London. To the west, the Elizabeth Tower that normally houses the great bell of Big Ben has its top severed just above its clock face, smoke rising from within like a giant, fat chimney. Below it, the Palace of Westminster is just a delicate façade, fire raging through each of its many windows. Westminster Bridge is no longer a bridge, just two stubby, smouldering protrusions on either side of the river, an abandoned 1940s red double-decker parked right up to the edge of the north side. In the east, the dome of St. Paul's Cathedral is intact, but bizarrely oversized and there are numerous structural interlopers added to this spectral version of England's capital; dark, twisted towers and jagged, crenulated fortresses that jostle for position amongst the Victorian buildings.

"Come, time to go," announces Jibarial sharply.

The Sleepwalkers find it hard to tear themselves away from the scene.

"We have to regroup with the others. I came to find you and now we must go a little way south and see Raphael. We have much to do. Our mission lies across the river, somewhere in the heart of that city."

"But how do you know?" Titus asks. "Before I dreamed this city up, presumably it didn't exist here? How do you know that our mission is here?"

"Just because there is now a city here does not mean that there was nothing here before, Titus. This heavenly realm is a constantly shifting landscape but relatively formless. We fight over territory for the sake of your world. You sometimes just bring form where there is no form. There is always north and south, east and west, up and down. And we know that the enemy and his growing power are towards the north. Thanks to you, Titus, we now just have a burning city to fight our way through. A burning city, no doubt full of marauding fiery demons."

Jibarial turns abruptly and marches off.

"It's my pleasure," shouts Titus after him.

Rissa and Rina play cards in the galley with the now teenage Almas, both trying their best to behave normally but slightly overdoing the laughter. Almas plays along in stunned, silence.

Murray finishes off making two mugs of coffee and gives an approving nod at the three of them as he shuffles past and up onto the top deck, where Yanni sits by the wheel.

"I need you to do me a favour, Yanni," he says, handing his Greek friend a steaming mug.

"Yes, I think you probably do. These are strange times, my friend. Maybe time for me to come out of retirement. Temporarily, of course."

He takes a sip from his mug.

"Not bad, Murray. Not bad coffee."

"I need you to go somewhere for me, Yanni."

"Don't tell me. It will be time consuming. It will be treacherous. It will be potentially life threatening."

"Nah, just a little trip. Easy-peasy."

"Oh, that's a shame."

They both laugh.

"I don't know what's going on here, Yanni. I'm not even sure Sanntu knows, either. So, it's something big and very, very strange. But one thing's for sure, Brax and his Night Reivers have been just one small step behind us this whole journey. They knew we were on Patmos. How?"

"Come on, Murray, the Reivers know where the *thin* places are. They know where The Sleepwalkers dream best. There are not that many of them in this world."

"But there are enough, Yanni. Too many to guess. Too many for them to just happen to be here at Patmos the day after we arrive."

"They could just be lucky. After all, there are Night Reivers all over the world. Maybe they just mobilised them all to cover as many locations as possible?"

"And Brax, of all people, struck that lucky? No, I don't buy that, Yanni. I don't buy it at all. There's something else going on and I need to prove it. That's why I need you to go back home and pack a bag."

"And what of you, Murray?"

"We need to move again. Change locations. If Almas can survive that fall into the sea, then so can Brax and he isn't going to rest until he has stopped Titus and Bina."

"When? Now?"

"Yes, as soon as you've left, we need to sail again. Get to another safe thin place. They're safely in Somnambula now, so it's okay, they've made the jump."

"But the sailing, Murray, you know it could upset them. What if you encounter rough seas? You know that could affect them as they sleep."

Murray sighs deeply, nodding.

"Yes, Yanni, I know the rules. I know it's not the done thing to move them while they sleep, but I can't risk staying in these waters, not with Brax and who knows how many other Reivers on the island. We couldn't withstand an all-out attack if they chose to come at us here. No, we have to sail. Somewhere that's just a couple of days away."

"Israel?"

"Yes, Israel. It should be a straight run from here."

"And you need me take a plane and fly ahead of you?"

"Sort of, but not quite. Now finish your coffee."

"What kind of *power* is the Hell Diamond?" Titus demands of Raphael as they sit around a charred kitchen table in the remains of a Georgian style townhouse.

"A growing one. One that, if unchecked, will wreak some kind of unspeakable havoc on earth, the like of which we haven't known for generations."

Raphael pauses, looks up to the sky, through the gaping hole where there should be a roof, and continues.

"Maybe ever."

"But you don't know exactly what it is? What it looks like?" Bina asks gently.

"No, but *you* will, when you find it. And what we do know is that The Spear will destroy it. No Keeper can remain in the presence of this power for long, unlike you Sleepwalkers. It will not harm you in the same way. All you need to do is get close enough to plunge The Spear's tip into it and destroy it."

Bina senses a weariness in the archangel's voice and in his slow methodical movements. The angel commander who seemed both ancient yet ageless when she first met him, now, to her, appears troubled.

"Do *you* think we can do this, Raphael?" she ventures.

"I do," he responds with no hesitation. "But I have lost many Keepers and this battle has been going on so very long. Besides, you will have the very best I have to protect you. Jibarial, Axyl, Amanthragan and Portiel will be with you. It will be better to move through the city as a small unit. You can travel quicker and go less noticed by Darkangel forces. I will send other units into the city, too, to distract the enemy. You just have to follow the glow that we see in the night sky and find its source."

Raphael pats the table, pushes back his chair and stands.

"Oh, and there is someone else here that would like to speak with you, Sleepwalkers," he says with a beckoning hand towards the kitchen doorway.

An angel who they have not seen before enters. He is slimmer, not as muscular as other Keepers they have encountered, with tightly cropped dark hair, beard and moustache, and wearing a lighter, less rugged version of the warrior uniform.

"Hello, Titus, Bina," he says with a familial warmth.

"Hello," they reply together.

"I have a message from a friend."

"A friend of ours? Or a friend of yours?" solicits Bina.

"Both. I have a message from Murray."

Sanntu steps closer to the Sleepwalkers.

"It is nice of you to see me. Literally. Normally you cannot. I have been in your presence before on earth but there you would never be aware of me. But here, you are."

"You know Murray?" Titus asks.

"Yes, I am Sanntu. I am, what you might call, a go-between, between here and your earth. I am a messenger angel, not a warrior like many others here. I liaise with the Sentry and keep them in touch with things here. I have known Murray ever since he first became a Sentry."

Bina is confused.

"And you have a message from him?"

"Feels like we've only just left him," adds Titus.

"Yes, I know," agrees the Sanntu, "but he and the crew have had to leave. In a hurry. And he wants you to know that things might get a little rough."

"Rough?" snorts Titus. "We're two teenagers fighting fiery demons in a weird nightmare. Rough?!"

"No, rough, as in literally rough. *The Dreamweaver* is at sea and the journey could get...."

Sanntu searches for the most effective yet least offensive word.

"Choppy."

"How does that affect us here, though?" asks Bina.

"If your sleeping bodies are experiencing discomfort or nausea then your brain will tell your spirit. And you will feel perhaps a little disoriented here. It is hard to say just how it will affect you as everyone is different. Not everyone gets seasick. But Murray just wanted you to know, so you did not get too worried. Now I must leave you."

Sanntu performs a polite head bow, first to Bina and then for Titus.

"Bina, Titus, it is a pleasure to meet you both."

He spins and exits the room.

"Great," pronounces Titus disdainfully. "Maybe our new secret weapon is that we can puke over Darkangels. Perhaps that would put them out."

Bina manages to smile and tut at the same time.

Jibarial enters, throwing down The Spear onto the kitchen table with a thud that makes them both jump.

"It is nearly time, Sleepwalkers. Darkness falls soon and we will cross the river at the place you know as Tower Bridge. Angel sorties have seen the pulsing glow of the power source to the west. We can work our way there on foot."

Titus counters his nervousness with a typical jibe.

"Don't suppose we could get one of those open-topped tourist bus tours, Jib? I've never been to London and it'd be nice to take in the sights. Maybe get a bit of commentary."

"He can't help it, Jibarial," says Bina apologetically.

"I understand."

"Or at very least, a gift shop. Take back a souvenir."

"I will see what I can do," Jibarial offers, going with the joke. "But now it really is time. The others are waiting."

The twin edifices of Tower Bridge rise up before them in the darkness; river sentinels that separate them from the northern bank of the Thames. The bascule bridge on the road ahead is not fully closed, locked in a position that creates a two-yard gap; the black river raging below.

There is a confidence to the way that Jibarial, Axyl, Amanthragan and Portiel strut, hands on sheathed sword hilts, up the inclined path towards the centre of the bridge. They have large, slender black graphite crossbows slung over their shoulders and each wear two crossed magazine belts of short, snub-nosed bolts. Titus and Bina shuffle more nervously behind them; Titus using The Spear as a large walking staff, glass blade pointed skyward.

"We will have to make the…you know….." Axyl points out, making a running and jumping action with his fingers, as they reach the central gap.

"Jump?" suggests Titus with trepidation.

"Jump, yes," agrees Axyl.

"We can make that," Bina encourages Titus.

"Or we could drift?" suggests Titus.

"No!" barks Jibarial. "You need to conserve your strength. We do it the easy way."

"Easy?" mocks Titus rather too loudly.

Axyl shushes him, patting his finger to his lips.

"Come on," Bina enthuses rushing towards the gap, leaping it cleanly and effortlessly. She spins around and beckons the others across.

Jibarial grins approvingly at Bina's display of bravado.

"She's good, huh?" Titus says knowingly, giving Jibarial a sly dig in his side with his elbow.

"She is."

Axyl, Amanthragan and Portiel all stand at the very edge of the bridge opening and, with the minimum of effort, hop over to the other side to join Bina. Jibarial waits with Titus and nods to him that it is his turn.

"Me, then? Okeydokey. Fine. No problem. No problemo," he procrastinates.

He hands Jibarial The Spear, walks to the edge and looks down towards the river. In the darkness, he cannot see it, but he hears its waters raging and racing below. He strolls slowly back towards the south bank and after twenty paces turns and takes a deep breath.

"Time may run very differently here in Somnambula, Titus, but we are still on the clock," chides Jibarial.

"Funny," replies Titus, unamused.

"You can do this, Titus. Here, in Somnambula, you can do this. Forget what you couldn't do on earth. Here, you can run and jump and..."

Titus explodes into a sprint before Jibarial can finish. He feels the chill evening air strike the back of his throat as he gulps in large breaths. The sensation thrills him as he nears his take-off point, but the roar of the Thames below unnerves him and he slows his pace, wanting to stop and try again, but he realises it is too late. His leap is half-hearted and his arms flail about him as he flies between the two bridge sections, across the void. His midriff thuds into the end section of the north half of the drawbridge, his hands instinctively searching for some kind of grip on the road surface above. In a moment of terror, he imagines his body dropping into the unseen river and being swept miles away in its fierce, turbulent current. Instead, he feels a jolting pain at his left wrist. Amanthragan kneels at the edge of the bridge, gripping Titus's arm and hauls him effortlessly up onto the road.

"Close," says the rescuer.

"Close to death or close to making it?" responds Titus shakily.

"Both."

Jibarial lands silently and places a hand on Titus shoulder.

"Do not doubt what you can do, Sleepwalker. You are capable of so much once you learn your identity here in this place."

"I just...I didn't..." Titus flounders. "I'm just a sick, crippled kid."

"That is not how we angels see you."

Jibarial delivers The Spear back into Titus's hands.

Axyl points to the north bank of the Thames and encourages Titus: "Let us keep...."

"Moving?" interrupts Titus.

"I was going to say *marching*," Axyl responds, indignant but unconvincing.

The Dreamweaver scuds southeast, away from Patmos, across the midnight Mediterranean waters. Lasaro and his daughters work wordlessly together on the floodlit deck, bringing the sleek yacht to its full speed. Murray looks in on the sleeping Titus and Bina, steadying himself in the doorway from the buffeting movement of the boat. He frowns as if to question his own actions and shakes his head. He wishes he just had his Sleepwalkers to worry about, but things are now far more complicated. He is running from Night Reivers, heading out into open sea in the pitch black, and he is confused by the supernatural growth of Almas and what that means. The voice behind him plucks him sharply from his concerns.

"We are sailing again?"

It is the voice of Almas, but with less of its previous, staccato broken English accent. It is now clearer, more developed, and more confident; yet still him. Murray closes the cabin door defensively and turns to the boy.

"I wanted to speak to you, Almas. Let's go and sit down."

"Why are we sailing, Murray?"

"The kitchen. Let's sit."

Murray brushes past Almas and goes to the small galley kitchen, where he pats a cushioned bench, encouraging him to sit. Almas obliges and Murray sits across from him, placing both arms on the table, interlocking the fingers of his hands.

"Almas," his tone is imploring but concerned. "Do you know what is happening here?"

"We are sailing again," he returns, as if it is obvious what is happening.

"I mean, what is happening with *you*."

"No."

"No? That's it? You fall off a cliff..."

"Pushed."

"Yes, pushed. Into rough sea and you miraculously survive, swim back to us...."

"Yes, I never learned to swim. That *is* strange."

Murray cannot disguise his growing frustration.

"Almas, that is *not* the strange part."

"Strange to me."

"Almas!"

Murray takes a breath and corrects his tone, trying again more patiently.

"Almas, you were a small child, just six years old, no more. And now, now, you must be fourteen. You've grown eight years in a few hours. Do you know how or why? Do you know who you really are?"

Almas looks thoughtful for the first time.

"What are your dreams like, Almas? What did you dream last night?"

"I dreamed of the bad men."

"The bad men? The ones who took you? The Night Reivers?"

"Yes, the Night Reivers. The one called Brax."

"Had you seen him before? In your dreams?"

Almas scowls as if thinking this hard pains him.

"Yes, I think I have."

"Listen to me, Almas, listen very carefully, it is very important that you think hard and work out why you are here and who you are. You are important

Almas. There is something very important about you. You are safe here with us, but you need to help us. Who are you, Almas? Who are you?"

"I am Almas."

Murray rubs his face with the palms of both hands, tired and discouraged.

"I have to go. I have to help the others crew this boat. We have a long journey. We'll talk again. But you should rest now."

Murray stands wearily.

"Where are we going?" asks Almas sweetly.

"We're going to Israel, Almas. A place called Haifa. It's a good place to dock and we should be safe there from the bad men. They won't know we've gone there."

"Haifa? Israel?" Almas plays with the sound of the words.

"Yes, that's right, Almas. Now, get some sleep. I need to help on deck."

On the deck of *The Dreamweaver*, Lasaro is at the large wheel, a small silver hipflask in one hand that he takes a sharp swig from. Murray appears beside him and takes the wheel, easing him out of the way.

"Go and help the girls, Lasaro. I've got this."

"Ay', Captain. You plotted a course?"

"Yep."

"Jaffa?" he whispers.

Murray nods knowingly to his old friend.

'Tell only your girls, Lasaro. Just you, Rissa and Rina."

"Ay', Captain."

Lasaro melts into the darkness towards the bow.

"Chicas, tu papi esta viniendo," he sings ahead of himself cheerfully.

The four Keepers and two Sleepwalkers step carefully through the war-torn debris of Somnambulan east London; Jibarial at the head, with Axyl and Amanthragan on each flank, crossbows raised and eyes scouring the scene

151

for trouble. Portiel keeps an eye at the rear, walking backwards and only glancing over her shoulder occasionally to check she is still keeping pace with the others. Titus and Bina are at the centre of the group; Titus still protecting The Spear and Bina delivering regular nods and encouragement that Titus responds to with his own simple, curt bow of the head.

"Saint Paul's Cathedral," he whispers, jabbing The Spear towards the looming dome just visible against the midnight blue-black sky. "Well, obviously not *the* cathedral, just my own bizarre sleeping projection of it, based on a television documentary I once saw. But it'll do."

Everywhere for hundreds of yards around the cathedral is laid to waste - a field of smouldering building rubble, fenced by the carcasses of bombed-out grand office buildings, warehouses and stores with their charred skeletal timber frameworks exposed. In between the more recognisable architecture, other demonic structures protrude skyward. Like evil weeds trying to choke a glorious garden, they spiral irregularly upwards and outwards in the gaps between rows of shops, homes and office blocks, warping and polluting the London skyline.

"A single Nazi bomb got through and destroyed the altar inside," Titus adds, suddenly remembering a detail from the blitz documentary. "But amazingly, the dome and the main structure survived all the bombing intact."

"Let's hope that's a good omen," Bina murmurs back.

Jibarial stops and turns back to the group.

"We head that way," he says, thrusting his crossbow westwards towards an opening between two large, crumbling buildings. "That road should lead us all the way across the city and take us to the Hell Diamond. Keep your eyes open."

"Or we could just take the Tube," Titus offers, dryly.

They continue to pick their way across the field of fragmented city aware of a faint cold, stinging on their faces. Jibarial is the first to look up and see the fat snowflakes filling the sky. Within seconds, their boots are crunching and squeaking in a fast-laid blanket of snow; their vision impaired by the dense flurry and the whole city takes on an eerie, dampened, deadened silence.

"Darkangels," announces Portiel without emotion.

"They love to play with the weather," agrees Amanthragan.

"Yeah, they created quite a downpour on Kerberos," says Bina.

"I suppose they never do hot sunshine?" shivers Titus.

Just yards from the beginning of a visible main thoroughfare, where the remains of two six-storey buildings nearly stand, a series of small bonfires still burn amongst the city ruins. The fires reach knee-high and the group feel the warmth of the flames as they approach them. Only Bina notices that the twelve neat, near-identical fires seem to make a perfect circle which they are all now right in the centre of; the Keepers being more preoccupied with their own specific viewpoint: front, rear, left and right. She elbows Titus and draws a circle with her finger in the air. Titus takes a second to decode the action and then, with eyes widening in alarm, slowly spins around to take in each of the fires.

"Jib."

He says it so timidly that he is not heard.

Bina reaches out to touch Jibarial on the shoulder. The angel spins and gives a questioning look.

"The fires," Bina says simply and softly.

It is all that Jibarial needs.

"Weapons ready," he commands as they all stop and draw closer together.

Through the blizzard, in the harsh cold, the twelve small blitz-damage fires begin to grow, altering shape from their nebulous flickering forms into human-like figures. As if emerging from invisible cellars below, a dozen Darkangels rise up to trap them.

The four Keepers instinctively pull together tighter to protect Titus and Bina and shield them as fully as possible from their enemy, each raising their crossbows to shoulder level and taking aim.

"Protect the Sleepwalkers and The Spear at all costs!" cries Jibarial.

The blazing torch figures rip through the snow-filled air towards their prey, scorching a black trail on the earth below them and emitting a shrill battle cry.

Four of the screaming demons are dispatched instantly with the bolts fired from the crossbows of Jibarial, Axyl, Amanthragan and Portiel; their flames dispersing and dissolving into the snowy air and the dark shapes within fizzling into grey ash that is blown away on the night wind.

The remaining eight Darkangels advance, giving the Keepers no time to reload their bows, just draw their large swords.

"You need to get to the safety of that building ahead," shouts Jibarial over his shoulder to Titus and Bina.

"We will make a way for you," adds Axyl.

The Keepers are swinging and slashing their broadswords at air in front of them, making the demons recoil.

The Sleepwalkers look to the building that Jibarial refers to. It is fifty yards away; one of the least blitz-damaged buildings on the road into the west of the city and it stands alone amidst the rubble.

"I don't think I can make it," Titus offers up nervously.

"You can make it," Jibarial affirms. "You have to believe that you are stronger than you know, here. Remember that."

In between each rhythmic swing of their swords the demons flare up and flick their tongues of fires. Each hot shard shrieks towards the faces of the Keepers as they form a protective group around Titus and Bina.

"When I say, you run. Run with all your Somnambulan strength," shouts Jibarial, protecting his face from the heat with his left forearm.

"We will focus on these four," shouts Portiel, pointing her sword towards the four Darkangels that stand closest to the beginning of the road where the appointed sanctuary lies.

"And we will force them back," adds Amanthragan.

"When the way opens up...." Axyl yells.

"Run!" Jibarial finishes.

Axyl, Amanthragan and Portiel move tighter together and begin to jab and swing more furiously at the demons on the west side of the surrounding group. Jibarial stays on the eastern side, widening the arc of his broadsword assaults, taking on four demons by himself.

Titus and Bina see a gap between the circle of Darkangels open up to reveal the road ahead and the blackened revolving doors of what looks like a grand department store. Bina grabs Titus's hand and takes The Spear from him.

"Time I carried that. Now you focus on running. Let's go. Now."

Titus takes a deep breath, closing his eyes as he does, as if about to dive into water. Bina tugs on him and they begin to sprint out of from the centre of their protectors and into the open London night.

"Run, Sleepwalkers, run!" roars Jibarial, his voice echoing off the shattered walls of the broken buildings.

They feel the sharp, painful stab of cold air digging into the back of their throats as they sprint for the cover of the Victorian store, moving as fast as they can over the slippery snow-caked rough ground. Although Bina is a few yards ahead, Titus is hitting his stride and growing confident in the strength of his legs.

"Don't look back, Sleepwalkers. Keep running," comes the booming voice of Jibarial behind them.

Halfway across the open ground, nearing their destination, Bina notices more fires either side of them, in the windows of the buildings that line the road. It is just the briefest of glimpses through the heavy snowfall and she does not allow it to slow her down.

"Nearly there, Titus," she manages through gasps for breath. But there is no answer from Titus or even the sound of his footsteps or panting behind her. Bina stops abruptly and turns. She can make out the slumped figure of Titus on the ground and, behind him, can see the eight remaining Darkangels swarming around Jibarial, Axyl, Amanthragan and Portiel; their blades flashing in the fierce fiery glow of the demonic dance.

"I....I....I.....feel.....sick," she hears Titus croak.

He is on his hands and knees convulsing and gagging.

'Just get up, Titus, we're there. We're nearly there. Get up!"

Titus tries to push himself upright, his hands deep in the thickening snow but his elbows buckle, planting his face into the cold with a crunch.

"Just feel nauseous," he says weakly to himself. He remembers what Sanntu had warned them of about *The Dreamweaver* being out in open water.

"Seasick," is all he can manage to cry out to Bina, as he lifts his face just enough to momentarily glimpse her.

Bina can only look on as the two fiery shapes she had seen in the windows of the nearby roadside buildings dart from their cover, one from the left, and the other from the right. Now in their full Darkangel form they fly with a snarling rush of blistering air towards Titus, picking up his limp body and carrying him, with his legs trailing through the snow, at speed through the night. It is all done in a second. One moment Titus is there in front of Bina, lying on the ground, and then the next he is gone; even the tracks his drooping feet had made in the snow are almost instantly covered by the night blizzard.

It takes Bina several seconds to realise what has happened, and a further few to understand there is nothing she can do. She turns in the direction of the old department store and jogs towards it, dazed, dejected and dumbfounded. The store's revolving doors still work but complain with a loud creak as she pushes them. Inside she collapses onto the marble floor. Around her, charred mannequins stand guarding the gloomy store, and shattered glass display cabinets spew their silk scarf, leather glove and perfume bottle contents. Instinctively she takes cover behind a sales counter and sinks down out of sight, sobbing and shaking.

The large, ornate store clock that hangs over the counter is no longer telling the time; it is transfixed at nine thirty-four; its second hand frozen at the quarter-past mark, and so Bina has no idea how long she has been slumped there when she hears the revolving doors creak into reluctant life again followed by echoing footsteps on the hard floor. She slows her breathing and sinks lower.

"Bina!"

It is Jibarial.

Bina leaps to her feet and runs to the angel, who stands with his three compatriots at in the middle of the store. She throws her arms around him and begins to cry again, this time openly and deeply, tears flowing.

"They took him. They took him and there was nothing I could do."

"I know, I know, Bina," comforts Jibarial, patting her tenderly on the back as she hugs him.

"We will find him, Bina," reassures Axyl.

"No harm will come to him," Portiel offers.

"No Sleepwalker will be harmed here, not while we still stand," Amanthragan delivers with menace, gripping the hilt of his sword for effect.

"Where have they taken him?" Bina says, trying to slow her sobbing and wiping her eyes with her sleeve and pulling back awkwardly from her embrace.

"We don't know, Bina, but we will track him. We will find him," answers Jibarial.

"And how did you escape those.....those..."

"Darkangels," says Axyl.

"We despatched several more but then once they had Titus the others just fled. That must have been their main goal. They did not need to keep fighting us, so they ran," explains Jibarial.

"They probably went wherever they took Titus," adds Amanthragan.

"Do not worry, young Bina," Portiel says, "they cannot kill him."

Jibarial flashes a disapproving glance at Portiel.

"Well, they can't," she pleads in response.

Bina looks nervously from Jibarial to Portiel and back again.

"Well, what *can* they do to him?"

The NINTH Chapter of the Sixty-Fourth Book of Dreams:

Where a demon mocks,
ravens scream,
and a friend reaches out.

Titus does not open his eyes for fear of what he will see, but he feels the faint undulations of something slimy moving beneath his prostrate body and hears a chorus of discordant hisses. An odour begins to fill his nostrils; a sulphurous, hot stench that causes his breathing to shorten. He only remembers falling in the snow, queasy and disoriented, and then the rush of hot, hot air that enveloped him. There is a dim recollection of Bina gesticulating ahead of him in the blizzard; urging him on, but then just blackness as his body became weightless. He shivers off the hazy memory and puts his mind to work on the here and now. Trying to stand, eyes still shut, he feels the ground moving; knees bent and arms outstretched for balance, he shakes and falls and the hissing volumes increases momentarily as he does. It is all it takes for Titus to now know where he is. At the very moment, he realises he is trapped inside a soul-cage, he hears a clear, deep baritone voice. The voice seems to come from all around; a three-hundred-and-sixty-degree projection that Titus not only hears, but feels with every bone and muscle in his body. With every syllable the voice conveys there seems to be an accompanying rush of wind.

"There will be several questions running through your human mind at this moment, Sleepwalker."

Titus finally, slowly opens his eyes.

Dawn is breaking over the Somnambulan London, bathing everything in a rich, sharp orange that reflects harshly off the limestone walls of the large tower that Titus's snake prison is suspended from. Through the writhing tightly spaced bars below him he sees the source of the smell; a broiling moat of red angry lava.

The Norman keep that he hangs from is square and wide, with four larger towers, one at each corner. There is a thick iron pole that protrudes from the pale stone outer wall, over and around which the snakes of his soul-cage slither, keeping it suspended over the open space.

"Firstly, you are wondering where you are."

There is no sign of the speaker, just the all-encompassing sound of his voice.

"Actually," Titus attempts shakily, in an effort to convince himself that he is not as scared as he is, "my *first* question is: where have you hidden the surround-sound speakers? I mean, it's got to be hard getting planning permission for that in an historic place like this."

There is an explosion of flames right in front of Titus on the top of the keep and the now familiar figure of a Darkangel; but this one is much larger, his flames redder and more vicious and the noise from his blazing form louder. It stands just feet away from the gently swinging soul-cage, looking out from the turreted ramparts directly at Titus.

This close, Titus can see the figure within the flames; the blackened, leathery human-like giant engulfed in fire but never consumed by it. It seems to revel in the heat, taking its energy and pleasure from every flicker and curl; breathing in its intensity. It speaks again, but this time the voice is direct and clearly sourced, each word hitting Titus with a hot blast that makes him recoil.

"You are in the place you might know as the Tower of London," it expels with a luscious roar and completely ignoring Titus's impertinence.

"Appropriate really. Your earth history shows this to be a place of imprisonment for many centuries. And your next question, I think, must be..."

"Where's the gift shop? I mean, it's the Tower of London. Got to get a memento."

Despite his attempts at flippancy, Titus's voice is tremulous with deep fear.

"Can anyone save me?" spits the demon.

"Tea towel, mug, little stationery gift pack."

"The answer is no, they cannot."

"T-shirt then?"

"None of your Keeper friends can save you now from the soul-cage. You will remain here, separated from your mortal bones. Without your spirit your body will die, wither. For some it is weeks, for others months. But die you will. And your spirit will remain here, trapped in an eternal sleeping state, imprisoned by my serpent friends."

As he says this there is a cacophony of ecstatic hissing from the snakes.

"Soon you will begin to succumb to the hypnotic powers of the serpents. A day or two, perhaps. And then, nothing. A comatose state, forever. Unable to move or react. Lost in your own useless, helpless thoughts for eternity."

"So that's a definite no on the gift shop, then?"

"Maybe you have another question?"

The demon leans ominously closer to Titus, tilting his head questioningly, almost imploringly.

Titus stops himself from letting loose with more sarcasm and allows dread to take control as he stares deeper into the featureless face of the creature. At this moment, he is uncomfortably aware that it is simply the adrenalin surging through his body that is causing his mind to pump out glib remarks like machine-gun fire; and, with that realisation, and with the realistic assessment of his dire circumstances, he falls back against the snake bars of his imprisonment, quivering.

"Who….who *are* you?" he asks after a pause.

There is a single, abrupt, guttural laugh and a violent snarl of flames being doused as the demon's fiery corona vanishes, leaving just the physical form beneath. Without his flames the demon is a muscular, towering figure of yellowy-brown, his skin cracked and broken all over. His face is just two dark hooded round eyes and two irregular holes where a nose should be. He rubs his chest with his vast hands as if the sensation of feeling his skin is not a regular one, and then smiles, his wide mouth almost reaching to the very edges of his broad face.

"I am Shadowmaster," he declares with unsuppressed joy.

"Sh....Sh...Shad...," attempts Titus, trying to stand.

Shadowmaster momentarily emits another sudden burst of bodily flames and the force of the hot blast pushes Titus to the floor of the far side of the soul-cage.

"You came here to destroy my Hell Diamond with The Spear," the demon challenges, his flames diminished again.

"Hell Diamond? I don't.....know.... No, not me."

"But you will not stop it. You cannot stop it. Nothing can stop it. It will continue to grow and when it has reached its full power, the final battle will begin for this heavenly realm and your earth. The Darkangels will triumph and all hope will be lost. Fire will reign and darkness will prevail."

Titus cannot help himself.

"You do realise that last sentence doesn't make sense?" he manages to chide, his voice still trembling.

"Even if your female friend reaches the Hell Diamond, she and your Keeper friends cannot destroy it."

"But we have The Spear. That can destroy the Hell Diamond."

Another sharp laugh from Shadowmaster.

"Yes, The Spear," Shadowmaster says slowly. "The only way to break the power of my Hell Diamond."

"You know you're doing the usual baddie thing, don't you? Revealing the story."

"Am I? Revealing the story? Well, most of it. There's still something I am not telling you. There is still a....."

Shadowmaster pauses, thinking of the perfect word.

"...twist," he announces with demonic glee.

"Twist? What twist?"

"It would hardly be a twist if I revealed it, would it? Now it is time for me to leave and head across this strange city to see how my Hell Diamond is growing. Soon you will be asleep and soon after that, you will be dead. On earth, that is. Here it will be more like a living hell. Call it the best of both after worlds. But I will not leave you alone. This Tower of London is famed for its ravens. Legend has it that six ravens must guard the tower at all times or the monarchy will fall. So, their wings are clipped so that they cannot fly. I will use them to guard you. Farewell, Sleepwalker."

Shadowmaster's blazing halo erupts again and he sweeps swiftly away, disappearing into one of the corner towers.

There is the sound of flapping wings and a waft of cool morning air as six huge ravens land on the tower's edge. Each bird is six feet tall from claw to head, and they perch with perfect equidistance staring out towards the river with glowing blood-red eyes that pierce the jet-black of their bodies.

The snakes hiss louder again and the ravens respond with devilish avian shrieks, one at a time as if counting off their arrival and making their presence known.

The panic that rises in Titus as his eyes flit from hideous serpents to devilish birds, tussles with a feeling of irrepressible drowsiness as the soporific effect of the soul-cage begins to take its toll.

"You're burning the street,
You're burning the ghetto,
With anxiety, with anxiety,
Babylon's burning,
Babylon's burning…"

Almas loudly sings along to the song playing on the old Sony Walkman portable cassette player that Murray had given him. With headphones clamped around his ears he is oblivious to the volume of his exuberant accompaniment

He sits on the deck, bathing in the morning sunshine as *The Dreamweaver* ploughs through the open sea.

Murray appears from the galley kitchen with a worried frown. He sees Almas.

"Don't break that," he enunciates with exaggerated mouth movements for Almas to lip-read. "It's practically an antique."

"I like this song," yells Almas. "The Ruts. I didn't like it much when I was younger. But now I love it."

"You mean when you were young just two days ago?" Murray mutters quietly, more for the ears of Lasaro, who is at the wheel.

"We're making good progress, Captain," reports the Spaniard. "We should be at..."

Lasaro pauses, glancing toward Almas.

"...our *destination* in another twenty-four hours." he completes.

"Good. That's good, Lasaro. I'll check in with Yanni when we arrive."

"And, how are *they*? Still sleeping?"

"Yes, still sleeping. That's the second night in a row. There must be something wrong. It's not unheard of, but it's still not good. There's only so long their bodies here can stay strong without food or water. Maybe something has happened to one of them".

"I don't know, my friend. I don't know much of the spiritual things. I stick to the nautical. It's all a deep mystery to me."

Murray laughs, although not enough to dispel the concern that is etched on his face.

"This is what I do, Lasaro. What I've always done. And it's all a deep mystery to me, too. I just know that in order for them to return here properly they both must be together. They must have been separated."

Almas continues to listen to Murray's old cassette tape, drumming on his thighs to the music, bobbing his head and joining in with the occasional lyric.

"And we still don't know why Almas is here and what is happening to him," Murray says conspiratorially out of the corner of his mouth, followed by a broad approving smile to Almas.

"*Another* deep mystery," sighs Lasaro, his eyes never leaving their fix on the horizon.

"It must be some element of Somnambula that is breaking in here on earth, via Titus or Bina, or both. Some element of their rules of time. I've never seen it before, but..."

Murray trails off, not quite knowing what he is saying or what he means.

"Anyway," he says more cheerily, trying to change the subject, "where are the girls?"

"Ah, they are sleeping, too. They had a long night navigating us through the storm. They worked hard. I am letting them rest."

"Oh, good. Good man," Murray says slapping his friend on the back. "And you must rest, too, now. Go on, go below and grab a few hours. I've got this."

Murray takes the wheel and Lasaro disappears below deck without a word. He begins to whistle a tune – 'Babylon's Burning' by The Ruts.

The paper airplane that floats onto Titus's chest goes initially unnoticed. His breathing is shallow and slow and he lies on his back succumbing to the soft rhythmic movement of the snakes, his eyes flickering.

As if sensing something untoward, one of the monstrous ravens lets out a harsh squawk, which the other five immediately mimic. Their heads bob and swivel erratically, looking for the source of their concern.

Titus stirs slightly at the sound of his bird sentinels and rubs his eyes in an attempt to wipe away the sleepiness he is feeling. As he does, his hand brushes the paper plane. Without looking, he fumbles at the item with the fingers of both hands until he understands precisely what it is. He sits up, still fighting the fatigue and unfolds the paper, looking all around him through the bars of the soul-cage, searching for whoever could have flown it to him. He sees no one; just the ravens on the ramparts of the keep, which have now settled down and resume their still, silent watch.

Titus looks at the unfolded sheet of paper. It is tourist map of 1940s London. Wiping his eyes again, he regards the map more closely. There are photographs of key attractions with a short, explanatory paragraph of copy with each one; Trafalgar Square with Nelson's Column, the Prince Albert Memorial off Hyde Park, the Houses of Parliament, Westminster Abbey and a shot of Buckingham Palace taken from the Mall. This last picture is circled with red ink; not a neatly designed and printed circle, but one that is drawn on roughly by hand. Underneath it is an arrow, drawn in the same red ink, pointing to the Mall just a few hundred yards in front of the palace. By the arrow is a red-ink message:

Think of this place now. I'm coming. Bina.

Titus's reads and re-reads the message, his foggy mind unable to make sense of it.

"Think of it? Think of it? Why, Bina? Why?" he mutters. Then he says it all again louder. This disturbs the ravens and they begin with a disgruntled cooing that builds quickly to shriller cries. The birdcall crescendo pierces the London morning and brings Titus to his senses.

"Of course!" he cries and he stands precariously to his feet, steadying himself by leaning as gently as he can on the disgusting, wet bodies of the snakes as they form the vertical bars of his prison.

Titus scours the whole scene for signs of a rescue. He sees the river beyond the walls of the Tower of London, and Tower Bridge rising from it, where he made his ill-fated leap. He looks below to see the steaming, spitting pool of lava and up to the fidgeting, flapping ravens on the wall. But he sees no sign of Bina or any Keeper; he just hears a long, faint whistle followed by a sharp crack of masonry. A heavy bolt thuds into the keep wall just several feet above the soul-cage, and just inches below where the now-shrieking ravens hop up and down, wings outstretched. Attached to the bolt is a cord that stretches towards the river and out of sight.

"Surely not!" shouts Titus in the direction of where the rope line points.

The line begins to bounce and shake and gives off a buzzing noise as the ravens become airborne and surround the soul-cage in a flurry of black hellish feathers.

Bina becomes visible as she clears the Tower of London's outer wall, travelling at speed as she grips the metallic trolley that rolls across the top of the rope stretching from the tallest part of Tower Bridge's north tower to the bolt on the keep wall. The makeshift zip wire is being pecked by three of the frantic birds while another pulls at the bolt in the wall; the remaining two hover menacingly above the soul-cage offering loud encouragement to their friends.

As Bina hurtles through the air and down the inclined line, her legs tucked up tightly to her body, she screams out to Titus.

"The picture! Focus, Titus, focus!"

Titus looks down at the image of The Mall and scrunches up his eyes picturing the scene in his still-lethargic mind.

The two ravens above the soul-cage wing their way with murderous squawking intent along the zip-wire to the fast-approaching human. Bina sees them hurtling toward her and instinctively tries to make herself smaller as she hangs from the wheeled trolley apparatus.

"Now, Axyl. Anytime," she mumbles to herself.

There is the whistle of another flying bolt as Axyl lets loose from his crossbow from his position at the top of the bridge tower, and one of the raven screeches with pain, its outstretched right wing punctured by the bolt, causing it to circle helplessly to the ground. The other raven responds ferociously trying to peck at Bina but unable to quite keep up with her speed.

Axyl releases a second bolt, narrowly missing the attacking bird.

"The Mall, The Mall, The Mall," Bina mumbles over and over, trying desperately not to allow the fact she is tearing through the air, one hundred and fifty feet above the ground, on a zip wire and being pecked at by a giant demonic raven, to break her concentration.

"The Mall, the Mall, the Mall," repeats Titus breathlessly as the dozen squirming serpents that encage him become more agitated and their geometric choreography less predictable.

"The Mall."

"The Mall."

Four ravens, increasingly enraged, continue to pull and peck at the bolt anchored in the wall and the rope line attached to it; the other changes tack and flies above Bina, keeping pace with her movement, its claws extended and picking at her hands, trying to loosen her grip on the short handles of the trolley.

"The Mall."

"The Mall."

"The Mall."

"The Mall."

Titus opens his eyes wide to see Bina careering towards the keep wall, realising her trajectory will take her just a few yards above him. He takes a deep breath and thrusts his arm between the snake bars, his hand splayed as wide as it can go. The snakes around his arm begin to bend and writhe to crush it and force it back.

The solo raven gets a lock over Bina's knuckles and she screams in pain, releasing her grip completely and falling away from the trolley and zip wire. Momentum continues her flight forward but gravity forces her lower, towards the soul-cage and Titus's free hand.

"The Mall," she screams.

"The Mall," Titus screams back.

Freefalling, Bina reaches out with her right arm, her finger ends ju
connecting with Titus's. The snakes unite in a deafening, dissonant, sizzlir
song of defeat and ravens flap and screech indignantly as the trolley strikes th
wall with a loud clack, and both their prisoner and prey disappear complete
from The Tower of London in a single spherical flash of imploding light.

Up high on the north tower of Tower Bridge, Axyl lowers his crossbo
and nods approvingly at what he has just witnessed from his upper windo
vantage point. He unties the zip wire rope from its anchor point around th
central window frame strut and lets it fall to the ground.

"Well I never thought *that* plan would work," he admits to himself an
starts to whistle a merry tune as he sets off down the tower stairs.

"I knew it would work," Jibarial announces joyfully to Amanthraga
and Portiel as they wait on their haunches in the undergrowth of parkland t
the side of the road.

Amanthragan and Portiel jump from their hiding place and rush out t
the middle of The Mall where Titus and Bina lie dazed and still glowing whit
from their drift out of The Tower of London. Without a word spoken, the tw
Keepers gather the Sleepwalkers, helping them to their stumbling feet, whils
spinning their heads continually in search of danger, and pulling them to th
cover of the park.

"Good work, both of you. No Sleepwalker has ever drifted successfull
from a soul-cage before," congratulates Jibarial.

"Yay," manages Titus with a half-hearted punch to the air and lyin
exhausted on his back.

Bina is just wide-eyed and still, sitting with her legs outstretched o
the grass and not quite able to take in the last few minutes of her life.

"You were very brave, Bina," says Jibarial.

Bina just stares impassively back at Jibarial.

"We spent several days tracking you," Amanthragan tells Titus. "It wa
Axyl that spotted you in the soul-cage from his bridge lookout and Jibarial'

idea to send Bina in on the wire so that you could both touch and drift out of danger."

"A few days longer and we would have lost you," adds Portiel.

Sitting up, Titus reaches out to Bina and rests his hand on her shoulder.

"Thank you, Bina. What you did was incredible."

"You would have done the same, Titus, if the roles had been reversed," reassures Jibarial realising that Bina is still shell-shocked.

"You know, I'm not sure I would, Jib. You saw me at the bridge when I couldn't jump. And then when I collapsed in the snow."

"You could not help that, Titus," responds Jibarial with a stern tone. "That was due to what was happening on earth affecting your body. As for the bridge, you just doubted yourself. And you needn't."

"But I'm still weak, Jib. I'm still weak here."

"You are as weak as you think you are. But you are a Sleepwalker. Your potential is almost limitless here and you just have to begin to believe that. When you do...."

Jibarial lets the sentence hang in the air to make his point.

"Where are we?" says Bina suddenly.

"The Mall, Bina, remember?" encourages Titus. "We drifted here. The Mall. From the picture. The one you flew in to me as a paper plane. And by the way, that was an amazing shot, getting that paper plane in through the bars of the soul-cage like that."

"Twenty-two," Bina responds.

"Twenty-two what?"

"That was the number of paper planes it took," laughs Portiel. "The other twenty-one landed in the lava pit below."

"I think you would say they crashed and burned," Jibarial deadpans.

"Was that a joke, Jib? Whoa, an angel just made a joke," announces Titus.

"The Mall?" says Bina as if now the word is vaguely familiar. "Yes, this is where we had to come. It's where the Hell Diamond is."

"The Hell Diamond? It's right here? Shadowmaster made out we didn't stand a chance," laughs Titus defiantly.

"Shadowmaster?" blurts Jibarial with concern. "You have seen him?"

The Keepers exchange worried looks, brows furrowed.

"Yes, he was there when I was in the soul-cage," explains Titus.

"You met Shadowmaster?" Amanthragan asks, almost impressed.

"And he spoke of the Hell Diamond?" adds Jibarial.

"Yes, and yes. He knows we were trying to destroy it with The Spear."

"Shadowmaster," says Jibarial, chewing the word slowly and quietly to himself.

"He must be scared if he spoke to you of The Spear, Titus," explains Portiel.

"He didn't seem very scared," responds Titus.

"We are nearing the culmination of eons," Jibarial muses philosophically, gazing into the middle distance. "The Hell Diamond has been a legend, a myth, for a long time. It is meant to signal the final escalation of the Battle of the Ages. A power so lethal, so wicked....."

"What?" implores Titus. "So wicked, what? Let's start getting a little specific about this thing."

"We do not really know," says Portiel softly.

"But we have found it now," Jibarial ruminates. "The growth of the Hell Diamond will not continue."

"But where exactly?" enquires Titus, looking around at the surrounding parkland.

"Just along The Mall," Bina says, pointing in a general westerly direction.

"Er...I'm no Londoner, but I've watched a lot of royal events on TV and isn't the thing that's in that direction along The Mall...."

"Buckingham Palace," reveals Bina.

"You're telling me that the Hell Diamond is in Buckingham Palace?"

The Keepers all nod.

"Well," says Titus with a world-weary groan, "that'll be another tourist attraction ticked off the list."

"And we haven't got long," says Bina, now collecting herself. "The power is almost fully grown. After the Darkangels took you, Amanthragan and Portiel managed to get through the city, following the glow and traced it here. I stayed with Jibarial and Axyl to free you and Portiel sent word back to us so that we could both drift here. Once the plan was set for me to zip-wire into the Tower of London, Jibarial headed here so that we could all meet up together and plan our attack."

"And I have brought The Spear," Jibarial announces, picking the weapon up from the leaf-strewn park ground.

"It was my idea to send the paper plane," Bina says proudly. "I saw a little tourist kiosk that had been destroyed and there were London maps everywhere. And then we came here so we can meet up with Raphael and the Keeper army, over the road there. It's their make-shift war room."

Bina points across to the opposite side of the Mall and to some steep steps that lead to an imposing large white building with Doric columns either side of broad red doors. But Titus does not look; he gets to his feet and wrestles with some of the parkland undergrowth to try and force a view of the Mall. Along the famous dead-straight, tree-lined boulevard, he can make out the unmistakable royal palace and the golden figure of the Victoria Memorial glinting in the sunshine just before it. But what draws him in more is the large, pulsing arc of cold blue light that sits over the palace building and surrounding courtyards. The very sight of it seems to emanate a freezing radiance that makes him physically shiver.

"That's the Hell Diamond?" he says, letting go of the foliage and slumping back to the damp ground.

"That is the Hell Diamond," affirms Jibarial.

"First mentioned way back in the Fifth Book of Dreams," says Portiel thoughtfully.

"The Book of Dreams?" Bina asks.

Jibarial looks uneasy but realises that it is time to explain.

"Yes, the account and testimony of the Battle of the Ages and the Sleepwalkers. Welcome to the story."

"The finale," adds Amanthragan.

"Finale? Book of Dreams? Come on, guys, we need more than that," Titus demands.

"Everything that happens here with us and with whichever Sleepwalkers are chosen for that time, is written in an angelic language," explains Jibarial.

"Right now, you are in the Sixty-Sixth Book of Dreams," asserts Amanthragan.

"Sixty-Third," corrects Portiel with a cough.

"*No*, it is sixty-six, Portiel," Amanthragan argues.

"Sixty-Fourth," contends Jibarial. "Everything is written as it happens and to those who are reading it, to those who are gifted to be able to read it....."

****

"... it is happening at that very moment," said Aleck, quoting Jibarial's words from the Sixty-Fourth Book of Dreams. He stopped reading and lunged back into his chair. Professor Pipkin did exactly the opposite and leant forward with excitement.

"So, it *is* all happening now, Aleck. I was right. The words you are reading, it is like they are alive, leaping from the page the very moment they are happening. And if that is true then these poor children, these Sleepwalkers, they are here in London right now," she expelled in one breathless flow.

"Not *here*, Venetia. Not this London. They're in some alternative dream-state, heavenly London. But it is happening now. But somewhere in the Mediterranean there is a boat sailing towards the coast of Israel right now. That's real."

They sat in silence for minutes, both unable to take in the temporal impossibility of what they were being presented with.

"But what if I was to stop reading?"

"What?"

"Well, if I stop reading from the book, do the events stop happening? It doesn't make sense."

Another few moments passed.

"We are outside of time, here, Aleck. There are larger forces at work. Eternal forces, heavenly forces, ways that are so high above our ways that we cannot possibly understand."

"But you're a scientist, Venetia, don't you want to understand this?

Venetia laughed, high pitched and sudden.

"Sometimes, as a scientist, you have to hold your hands up and say you just do not know. And I am pretty sure that not many scientist have come face to face with the eternal battle between angels and demons before."

"But why us? Why me? Why am I reading this book? Jibarial says that some are gifted. Why me?"

"I think there is only one way we will know that, Aleck."

Aleck knew what she was saying and leant forward and began to read again from the book....

The TENTH Chapter of the Sixty-Fourth Book of Dreams:

Where a deception is revealed,
an army gathers,
and a plan fails.

The Israeli port of Haifa is a riot of morning activity, warmed by a pleasant fifteen degree Celsius and a clear blue sky. Yanni, wearing a Hawaiian shirt of tropical skies and palm trees, steps into the public telephone kiosk on the seafront at Bat Galim Beach. Skaters, dog walkers, joggers and cyclists busily vie for space along the esplanade. He opens his book of poetry and takes out a loose piece of lined notepaper held in its back pages. Squinting at the paper, he picks up the receiver, clasps it under his chin and begins to type in the telephone number whilst fumbling for coins in his trouser pockets. There is a complex series of clicks, whines and buzzes before he eventually hears a recognisable dialling tone and then the sound of Murray's voice. Yanni feverishly begins to feed all his loose change into the telephone's slot.

"Murray, it's Yanni. You were right," he blurts loudly. "They're here The Night Reivers are here, in Haifa."

Murray is stood on the deck of *The Dreamweaver*, the large satellite phone pressed close to one ear and his left hand cupped over the other to block out the sound of the buffeting sails and waves. The reception is poor but Murray can hear enough of Yanni's message to understand it.

"Brax? Is Brax there, Yanni?"

"Brax? Yes. Him and his team. They arrived on their bikes and they're scouring the whole place - the industrial port, along the beaches, the marinas everywhere. You were right, Murray. It has to be the boy. He must be telling Brax somehow of your whereabouts. That's how they knew about Patmos."

"OK, Yanni. You need to lay low. Don't let them see you. Stay out of sight and keep track of them but, whatever you do, don't let them recognise you. Bra and his henchmen haven't ever actually met or seen you before, but the demons that control them have, so it's likely they'll know who you are. Do you understand?"

Murray speaks louder and more emphatically into the satellite phone.

"Do you understand, Yanni?!"

The phone connection crackles with static and Yanni cannot quite make out what Murray is saying. There is a tap on the telephone kiosk window from someone standing outside on the seafront, and Yanni waves a dismissive hand in the air without turning.

"I've got to go, Murray. There's someone waiting for the phone. Be careful."

"Yanni, Yanni…"

The connection is lost and Yanni puts the telephone down and turns to open the kiosk door to see Brax standing there. He instinctively tries to keep the door shut but Brax pulls it open violently, dragging Yanni out into the open to be surrounded by five other Night Reivers.

"It appears that old Sentries never die, they just crop up in unexpected places," rasps Brax.

"I don't know who you think I am, young man, but I was just making a phone call home to check on my sick mother in Athens. I am on holiday with my grandchildren…"

There is a sharp blow to the back of Yanni's head from a truncheon wielded by one of the Night Reivers and he crumples to his knees.

"Your name is Yanni and you are, or rather *were*, a Sentry. You guarded two pairs of Sleepwalkers in your time and were responsible for overseeing them do great damage to our side. And you will suffer for that. But first you will tell me where your colleague Murray is and his new protégés."

"You can go to hell, Brax," Yanni groans, still reeling from the pain of the blow.

"No, I've come *from* hell, Sentry. I'm not going back just yet. Not until I've destroyed the Sleepwalkers."

Brax signals to his gang.

"Take him. Get him ready."

"You know what this means, Captain?" Lasaro says with a worried tone.

"Yes, Lasaro, I know."

Murray is still holding the satellite phone in his hand, staring at it as if he still does not believe what he heard and what he now has to do.

"He is still sleeping. He's still in his cabin. I'll go down. I'll do it."

Murray slowly makes his way below deck and stands outside the cabin where Almas is asleep. Taking a key from his pocket he quietly inserts it into the keyhole and turns it, locking it with a gentle click, then he turns and walks away.

As he climbs the ladder steps from the kitchen back up on deck to join Lasaro, he can hear Almas' cabin door handle being turned and several taps on the door.

"Hey, someone. The door is locked. Hey. Anyone? Let me out."

Murray ignores the plea and takes the wheel from Lasaro, who gives him a friendly, reassuring pat on the back.

"Let's take her in to Jaffa. We should be there within a few hours now and we should be able to rest there uninterrupted. It should take the Night Reivers a while to figure out we're not in Haifa."

"Let's hope so," mutters Lasaro.

Under the cover of darkness, Titus, Bina, Jibarial, Axyl, Portiel and Amanthragan cross the Mall and scuttle up a marble staircase towards the entrance of a grand Georgian building. In the echoey, cold magnificence of its hallway, battle-weary Keepers sit in groups on the stone floor. As they notice the Sleepwalkers they stand and deliver respectful nods; some smiling warmly, others looking more concerned than pleased, a few seem astonished.

"They have fought their way through the city to join you here," announces Jibarial to Titus and Bina, marching them purposefully through the building and up a sweeping staircase that splits both left and right.

"They had faith you would make it and now they are here for the final push."

"Where are you taking us, Jibarial," wheezes Bina, stopping to catch her breath halfway up the staircase. Both she and Titus are aware now that they are exhausted; that their earthly bodies are tiring from lack of sustenance combined with the activity of their brains and their adventuring Somnambulan spirits.

Jibarial stops, too, and turns to the teenagers.

"I know you are tired, Sleepwalkers," he sympathises. "But we are close now. You can rest briefly but we must stop the Hell Diamond. Come, Raphael is here, upstairs. He wants to see you before you take The Spear to destroy it. Come."

Titus and Bina stare at each other blankly for a few moments and then Bina flashes Titus an encouraging grin.

"Fiery demons, cages made of snakes, giant hell birds, street battles in bomb-damaged streets. We've done the hard bits. All we have to do now is raid Buckingham Palace and destroy the pulsing diamond that threatens the end of the world. I feel good about this," Titus fires sarcastically before trotting past Jibarial and then up the flight of stairs.

"Anyone coming?"

"It must be done now, my children," delivers Raphael portentously, standing up from behind a desk littered with unfurled charts.

"We cannot wait for you to go back to earth and rest. I know you are feeling weak and you have been sleepwalking now for days aboard your

Sentry's boat, but the power of the Hell Diamond is reaching its peak and if we are going to destroy it with The Spear then it has to be tonight; it has to be now."

"We're ready," Bina affirms as they stand together across from Raphael.

Titus strikes the stone floor with the base of The Spear to confirm that he is ready also.

"Good. Only you two can approach the Hell Diamond. It is too powerful for Keepers to draw near to for long. That is why it has to be you. We will go with you to the Palace and put up a fight but it is up to you to get as close to the thing itself and then thrust the weapon directly into it. It will destroy its power forever. Sadly, you cannot drift there because you need The Spear. We have to escort you through whatever defences Shadowmaster has...."

"Er, about Shadowmaster," interrupts Titus.

"Ah yes, you two have met."

"Yeah, and he...well, he seemed to hint at some kind of twist. Like there's something we don't know. Something we've not anticipated."

"Titus, the forces of Hell and all its demonic puppets are masters of deception and lies. They manipulate and prey on your fears to make you feel weak and powerless, and to doubt your purpose in life. You cannot trust anything they say, particularly Shadowmaster. It is alright, we have thought of everything and now it is time to finish it."

"But what if something *else* is the lie?"

"Like what?" implores Bina, turning to Titus.

"Well, it just seems......oh, I don't know. It was just the way Shadowmaster said it and how he looked at me. Like there's something missing."

Raphael moves from behind the desk and towards the Sleepwalkers. He places a hand on Titus's shoulder.

"Titus, that is precisely what he wants you to think. He wants to cause you to pause, to doubt, to surrender."

Titus stares into the depths of Raphael's warm, eternal eyes and relinquishes his uncertainty with a nod and a smile.

"Okay, Raff, you're right, you're right, let's do it."

Raphael's look turns quickly from affectionate to stern.

"You know that you are the only person in all of Somnambulan history that has ever called me Raff."

Raphael holds the stare and Titus gulps a deep, nervous gulp before the archangel breaks into a laugh.

"And I quite like it."

Jibarial breaks the moment with a sharp clap of his hands and the room empties; the whole building erupting into a bustle of angel army preparation. Within seconds the hallway of the great building is filled with several hundred Keepers.

"We do this fast and we do it now," commands Raphael from the centre of the stairway towards his gathered troops.

"For Somnambula, for truth, forever!"

"For Somnambula, for truth, forever!" repeats every Keeper as one glorious voice.

He draws his sword and turns to Jibarial, Axyl, Portiel and Amanthragan, who stand now immediately at the base of the stairs; pointing his sword at them, he gives them their own specific command.

"Protect the Sleepwalkers at all costs. That is your only job. Get them to the Hell Diamond. We will do the rest."

They place their splayed hands across their hearts and bow in compliance. When Jibarial raises his head, he catches Bina looking to him and they hold each other's glances for several seconds. Axyl notices the shared moment and breaks it with a harsh slap on Jibarial back.

"Come on, my friend, we have a job to do. No time for ...oh, what's the word?"

"Sentiment," offers Titus, cheekily.

"Sentiment?" queries Jibarial unconvincingly.

The doors of the building are opened and the angel army spill out into the night and down on to The Mall. Forming neat columns with Raphael at the head, they break into a brisk march; Titus, Bina and their Keeper protectors bunched together at the rear.

Ahead, along the straight stretch of clear road is Buckingham Palace, swathed in a blue aura that throbs against the ink-black sky. The light emanates from somewhere behind the royal palace, piercing every window and doorway, creating hundreds of laser-like shafts pointing both upwards to the sky and out towards the approaching angel army.

There is no sign of fiery demon figures anywhere along the Mall or outside the palace and the night is quiet, save for the rhythmic pounding of Keeper boots on the road surface.

Bina notices a white light striking the treetops that line the Mall and as she tries to keep pace with the marching army she looks up to see if there is a moon in the Somnambulan sky.

Portiel sees her and realises what she is doing. She points behind them to the low part of the horizon. Bina follows the direction of her finger and sees planet Earth hanging there, low and large in the night sky; so huge she can make out the recognisable shapes of continents and seas. Titus turns and notices it, too. It is the most awesome and beautiful thing that they have ever seen but it unnerves and unsettles them also.

"Are we on another planet?" asks a stunned Bina.

"No," laughs Portiel. "You are in Somnambula. You are not on any planet."

"Then why are we looking at the Earth?" says Titus.

"Your world is breaking in to ours. Both worlds affect each other and right at this moment our two worlds are colliding in a terrifying way. Sometimes we see it, mostly we do not. But it *is* beautiful. Come on, we must keep going."

Bina stops for a moment and looks at the sphere of humanity against the Somnambulan London horizon. Her eyes pick out the unmistakable 'boot' of Italy and then follow the contours of the Mediterranean. She imagines *The Dreamweaver* somewhere up there and her and Titus's earthly bodies sleeping in their cabin; she thinks of Almas and how much she misses him and of how she is going to explain any of this to him if she ever returns across that enormous void to her home.

"Bina, don't look at it. It'll drive you crazy," shouts Titus, grabbing her by the arm and urging her to join the march.

"How many nights have we been sleeping up there, Titus," she says mournfully.

"I don't know, it's hard to say, Bina. But we're nearly there now. We can go home soon."

Titus is trying to urge her along, pulling at her arm but Bina drags her feet and continues to look over her shoulder to the setting Earth.

"It's been days. Nights. We haven't eaten."

"Don't do this now, Bina. Not now. We're close."

Jibarial breaks from his swivel-eyed vigilance ahead of the Sleepwalkers and confronts Bina. He stops her, takes both her hands and looks deep into her eyes.

"I will get you through this, Bina. *We* will get you through. Titus will get you through. You will be home soon, I promise. I won't let anything happen. Now, come on, we must not split from the army. Yes?"

Bina does not answer; she is just absorbed by Jibarial's gaze.

"Yes?" repeats the Keeper.

Bind nods.

"I say it, and nothing. You say it, boom, she's off," tuts Titus, setting off again towards Buckingham Palace.

The Keeper army reaches the Victoria Memorial monument directly in front of the palace gates and instinctively they split into two even columns that march either side of the edifice.

"I'm not sure that's quite right," Bina says pointing up to the top of the monument.

"It should be an angel," Titus responds. "It's supposed to be called Winged Victory. But that's no angel and it's not my idea of victory."

Atop the Victoria Memorial is a grotesque, twisted demonic figure in gilded bronze, its clawed feet digging into a globe below it and two pitiful, emaciated human beings cowering beneath that. The golden sculpture glints and flickers in a combination of the Hell Diamond's blue glow and the reflected light from the low Earth. As Titus and Bina look closer at the perverse landmark they make out the faces on the subjugated human figures; and in one dread moment they can plainly see that the carved visages are their own; grimacing and fearful, their own faces imposed there on the golden statue.

Jibarial and Axyl see it, too and quickly usher the Sleepwalkers forward without saying a word. No one speaks of what they are seeing, their minds warring with the choice to, at once, comprehend it and ignore it.

The army amasses in front of the palace gates, Raphael still at the head and stood at the central black gates. He turns to face his troops and raises his sword above his head. The dense, pulsing blue from within the palace continues to pierce the darkness with shafts of horizontal light firing from every window and with one large arc from the roof whose reach grows outwards with every second.

"They know we are here!" growls Raphael to his army. "Now it is time to let them know *why* we are here!"

The army roars in response, not a tuneless warrior's cry but a perfect choral, multi-pitched sonic display of unison and intent that fills the night air and seems to cause the ground to resonate beneath their feet. Each Keeper holds their note for an impossibly long time and then, with a final, awesome emphasis, they stop abruptly at exactly the same moment, forcing an invisible audio wave of power to sweep through the gates, blowing them to the ground and sending them twisted and bent, flying across the palace courtyard.

Raphael leads them and they run across the destroyed threshold; two hundred fearless angel warriors charging, swords aloft as the night suddenly erupts with the shrill cries of Darkangels that rush with an outpouring of fire from the palace. They come from the doors on the ground floor; they come from sentry boxes; they come from around the sides of the building; and some even leap from upper windows and the roof until there is a wall of fire that obstructs any view of the palace; a wall of demonic fire that is shot through with the sharp blue rays from the Hell Diamond.

"I think I saw a Pink Floyd concert on TV once that looked like this," shoots Titus to Bina with a flippancy that cannot disguise his terror.

"We wait," says Jibarial. "We wait for our chance to break through, but not yet. We hold back."

"I'm happy with that plan, Jib."

Keepers and Darkangels engage in a gluttony of combat as blades of steel clash with blades of fire. Demons detonate and dissipate with a thrust to their hearts and angels fall to fatal blows to theirs, as heavenly war breaks out and all hell is let loose at the far western end of The Mall in the Somnambulan facsimile of London, England.

"We start edging forward now. We have to find a way in to that palace," commands Jibarial.

Axyl, Portiel and Amanthragan gather tightly around Titus and Bina and they begin to make their way through the warring mass.

"The fighting looks lighter here, Jibarial," offers Axyl.

"Good, that way."

They shuffle towards the south of the palace building and as they do, the demonic throng seems to sense their movement and they send a wave of hateful, hot anger that makes the group recoil and crouch for protection.

"They know you're here," Portiel shouts to Titus and Bina.

"Yeah, I think the fact they built statues with our faces on was the fir[giveaway," retorts Titus.

"We keep going. Our only way is to get around the side or back and fir some way to break in," Jibarial orders, standing.

The group benefit from a surge of Keepers, led by Raphael, who mo to protect them and form a barrier from the Darkangels, and they break into run, but a single demonic figure breaks through the lines and flies towar them as they are just about to clear the side of the building. Portiel brea] formation and stands firm to face her foe.

"Portiel, no!" cries Amanthragan. "Stay with us!"

"Go on, you are nearly there. I will take this one," fires Portiel back ov her shoulder and raising her sword with a broad smile of warrior satisfactio

Amanthragan pauses and is torn between supporting his friend ar continuing the mission. It takes just a word from Jibarial to make up his min

"Come."

He catches up with the others as they clear the side of the palace ar Portiel and her adversary disappear from sight.

On the other side of the palace building, the three Keepers and tw Sleepwalkers stop, searching for any way to get inside the palace building.

"There?" fires Bina, suddenly pointing. 'What about that?"

The heavy tar-coated oak door is deeply set into the palace's souther wall, a vast iron padlock and chain locking it. Jibarial just nods towards Th Spear in Titus's hand and the Sleepwalker obliges, thrusting the weapon's ti into the padlock's rusting keyhole. The lock and mighty chain glow instant] white hot, melt and drip fizzingly to the floor.

"Quick, quick," intones an agitated Amanthragan, still looking for an Darkangels who might have followed them around the side of the palace, an still thinking of Portiel and her seeming sacrifice.

Jibarial grasps the door's ring handle and pauses deliberately, turnin to Titus and Bina.

"When we go through this door, we are in the heart of the wolf's lair. So, things will get very strange for you."

"Things already *are* very strange, Jibarial," chides Bina.

"Stranger," warns the angel.

"Come on, Jibarial! Let's go!" barks Axyl, unappreciative of Jibarial's last-minute lecture. But Jibarial ignores him.

"You cannot trust anything you see or feel in there. Everything you experience could be a lie."

Neither Titus or Bina know how to respond; they just stare blankly back at Jibarial, chests heaving in and out with their deep, nervous breathing.

"Just keep listening to my voice. Stay focused on *my* voice."

With his final instruction given, Jibarial twists the hooped handle, pushes open the enormous door and steps in. Titus and Bina do likewise, followed by an exasperated Axyl and Amanthragan, both edging in backwards, still vigilant to any pursuit.

Inside the palace, the blue light is all pervading, consuming every part of what looks like a wide, long corridor stretching out before them. The air is thick with the smoky light, making it impossible to make out any detail to the walls, floor and ceiling. As they inch forward, trying to become accustomed to the eerie light, they can feel the ground below them creak and crunch. Jibarial sinks slowly onto one knee. His eyes still fixed forward, he feels the ground and makes out the unmistakable contours and textures of human bones – skeletal limbs, ribs, skulls all tightly packed to form a rough, undulating surface. Unflinching, he simply rises and does not share his findings with the others. He just shouts another order to his comrades.

"Axyl, Amanthragan, brothers, I need you to close the door and remain here, standing guard,"

"But..." starts Axyl.

"No!" Jibarial interrupts. "There's no point us all continuing. The Hell Diamond is too strong. I will go as far as I can with Titus and Bina. You must make sure nothing follows us through that door. Do it!"

They both deliver curt nods of agreeance, shutting the door and standing either side of it, swords drawn in readiness.

"Let us continue," Jibarial encourages quietly to the Sleepwalkers.

"Let's," gulps Titus.

"Stay close," the angel offers.

"We will," Bina says, almost tucking herself completely beneath Jibarial's outstretched, sword-wielding arm.

"Er...should the corridor be all...er, wobbly?" enquires Titus.

As both Titus and Bina stare forward, they begin to experience the same sickening sensation of the glowing passageway starting to bend and stretch. Like being inside a giant flexible tube as some external force flexes and flicks it, the way ahead dips and rises, rotates and shifts in quick, disorienting succession. An unsettling nausea hits them hard and their arms reach out instinctively to steady themselves against the walls.

Jibarial, unaffected, knows that something is happening to his friends.

"Stay with me, children. It is all an illusion. Whatever you are seeing is not happening. It is a lie. Stay with *me*."

They can hear Jibarial's encouragement, although it feels distant and echoing, but neither of them can respond for feeling dizzy and sick. And as they continue to look into the now convoluting, hazy cobalt-blue passageway ahead of them, they each begin to see other things.

For Bina, the corridor begins to form into a blurry amalgam of many of the middle eastern city streets and alleys that she had spent so many of her previous months navigating. Contorted human faces, representing the people she had been accosted by in her vagrant state, push out from the walls to berate her. Their angry voices overlap, build and tumble just as violently as the corridors physical gyrations. Ahead, through the faces, and the grasping arms and hands that protrude from the living walls, she sees a car, crumpled and in flames. Two figures slowly open the passenger and driver doors and step out calmly from the wreckage. They carry the cuts and marks of a terrible collision but yet their all too familiar countenances are peaceful and unpained as they reach out imploringly to Bina through the blue gloom.

"Mother! Father!" she cries at the apparitions.

"No, Bina! It is a lie!" Jibarial yells.

But Jibarial's voice is a distant, muffled and indistinguishable against the chaos of Bina's vision.

"It can't be you.....can it?" she calls out.

"It isn't, Bina! It isn't!" Jibarial growls, growing angry, but still not getting through to her.

"It's ok, my darling," says Bina's mother gently, reaching out further to her daughter.

"Yes, my Bina," adds her father. "Come with us and end this. You don't need to do this. Be with us. Together with us."

"We can all be a family again, Bina. No more running," her mother continues.

Bina sobs uncontrollably and falls to her knees, both hands sinking into the sea of bones beneath her.

Titus sees none of this. What he is experiencing is his own personal nightmare. All around him he feels thick, plastic translucent shrouds crowding his face. He tries to flick them away, but they press in even more, each sheet pulsing in and out like living, breathing membranes, each one sticky and wet against his cheeks. Beyond the sheets loom grotesque visions of the hospital machines and electronic monitors that used to surround his hospital bed. Exaggerated, blinking LED numbers and flickering electrocardiograms grow to outlandish sizes with burning, blinding intensity. He also sees Nurse Sascha, forlorn at the foot of a bed, slowly shaking her head.

"I'm so sorry, Titus," she offers. "There's nothing more we can do for you. You're just too weak now. I'm sorry."

In his vision, the nurse is suddenly joined by an army of doctors and hospital officials, all sad-faced and shaking their heads in unison. Their chorus of 'so sorry, Titus, so sorry' builds and builds until he does not know whether to use his hands to cover his ears or continue to push back the oxygen tents walls that threaten to suffocate him.

Jibarial watches his Sleepwalkers struggle against their demonic hallucinations; Bina prostrate and weeping ferociously, Titus desperately flailing and screaming for the onslaught to stop. The angel is feeling the sapping effects of the Hell Diamond now, drawing strength from his body and causing his breathing to become shallow and difficult. But he summons everything he can, closing his eyes and stilling himself. Both hands gripping the hilt of his sword, he thrusts the blade downwards with unearthly force into the bone-formed ground, piercing a single skull and crying with all his gathered strength.

"LIARS!"

With a single deafening crack and a white light that momentarily overpowers the Hell Diamond's extended blue glow, both Titus and Bina's nightmares vaporize and vanish, leaving them drained and shaking on the floor.

"Come," he says briskly but with concern, holding out a beckoning hand.

Wordlessly, hesitantly, the Sleepwalkers stand and stumble forward following Jibarial along the foggy corridor that now seems stable.

"The light seems stronger. We must be near...."

A sharp, pained convulsion causes the angel to cut short his encouragement, and he doubles up, but only for a moment. Gathering his composure, he stoically shrugs off the interruption and swallows hard.

"Is it the Hell Diamond, Jibarial? Is it effecting *you*?" asks a concerned Bina.

"It is alright, Bina. I have to get you close, but then I can go no further.

"Go back now, Jib. We can do this," delivers Titus earnestly.

Jibarial smiles and nods.

"Just a little closer, Titus. And then, yes, you *can* do this."

The trio continues to shuffle ahead. In the swirling, misty light, it i impossible to tell how much ground they cover, but, all the time, the intensit of the blue light grows, until they are aware that there no longer appears to be any walls either side of them or ceiling above them, just mammoth double doors directly ahead of them. In their disorientation, they cannot tell just how high or how wide these wooden doors are, only that they tower above them.

Jibarial puts a flat hand on either side of the slim crack where both doors meet. From behind, Titus and Bina can see his broad angelic shoulders rise as he fills his torso with a deep, deep breath and pushes hard, leaning in and walking forward for the gateway to open with a roar of ancient, heaving oak.

They stand at the threshold of an immense palace hall and regard the sight of an abyss, a hundred feet in diameter, that appears to have ripped open the ground. From out of the hole pours the purest and thickest beam of the Hell Diamond's blue light. The light not only fills and swirls around the hall but it also shoots vertically towards the ceiling and has ripped an equally sized aperture in the palace roof, allowing the beam to illuminate the London night sky.

"There!" chokes Jibarial. "It...is...down...there!"

He cannot take the intensity and steps backwards, covering his face with his forearm.

"Go, Jibarial! Leave, now!" commands Bina.

"Quick, Jib. Do as she says. Go!" adds Titus.

"Go and join the others at the door."

"Yeah, we'll be fine. We know what we have to do."

Jibarial cannot speak now, he just manages a reluctant, faint bow of his head and backs sluggishly away and into the corridor. He disappears into the blue haze, out of sight of the Sleepwalkers, leaving them alone in a vast hall, near the edge of demonic pit spewing apocalyptic light.

"I guess we climb down," Titus says, gripping The Spear with both hands and shaking it dramatically.

"Are you feeling alright," asks Bina tenderly.

"I'm.....tired," sighs Titus. "But thanks for asking. You?"

"Tired, too, Titus."

"Alliteration."

"What?"

"Been better, Bina," Titus fires back.

"Oh, yes."

Alone, frightened and drained, the two enjoy the moment of friendship and connection.

"You know, I've spent my life in a hospital bed, shielded from everyone by a plastic sheet. Anyone who ever said anything nice to me was just a medical professional, paid to say nice things. But here, on the edge of hell in some nightmarish life and death dreamscape I'm knowing what it's like to have family," delivers Titus at his most guileless.

Bina moves towards Titus and envelops him in a fierce sisterly hug.

"I've spent the last years of my life running," she says through tears. "Running from tragedy and pain. But I think I was running always to this moment. This is where we both have been heading, Titus."

She breaks violently from the hug and stands back to face Titus.

"No more running, though. This is where we stand," she announces firmly.

They move to the very edge of the pit and stare down into the intense blue glow, unable to determine the depth.

"The power of the Hell Diamond won't allow us to drift down there," says Bina.

"I know, and we would have to throw The Spear down and we can' risk losing it."

"We climb."

"We climb."

Titus secures The Spear through his trouser belt behind him and they both lower themselves down, kicking holes into the soft earth and clay of the pit wall. There are rocks and gnarly tree routes protruding through the earth lit up in the blue glow, and they gratefully grasp them as they descend into the unknown.

"How far?" asks Titus, fairly sure of the reply.

"Who knows."

"Thanks."

"What do you want me to say?"

"Say 'not far'."

"Okay, not far."

"Really?"

"I don't know."

"No, you say 'really'."

They continue to edge precariously down the slippery wall, taking hold of what they can, forcing tiny ledges for their toes wherever the surface is soft.

"Why don't you just tell yourself what you want to hear?"

"It's not the same. I need my big sister to tell me."

"Is that what I am? Your big sister?"

"Well, I've never had one. And if I were to have one, you'd make a pretty good one."

"And you'd be a great little brother."

"Younger brother."

"Okay, *younger*."

There is a few second's pause before Bina speaks again.

"Although you are quite little."

"Why don't you just say stunted."

Bina laughs which makes her lose concentration and misplace her right foot. She slips with a jolt but manages to regain her poise by reaching out with her right hand to take hold of a large, pointed rock.

"Was that our first brother-sister row?" asks Titus through gritted teeth as he conserves his energy to reach for his own secure hold.

"Maybe we should just stop talking altogether," offers Bina.

"Yeah, prob...."

Titus completely misjudges his handhold and his arm recoils into space causing his feet to give way below him.

"Titus!" Bina yelps, instinctively reaching out a hand to help him but triggering her own disconnection from the wall.

They both scream as they freefall through the bright cerulean haze and land with a splashy thud on their backs in a pool of thin, watery mud.

"Oh-ow," howls Titus, part moan, part laugh of relief.

"I guess it wasn't that deep," says Bina.

"Really?"

"Really."

"It's strange that there's no one here. No Darkangels," says Titus suspiciously.

"You complaining?"

"Not complaining, just curious."

The pair stands up, trying to wipe the excess mud from their shoulders and arms and begin to wade through the ankle-deep waters. Ahead of them is a large opening in the pit wall and a short corridor that opens out into an underground cavern. They trudge through the opening and along the corridor bathed in the light. In just twenty yards they are there, in the vast cavern flooded in the blue light which now pulses faster and stronger than ever. Staring into the light they begin to make out the multifaceted surfaces of a vast arcing gemstone set into the cavern's floor. The thousand lustrous, dazzling crystal surfaces of the Hell Diamond seem to screen a faint, dark movement inside its structure; a shadowy, serpentine flicker of life. Not only does it project an almost blinding light, but also it emits a deep sense of palpable dread. Titus and Bina stand at the Hell Diamond's edge, drenched and filled with a fear that makes them sick to their stomachs.

"The Spear," Bina says through choking terror.

Titus reaches over his shoulder and draws it from behind his belt. He grasps it in both hands.

"You or me?"

Bina shrugs.

Titus closes his eyes and tries to shield his mind, his body, his soul from the crippling panic that the Hell Diamond is instilling. He thinks of his bed in his Gibraltan hospital and of his previous life of inertia and boredom; he channels all the frustration of over five thousand days of relative solitude behind a screen; and then he opens his eyes wide and runs out and up over the rising arc of the Hell Diamond; ungainly at first, his wet shoes not gripping the glassy surface well, but quickly gaining momentum and balance, he gets to what feels like the apex of the curved gem, lifting The Spear as far as he can above his head and down violently, swiftly, hard into the Hell Diamond's heart. The Spear's tip glows white hot as it meets the Hell Diamond and then dims instantly and shatters. The blue light remains undimmed and the surface of the Hell Diamond lies unbroken and unaffected.

Titus lifts the broken weapon to examine it; all that is left is a wooden shaft, just a useless pole, and he drops it, letting it role ineffectually down the slope of the Hell Diamond where it stops at Bina's feet.

A laugh begins quietly somewhere in the cavern; it is distant and unplaceable but to Titus it is vaguely familiar. The laugh grows in intensity and heartiness and begins to bounce off the walls of the cavern and the surfaces of the Hell Diamond until it is a deafening chorus of fiendish joy.

"And there, my friends, is the *twist*."

Shadowmaster chews on his words with cackling delight as he emerges from the dark far edge of the cavern, his flaming hulk hovering across the surface of the Hell Diamond towards Titus who sinks to his knees in miserable defeat.

"Titus," cries Bina pitifully from her viewpoint.

"The Spear was just a lie. It was always a lie. A lie we planted centuries ago. A lie that grew and grew and became a legend, a pathetic hope for the gullible sinless."

Shadowmaster looms closer to Titus and powers down his fiery glow to reveal again his broken, jaundiced skin and his wide black, lifeless eyes. He is all bulk and deformed muscle, singed and smouldering and with a fearsome breath of brimstone and decay.

"But why bother with all that?" manages Titus, recoiling from the stench.

"Because it is... fun."

Shadowmaster seems pleased with his answer and laughs again.

"Fun to give false hope. And even more fun to then dash those hopes. Fun to lie and fun to watch as stupid people realise the lie too late. But most of all, it is fun to draw innocent, naive young Sleepwalkers to their doom and have them completely exhausted at the end of their tether. Did you not wonder how pathetically easy it was for you to escape from Kerberos with The Spear? Did Raphael not marvel at how simple it was to nullify the island's defences? Nice fortresses, by the way. I assume that was you or the girl who dreamed those up. I liked them. Very..... *demonic.*"

"What now?" asks Titus weakly into the ground.

"What now?" muses Shadowmaster cheerily. "Well, your friends are putting up a good fight upstairs but losing none the less, so that will not be long. The Hell Diamond is about to reach its full potential and then unleash...."

Shadowmaster pauses and ponders.

"...well, I will not tell you what it will unleash on your earth, mainly because I am not quite sure. But it will be the greatest outpouring of evil your world has ever known. And now there is nothing to stop it. Your useless Spear has not stopped it. You two cannot stop it because you have no weapon. So, it is finished. I will just imprison you both here in this cavern and let the Hell Diamond consume you completely when it reaches its full power. Absorbing your heavenly powers will give it even more dreadful energy. How ironic. You came to destroy it but you end up making it more destructive. Meanwhile, as my hellish cohorts sacrifice themselves to Raphael's Keeper army, I will make my way to Somnambulan safety to enjoy the ensuing chaos and do battle in other quarters. There is always more havoc to wreak in an infinite spiritual realm. It is such a shame you did not last any longer here, young Sleepwalkers. It was such a fleeting adventure. It only goes to show how merciless the forces of so-called good are, sending children with so little experience to do a job like this. Anyway, time to leave."

Shadowmaster reignites and is gone, ripping through the cavern, leaving a trail of fire and vapour.

Titus clambers slowly down towards Bina, who is sitting at the edge of the Hell Diamond and gathers her in his arms.

"It's over, Titus," she sobs.

"I know."

"You're supposed to say *no it isn't*," she says trying to laugh a little through the tears.

"No, it isn't."

"Really?"

"Really."

Two Darkangels approach them from either side; their flames reduce to reveal similar forms to Shadowmaster, only smaller, slighter and more sinewy. Picking up the limp bodies of Titus and Bina they drag them to the cavern walls where there are chains and manacles hanging. Without struggling, demoralised and devoid of hope, they allow the demons to shackle them to the wall, arms stretched upwards and clasped together at the wrists. The demons ignite again and stand guard either side of Titus and Bina as the Hell Diamond pulses to its apocalyptic climax.

"Sorry, little brother."

"Sorry, big sis."

The ELEVENTH Chapter of the Sixty-Fourth Book of Dreams:

Where enemies collide,
a Sentry has to fall,
and a shocking realisation is made.

The sharp, rusty metallic slam of the door brings Yanni around from his unconscious state and he regards his surroundings through eyes that struggle to focus. He can just make out the shadowy outline of three tall, broad figures several feet away. As his faculties return, Yanni senses that he is sat on a plastic chair, his hands bound together before him with a red neckerchief. He starts to feel the pulsing pain caused by a blow to the back of his head and knows that he is now in the custody of Brax and his Night Reivers. The room he sits in is dank, narrow and rectangular with corrugated metal walls. The floor has pools of water that reflect from the light of two powerful battery lanterns that his captors have placed on the floor.

"It's a shipping container."

Brax's deep growl reverberates in the metallic space.

"And, ironically, it is bound for Greece later today. Maybe we'll send you back home in it."

The other two Night Reivers laugh obediently.

"Dead, of course."

They laugh more heartily.

"But before that we just need to extract a little information from you Sentry."

Still groggy and pained, Yanni manages a mumbled response.

"You do not really want to start with the death threat and *then* say you are going to get me to confess. There is no real bargaining power in that, is there?"

Yanni winces from the effort of speaking.

"True. But then I'm not going to make you confess....as such."

"Well, we are done here, then. Just untie me and I will be on my way," Yanni dryly responds.

"My other Reivers are still out looking for the boat with the other Sentry and the Sleepwalkers. They might be here in Haifa. But then again perhaps they are not. But one thing is certain, *you* know exactly where they are. And you *will* tell me. And then I *will* kill you. It's all quite simple."

"Well it would have to be. It must be tiresome trying to explain complicated things to your colleagues."

Brax sighs wearily and steps forwards, leaning closely into the seated Yanni.

"We've searched this whole port and scoured the horizon and there is no sign of your friends. But we found you, Sentry. And we even found your car keys and your car. Nice rifle, by the way."

One of the Night Reivers raises Yanni's gun above his head so he can see it.

"What were you going to do with that? Is that the same one you shot me with back on Patmos?"

Brax raises a heavily bandaged hand and slowly strokes the side of Yanni's face with it.

"I hope that hurts too much," Yanni says, moving his head away from Brax's loathsome touch.

"It hurts enough. But not as much as what is about to happen will hurt you."

"You can torture me, Brax. You can do what you like to me, but I am too old and too tired to be bothered. I will not tell you a single thing."

"Torture?" Brax spits dismissively. "What do you take us for?"

"Violent, blood-thirsty, cruel demon-possessed lunatics?" Yanni responds.

"Oh no," Brax says slowly, ignoring Yanni's jibe. "No, not torture. Something far more effective. Something I've always wanted to try."

Yanni fixes his eyes on Brax for the first time and is suddenly concerned. All his flippancy and defiance is gone as he begins to realise what Brax might be suggesting.

"Yes, you know what I mean, don't you, Sentry?"

"You cannot do that? Only an angel can do that?"

"The soul bridge? You think the Darkangels that dwell in me can't mimic that simple party trick? I mean, it won't be *exactly* the same. It might have some slightly more.....er, lasting effects...."

Brax leans in even closer so Yanni can smell his hot rancid breath.

"...like completely destroying your mind. Or death. I'm not sure which. And not too bothered either."

Brax brings both hands slowly down to the side of Yanni's forehead and grips tightly, screwing his eyes shut and grinning ecstatically.

"Powers of the dark realm, search this mind," he screams in a shrill piercing voice that does not seem his own. Even Brax's two fellow Night Reivers share a glance of uncertainty with each other.

"Flow through me now! Flow through me now! Flood this weak human mind! Illuminate with your darkness! Find its secrets. Find the Sleepwalkers!"

Brax's skin begins to glow red and take on the beginnings of a fiery glow as he stands over Yanni, cupping his head in his vast hands. Yanni convulses, his feet pounding the wet floor of the shipping container in fast metrical splashes. He is groaning and trying to twist his head but Brax's vice like grip is too strong and it only makes the veins and sinews of his neck stand out. Yanni's groans turn from something low and rumbling into open-mouth wailing as his body is slowly, systematically occupied with a demonic power.

Brax laughs in hysteric, manic bursts; joyful salvos of evil bliss as he sees what Yanni knows.

"I see it! Thank you! Thank you! I see the boat. *The Dreamweaver*, yes Murray! The Sleepwalkers! I see them both. And...."

Yanni is shaking violently, the legs of the cheap plastic chair dancing and rattling on the floor.

"....and...the boy!" Brax concludes with a combination of surprise and delight. He relinquishes his grip with a dramatic flourish and Yanni's body gives a final massive spasm that causes his tied hands to rip the fabric bonds. His chair topples and sends him hard to the wet floor, facedown and inert.

"They are in Jaffa!" Brax announces jubilantly. "Ha, ha! They thought they had tricked us. But I know where they are!"

He turns to his demonic colleagues, regaining something of his normal semi-human composure.

"I can be there in less than an hour. I'll go on the bike. You two, stay here and finish him off and join me at the port in Jaffa. I can't waste a moment."

Brax unlocks the large container doors and rushes out in to the sunshine of Haifa's industrial port. Three red Harley Davidson '48 Panhead motorcycles are parked between the towering rows of shipping containers. Brax straddles one and brings it to life with a deft flick of his heel, roaring out of the port and towards the main Kvish Ha Hof road that leads to Jaffa.

After a cursory glance left and right at the outside world, one of the Reivers closes the heavy container door and the other moves closer to Yanni. He lifts Yanni's old Greek army issue rifle and places the muzzle to the Sentry's right temple.

"Quick, do it," encourages the first Reiver.

He pulls the trigger sharply and there is just an echoing click.

"Those old rifles can be a bit tricky," Yanni quips, rolling hard and quick to his assailant's feet and grabbing the rifle's barrel. Tugging sharply, he brings the big Reiver to the floor, taking full possession of the firearm and spinning it around to let off a round into his thigh. The Reiver shrieks as the hot, sharp sting of the bullet wracks his body.

Yanni is up fast and pointing his rifle directly at the second Reiver, who goes to make a move but thinks better of it, glancing at his partner who is writhing in agony on the puddle-strewn floor.

"The soul-bridge should have killed you or scrambled your brain," says the confused henchman.

"What is your name," barks Yanni.

"What?"

"Your name? You have a name. What is it?"

"Naquin," he responds shakily.

"Naquin, Naquin, Naquin....." Yanni chews the name over and over, trying to get the measure of it. "Well, Naquin, I am going to leave now. But first you will tell me where my car is. *And* give me my keys."

Naquin points to his fallen comrade.

"But how did you defeat the soul-bridge?"

"Well, Naquin, one thing I have learned from a lifetime of fighting evil is that you do not defeat the devil, you just resist him. And besides, I have undergone enough soul bridges in my time to build up an ability to withstand the side effects. I am a Sentry, Naquin. Always was and always will be. It is just that now I am having to learn to be a twenty-first Sentry."

The joke is lost on the Night Reiver.

As a sailor, Murray knows the term *doldrums* in its true nautical sense, a word used to describe a low pressure in the Atlantic and Pacific Oceans, near the earth's equator, where sail-powered boats can sit becalmed for weeks creating a sense of frustrating inertia. But he also knows it well in its more colloquial usage; that creeping feeling of ill-ease, listlessness, depression, even uselessness. There were often moments during his Sentry duties where he felt in the doldrums. And this is precisely one of those moments. Although Jaffa was a place he fondly remembers, he stands now on the deck of *The Dreamweaver* in the ancient Israeli port, unable to really enjoy its unmistakable exotic ambience and take in the lovely mound of yellow-stoned buildings that overlook the harbour. It has been many years since he last visited here in his yacht, and he would love to simply dock and then take a leisurely stroll through the old town's streets and catch up with an acquaintance or two, but he carries the weight of this, and another heavenly world, on his shoulders as he worries about the fate of Titus and Bina and what they are currently going through. There is no way he can escape the memories of his previous Sleepwalkers either; their faces and their voices flood into his subconscious uninvited and unwanted. He cannot control when the recollections strike and he has grown almost used to the random attacks and the surge of regret and near self-loathing they generate. But he also does not try too hard to stop them or deflect them, thinking that, somehow, he deserves to feel this way and experience these crippling bouts of penance. All he can do is busy himself and try to stay focused on the task in hand and the safety of his current charges. Alone, he secures *The Dreamweaver* to her berth at the end of a long wooden jetty. The marina is crowded with other yachts of varying sizes and types and Murray takes what little pleasure he can in the fact that his boat is not immediately obvious amongst the plethora of craft as he pulls out the large, bulbous plastic fenders from a hatch in the deck and begins to position them along the side of his boat to protect its hull from the jetty. It is these necessary, methodical processes that give relief and prevent Murray from totally surrendering to the doldrums.

If only Murray knew more about motorcycles, and specifically the distinctive engine sound of a Harley Davidson '48 Panhead, then his melancholic reflections would be interrupted and his attention drawn to the far side of the marina, where a lone biker is riding slowly along the edge of the harbour wall.

Brax searches the mass of crowded boats that all bob and creak in the morning swell, scrutinizing each hull for a specific name; looking for any sign of Murray. He brings his bike to a standstill, turning the key to halt the engine and stepping away, releasing the stand to keep it upright. Away from the noise of the engine, Brax drinks in the sea air as if trying to detect *The Dreamweaver* on the wind.

Murray finishes lowering the final fender and, standing by the yacht's wheel, steels himself with a deep sight, picks up a morning mug of tea and begins to stir it thoughtfully. The teaspoon tinkles against the mug and he allows himself a long, slow examination of the port he knows so well.

Across the marina, through the random matrix of gently waving masts and beams, the Night Reiver and the Sentry identify each other at the exact same moment and both pause for just a few seconds. They both feel the peaceful, warm breeze on their cheeks as it blows across the harbour and both take in the faint bustle of a port waking to a new day and the gentle chiming of ship's bells; but those are the only sensations they share. Brax feels the sudden sting of hatred and malice rise within him, whilst Murray is filled with a familiar sadness. Murray slows his tea stirring, lifts the spoon and takes just one short, comforting shot of the liquid, Brax leaps back onto his motorcycle and kick-starts it. Slamming down the mug, Murray calculates there is no time to take *The Dreamweaver* out to sea again and looks around him for any kind of weapon.

The Night Reiver opens the throttle of his Harley and speeds along the wooden jetty, his wheels thudding the tiny gaps in the slatted structure, the racing engine escalating Brax's rage to a point of not even knowing what he is going to do when his bike reaches his target.

Murray pulls a distress flare gun from beneath the wheel, cocking it with a sharp push from the heel of his hand and spins towards the onrushing Brax. He waits until his target is just a few yards away, steadying his shaking right hand with his left and pulling the trigger. A fizzing, bright red trail bursts down the jetty on an inexact, spiralling path that strikes the bike's front tyre causing Brax to lose control of the steering. The bike careers at sixty-three miles per hour into the port side of *The Dreamweaver*, crumpling and puncturing the pine hull just above the waterline. Brax summons all his demonically-imbued strength to leap from the collision and up towards Murray on the deck of the yacht. The rare Harley Davidson bounces off the broken hull and spins uncontrollably across the jetty and into the water, disappearing almost instantly.

With an awkward roll, Brax is up on his feet and bearing down on Murray, who fumbles for another flare to load into his pistol. Brax swats the gun away with a powerful, still-bandaged hand and it flies through the air to join his bike in its watery grave.

"First you, then the children," Brax growls, pulling a large hunting knife from a sheath on his belt. Murray steps backwards, trips on fender and collapses to the floor. Brax thinks about delivering a triumphant speech but decides against it. Kneeling over Murray's prostrate body, he brings the knife up above his head with both hands, taking a deep breath as if to maximise the joy of the moment. The long, broad blade reflects the glorious morning sun, its point glistening with sharp, deadly menace as it is about to be plunged down into the helpless Sentry. Then a single shot rings out across the Jaffa morning. Holding his pose for a moment, Brax pauses to take in the significance of the gunshot and then gently releases his grip for the knife to fall to the deck, just missing Murray's face. Swallowing hard and peering down to the crimson flow that is now smothering the blue-ink tattoos on his bare chest, Brax falls forward and across Murray. It takes all of Murray's strength to push the heavy, torpid bulk of his nemesis away from him and roll it across the deck. Brax lies face-up, his ribcage convulsing quickly.

Lying, breathless and disorientated with his back up against the wheel, Murray sees the welcome figure of Yanni, still carrying a smoking rifle, clamber aboard *The Dreamweaver*.

"Is he...?" Yanni asks.

Brax splutters and twitches suddenly.

"No, he's alive," says Murray, who pulls himself over to kneel by his side.

"Where...where am I?" Brax gargles through lips that are covered in bubbled blood.

"You're....somewhere safe," assures Murray softly.

Brax's demeanour and countenance are changed; gone is the brooding, frowning menace and the permanently narrowed eyes. Both Murray and Yanni recognise the signs of a body that, in its dying state, is abandoned by its demonic possessors. Like rats from a distressed ship, the powers that had controlled the Chief of Night Reivers leave him in peace.

"They're gone, Brax. It's ok. It's just you now."

Brax makes to speak but nothing comes out from his mouth other than more gurgling red. He tries again and manages one single, blood-distorted word.

"Sorry."

He shakes his head as if not content with that and summons up enough energy to lift his head and speak again.

"I killed your other Sleepwalkers….it was me."

"I know, Brax. I know. But that wasn't you. You didn't do those things."

Brax drops his head again.

Murray leans in close to Brax's ear and whispers slowly and methodically for only him to hear.

"How can….you…forgive me?" Brax mumbles.

'Because you need me to, Brax."

A smile materialises on the ex-Reiver's face; a smile of peace and final contentment and he dies there on the deck of The Dreamweaver with that smile still fixed.

"Thank you, old friend," says Murray sadly, looking up at Yanni but still holding onto Brax's bandaged hand.

"Don't thank me, thank my old friend," Yanni responds, patting his trusty rifle.

"Any more Reivers?" asks Murray.

"No, they are back in Haifa. Two of them locked in a large metal container and possibly headed for Greece, the others probably still scouring the port and marina for you, but with no idea you are here in Jaffa."

"Good, that buys us some time."

"Where's your crew? The Spaniard and his daughters?"

Murray looks rueful.

"Hopefully safer than here. Before we came into the marina this morning, while it was still dark, I took a risk."

"What risk?" Yanni inquires, sounding like he already knows the answer.

"Lasaro, Rina and Rissa carefully stretchered Titus and Bina onto the dinghy and took them to shore. They were still sleeping but they'd been under for so long that I thought they should be okay being moved."

"As you say, risky," chides the elder Sentry.

"I know, I know, but something terrible must be happening to them, Yanni, and I don't know what. I just figured that moving them while they slept was the least of their worries right now. And with the boy, Almas, well....I don't know. There's just too much going on here...."

"And where is the boy?"

"Still locked below in his cabin. He was frightened at first, of course, but then he went quiet. I think he is sleeping."

"Was sleeping," announces Almas bursting from below deck. He stands in the sunlight transformed into a handsome young man in his early twenties, tall, slim and with long dark, flowing hair. He regards the palms of his hands with a pleased but curious look. They are both glowing brightly; a multi-faceted orb the size of a tennis ball hovering over each hand, pulsing and spinning.

"And it was a good sleep. Dreamed a lot, too. Interesting dreams. You see, I think I now know who I am, Murray," reveals Almas in now fluent and unbroken English.

"Not everyone knows what they want to be when they are young. Sometime you have to live a little, travel a little. Well, thanks to you, I have done that. And now I have grown up."

"So, who are you?" asks Murray, slowly standing.

"Someone important, I think. Or at least I can be. In fact, I think I can be anything I want to be. A politician perhaps. Yes, someone on the world stage. Someone that people can get behind."

Almas chews each word with a newfound relish for his fluency and erudition.

"Not for good, I think," ventures Yanni.

"One man's good is another man's...."

Instead of finishing his sentence, Almas thrusts his right palm towards Yanni and a ferocious bolt strikes him like blue lightening in the chest, forcefully throwing him to the deck.

"Yanni!" screams Murray, looking at his friend's still body.

"Oh, I think he's alright, Murray," Almas explains cheerfully. "I'm just getting used to these new powers. Very interesting," he says, regarding his hands again. "And I don't really see myself as a killer. No, more of a......manipulator. That's going to be more my style."

"Manipulating what?"

"Everything. "

"This isn't you, Almas. This doesn't have to be you."

"This is exactly me. This is who I was born to be. I just didn't know it yet. Anyway, where are the Sleepwalkers? Where did the others take Titus and Bina?"

"Safe."

"Not from me, they're not."

"I thought you weren't a killer?"

"Oh, I have to make an exception for them. They have to be stopped. Besides I had a dream where Titus was trying to kill me. Trying to stab me with a sharp stick. Now that's not very nice, is it? Anyway, it doesn't matter. You don't have to tell me. I'll find them. I can even sense them."

Almas closes his eyes and slowly makes circles with his head as if tuning in to some invisible signal.

"Roof top in the old town. Got them."

He lifts his hand again and releases another powerful bolt into Murray's midriff. Almas carefully steps across the three slumped bodies on the deck of *The Dreamweaver* and climbs down onto the jetty.

The Hell Diamond's growing aura is now fizzing and crackling with a fiendish energy and nearly at the feet of the captive Sleepwalkers.

"It's going to swallow us," Titus shouts, tugging desperately at the large pin that anchors his manacled, up-stretched arms to the cavern wall.

"I know. Maybe we will wake up," Bina responds, too exhausted to do the same.

"And maybe we won't."

Their two Darkangel guards are standing closer to the Hell Diamond and they begin to roar with nervous excitement at their imminent doom, taking demonic, masochistic pleasure at being consumed by the purist of evil that now laps at their fiery feet. Their exclamations move through the scale, leaping octaves in a single second, from hoarse, throaty growls to shrill, hysterical cries of something between ecstasy and agony, as the gem extends spiky blue fingers to suck their flaming hulks into its glow. The last thing Titus and Bina see of the demons are their contorted faces, mouths agape and gasping and still spitting fire, like two people drowning frantically in a turbulent ocean.

"Just us now," says Titus as jauntily as his desperate situation now allows and he gives another sharp yank of his chains.

"I would like to say it's been fun," says Bina, turning to face Titus and delivering a sweet smile.

"Yeah, but it totally hasn't, right?"

She nods and they both laugh a little and then they bow their heads in exhausted submission.

"Sleepwalkers!"

The cry comes from the cavern entrance and it is Jibarial, followed by Axyl. They wear glistening silver armour plating on their arms, legs and chest as well as helmets that cover their heads and half their cheeks, but they still cower and stoop in the presence of the Hell Diamond's energy. With arms covering their faces and taking laboured, sluggish steps, they progress as if they are struggling against some unseen and powerful elastic that is pulling them back.

"No!" cries Bina. "It will destroy you."

The Keepers pay no heed to Bina's protestation and continue to edge their way forward, circumnavigating the cavern wall, at the outermost edge of the Hell Diamond's reach and towards the Sleepwalkers, clearly pained and drained of their heavenly strength.

"We are coming, Bina," manages Jibarial, although too weakly for her to hear.

"Keep an eye out, girls, but don't let anyone spot you," instructs Lasaro

Rina and Rissa scurry on their haunches to opposite sides of the flat rooftop and hide behind the low wall that surrounds it. Their vantage point looks out on an old town square, now busy with traders and tourists in the mid-morning sunshine.

Lasaro extends a fatherly arm to the sleeping Titus as he trembles on the stretcher on the rooftop floor. Bina lies beside him, her face twitching and fists rapidly clenching and unclenching.

"Poor children," he whispers. "This is too much."

"All clear, papi," fires Rina.

"This side, too, papi," agrees Rissa.

"And hopefully it will stay that way until these children awake from whatever hellish nightmare they are undergoing."

"Is Murray meeting us here?" asks Rina without taking her eyes off the square below.

"Yes, when he is convinced that it is safe, he will come to us," responds her father, stroking Bina's brow softly.

"Then what?" Rissa solicits.

"I just captain the boat, chica. I do not make the plans. I will leave that to Murray. Let us just hope he has a plan."

There are screams from the Jaffa square below.

"Papi!" cries Rina.

"What?!"

"Look!"

Lasaro scurries towards Rina's position and looks down to the open square to see the people in a blind panic, chaotically running in all directions for cover and a lone man with long dark hair standing in the centre and indiscriminately firing something blue and destructive from his hands; upending market stalls and obliterating displays of produce and tourist souvenirs.

"Sleepwalkers!" Almas yells, his face to the sky. "Time to stop napping!"

"Get down," Lasaro barks, signalling his girls to disappear behind the rooftop wall.

"He looks like..." says Marina shakily, not quite able to believe what she wants to say.

Lasaro just nods sagely to his daughter.

"It is, chica. I think it is. Now stay low. He mustn't see us."

The square clears of people and Almas ceases his bombardment, beginning to take in the surroundings, scouring it for signs of his prey, eyeing each flat, ancient sandstone rooftop. But what he senses instead is the presence of a lone figure, standing directly behind him and just twenty feet away. Almas does not turn to face the stranger; he just closes his eyes and waits for him to speak. When he does, it is a soft, relaxed and peaceful purr.

"You were a puzzle, Almas," says the purple suited Sanntu. "You still are. But one thing is now clear. You are half of this world and half of the other, unlike anything before. And that makes you dangerous."

"Ah, a sinless, at last," Almas says, eyes still closed."

"You know, that sinless title is a total misnomer. It's not like we angels can't do anything wrong. We can choose to if we want, but most of us know the right path. Unlike you. Anyway, sorry about the delay but I was tied up with other battles in other places. But it seems like this one might be more important than I thought. Anyway, here now."

"Just you?"

"Just me."

"And that is all that stands between me and the Sleepwalkers?"

"That is all."

"Then let us get started."

Almas opens his eyes wide suddenly, spins, and crouching, releases a double shot of energy from both hands that strike Sanntu, sending him hurtling to the far side of the square and sprawling across a stall of oranges.

Lasaro, Rissa and Rina look on confused.

"He seems to be fighting and talking to someone that I can't see," murmurs Rina.

"I think the reinforcements might have finally arrived," responds her father knowingly.

"Quick, hurry, Axyl!" orders Jibarial, looking down at his feet and the imminent arrival of the Hell Diamond's fatal touch.

Axyl unsheathes his sword but it feels heavy in his hands and he struggles to lift it. He swallows hard, grits his teeth and, with a thunderous frustrated battle cry brings the blade down on the chains that hold the Sleepwalkers to the wall; first Titus's and then Bina's, whose bodies both immediately slump forward. Axyl catches Titus and Jibarial turns around to halt Bina's fall.

"Now, let us go, quick. There is nothing we can do about the Hell Diamond now," Jibarial orders.

The four shattered figures start to shuffle sideways along the cavern wall; Titus and Bina still wearing the iron manacles that clasps their hands together at their wrists. Jibarial leads the way and, arriving at the cavern entrance, reaches out to Bina, imploring her to hurry. Axyl makes up the rear of the quartet and looks anxiously down.

"I think you might have to go on without me," he announces calmly and gives Titus a reassuring pat on his shoulder. As Bina and then Titus fall towards the cavern opening, safely onto the rocky ground at Jibarial's feet, and out of the immediate reach of the deadly blue aura, they hear Axyl's final words.

"Fighting with you both has been a..."

Axyl pauses, again, seeking the perfect word. But this time, after a second and a smile of satisfaction, he finds it.

"Privilege."

The Hell Diamond pulls him under and he is gone, but from beneath its glowing deadly blanket they hear Axyl's final muffled encouragement.

"Fight on!" he cries.

Jibarial simply bows his head in sorrow for his old friend.

"No!" screams Bina and scurries back on hands and knees as if to try and drag the poor Keeper from his blue torment. Instinctively, stupidly, she reaches into the stream of light to take hold of Axyl's outstretched arm that thrusts his sword upwards in a final defiance.

"Bina, no!" scolds Titus.

Bina does not scream in pain or fear and she does not get pulled into the Hell Diamond's thrall; instead she just stares intently into the pulsing blue depths, hypnotised by some far-reaching epiphany. She stands slowly with renewed energy and a mesmerised conviction, giving one short glance over her shoulder to Titus and Jibarial.

"Don't you dare, Bina," says Titus, not really sure of what he is forbidding her to do.

"No, Bina, you cannot," Jibarial decrees with a fear in his voice that they had not previously heard.

"It is alright. It's okay. I know. I know what to do. I know what it is. I know *who* it is. I know what the word diamond is in Arabic," she proclaims serenely, looking straight ahead and starting to wade into the glow.

Lasaro immediately notices that Bina's convulsing fists and facial tics have suddenly stopped and that she is now sleeping more peacefully. He only hopes to himself that it is a good sign. He turns back to the scene below in the Jaffa square as Almas continues to battle with something that they cannot see.

With every violent strike to his body, Sanntu merely takes a moment, brushes debris from his velvet jacket and trousers and stands up again.

"We could do this for eternity, Almas," chides the angel.

"You are right, sinless. I will just get the children."

With a moment of realisation, Almas looks up directly to the spot where Lasaro and his girls cower and the three of them duck completely behind the wall.

"There you are."

"You're not having them, Almas," shouts Murray, arriving on the south edge of the square. "I am their Sentry and you are not touching them."

His commandment is accompanied by the sharp click of a rifle as it is cocked and Yanni stands on the opposite side of the square, behind Sanntu.

'Keep him there, Yanni. I'm going up to check on them."

Murray runs to an open doorway and up a stone staircase. Almas runs after him and a shot immediately rings out from Yanni's gun. Almas stops in his tracks and looks down at the bullet hole on the left side of his upper chest.

feeling it gently with his finger he looks to Yanni and shakes his head in calm disapproval before dispensing a single bolt from his right hand that sends the Sentry hard against a wall, concussing him. Undamaged and undeterred, Almas follows Murray up onto the roof, Sanntu in pursuit.

Bursting through the wooden doorway on the rooftop, Murray dashes to Titus and Bina and kneeling breathlessly behind them he places a protective hand on both their heads and waits for Almas to arrive. Lasaro, Rissa and Rina join him, standing behind him in a show of solemn solidarity.

Almas appears in the doorway and steps out onto the hot, sun-drenched rooftop. He strides up to Murray and with inhuman strength lifts him up off the ground by his jacket lapels and takes him to edge of the rooftop.

Sanntu arrives on the roof and goes towards Almas.

"Uh-uh, sinless. I will drop him," he warns, making as if to throw Murray down into the square.

Sanntu abruptly stops and raises his hands to Almas in a show of restraint.

"And I never got to share my whole Ramones collection with you, Almas," chokes Murray awkwardly as Almas's clenched, gripping fists dig into his throat.

"Oh, I think I can check them out later for myself."

"Makes sure you hear 'Rocket To Russia'. That's my favourite."

"Stop it Murray, you are only playing for time and there is nothing that can stop the inevitable."

"You're right there, Almas. Technically speaking, if it's inevitable then nothing *can* actually stop it."

"The children have to be stopped. I have to stop them."

Murray forgoes his flippancy and becomes imploring.

"Please, Almas. Think of Bina. She looked after you. She was a like a mother to you. All those adventures you had together."

"She played her part. She brought us all together in this one place when my powers arrived and I learned my destiny and my potential. And now she is not needed."

"I'm sorry," Murray says forlornly over Almas' shoulder. He aims it at the whole gathered group; at Sanntu for not being able to complete his mission; to his loyal crew for dragging them into such danger; and to his Sleepwalkers for not getting to know them better and seeing them do more for the sake of the great Battle of the Ages.

"You should be," spits Almas as he flings Murray's body over the edge of rooftop to fall fifty feet to his instant death on the stone square below.

Before either Jibarial or Titus can do anything to stop her, Bina is taking large sweeping strides towards the epicentre of the Hell Diamond, forcing her tired limbs upwards over the radiant mound, now swathed entirely by its glow. She becomes barely visible to her disbelieving friends as she reaches the zenith of the gem. She kneels, pauses briefly and places both hands flat on its cold, smooth, glinting surface.

"Almas!" she wails and begins to sob uncontrollably. "Almas, my little Almas. Why? You were *my* little diamond. I loved you. I love you, Almas. My diamond, my little diamond, my precious little Almas. I love you."

Her tears flow and fall and strike the Hell Diamond; each one fizzing and vaporising, but Bina does not notice; she simply continues her sad lament for her little Almas, crying and pouring out her affection and unaware that with every proclamation of her love and with every tear, the Hell Diamond flicker and fades.

Jibarial, now on his knees, immediately notices strength return to hi body as the Hell Diamond's power drains.

"How is *this* possible?"

"The Spear was a lie, but love isn't, Jib," bellows Titus joyously.

"But it is the Hell Diamond."

"No, Jib, it's Almas. It's the boy on earth. Bina's friend. The Hell Diamond represents him on earth."

Bina is now completely prostrate across the top of the Hell Diamond, which is now just a white, jagged, glassy rock, bereft of all power and brilliance. She cries more tears until she can cry no more and until Jibarial gathers her up and carries her limp body to the cavern's entrance; there, he lays her down against the wall, draws his sword and, with both hands, plunges it down into the outer edge of the now lacklustre gem. The crack made from his angelic blade spreads out in a thousand fissures across the entire mound, fracturing it with a creaking that fills the cavern, bouncing off the walls and building to a deafening racket.

"Time to go," says Jibarial, returning his sword to its sheath.

"Yeah, let's get out of this cave," says Titus.

"No, it is time for you two to *go*."

Almas is a six-year old boy again, slumped against the wall and weeping softly as Titus and Bina awake and stand awkwardly in the sunshine.

"I am sorry, Bina," he says through heaving sobs.

Yanni, still visibly dazed and panting, stands at the rooftop doorway and simply shakes his head sadly to Lasaro.

"He is gone," he says.

"What?" Titus asks, looking at everyone in turn for clarity. "Who's gone? Gone where?"

Yanni just moves to one side and extends an arm towards the stairway. Titus tears past him and down onto the square as Bina kneels expressionless before Almas and grips his arms, not knowing whether you shake him or embrace him.

"I couldn't help it, Bina."

"Yes, you could, Almas. But I wasn't there to help you."

On the square, Sanntu crouches by his human friend's body, placing a hand across his now unbeating heart.

"Thank you, my friend. I will see you again."

As Titus emerges from the building and onto the square, for a brief moment he thinks he sees a purple figure with a vaguely familiar face looking up at him and smiling a sad smile. It is like a split-second ghostly image burned into his retina but yet not actually there and he shakes it off, collapsing to his knees at Murray's side, unable to comprehend his Sentry's death.

The TWELFTH Chapter of the Sixty-Fourth Book of Dreams:

Where answers are sought,
a journey ends,
and another begins.

"We are here," announces Jibarial, bringing Titus and Bina out into a familiar woodland clearing.

"Why here, Jibarial?" asks Bina.

"Well, this is where we first met. It seemed appropriate."

"Why not give us a flash of lightning, Jib. You know, for old time's sake," kids Titus delivered with a grin.

"Maybe no lighting, Sleepwalker, not today. But how about settling for this."

Jibarial walks over to the large pile of wood at the centre of the clearing and, extending his sword to it, causes it to burst into flames, instantly creating a roaring bonfire.

"That'll do," declares Bina.

He points to the log on which they sat with Pure, Faith and Hero. They all sit and, for a while, say nothing, just enjoy the warmth of the fire.

"You would think we'd had enough of flames," says Titus and they all laugh, followed by another long pause.

"Yanni sent you back here again so we could talk. Raphael wanted me to thank you for all you have done. He wanted to speak to you in person, but the battle rages on and he was called elsewhere," says Jibarial looking directly into the bonfire.

"It's alright, Jibarial, we spent a day recovering on *The Dreamweaver* with others after...."

Bina cannot finish.

"After the death of your Sentry, Murray, yes. He was a good man and he did everything he could to protect you. That is why you are still here."

"So, what now?" asks Titus.

"You carry on. You continue to help. You were born to be Sleepwalkers, both of you, and that is what you must do. But first you must rest properly. You will go back to your earthly bodies now and you will gather your thoughts and your strength."

"But who will be our Sentry?" Bina implores.

"Yanni?" suggests Titus.

"For now, perhaps."

"*Then* who?" sighs Bina.

"Do not worry, there is always a Sentry. There will be another and they will find you. A Sentry always finds his Sleepwalkers. Murray found you both after all. Just return to your boat with your other friends for now."

Bina still seems confused.

"Are we safe from the Hell Diamond now?"

"Sanntu tells me that your friend, Almas, ran away. That he escaped in Jaffa?"

"Yes," Bina admits. "I was holding him but he just wriggled free and ran into the streets. You should have seen the look on his little face. So confused and so scared."

"We looked for him for as long as we could but the whole commotion and the gunshot had brought the police and Israeli soldiers out. We had to leave Murray's body and lock ourselves away in the boat," explains Titus.

"When we go back again now, we will set sail and get away from Jaffa as long as Lasaro has repaired the damage to the boat," adds Bina.

Jibarial nods as if he knows it all already.

"And then?"

"I don't know," says Titus.

"Me neither," says Bina.

"Back to Venice perhaps?"

Jibarial says it in a way that sounds more like a suggestion than a question.

218

"But tell me, Jibarial, tell me what will happen to my little Almas?" implores Bina.

Jibarial simply moves his head from side to side, unsure of how to answer.

"Is he still a danger now the Hell Diamond is destroyed?" she presses.

"I think…" Jibarial begins ponderously, "…I think that Almas knew very little of the power that had taken hold of him from an early age. At some stage, in some subconscious way, he gave in to it and gave it permission to start to control him and make him grow supernaturally, even though he did not know what it was. Who knows what he would have become in your world if he had been allowed to continue, but whatever he grew to be he would have been immensely powerful, *and* a manifestation of terrible evil. And that is never a good combination. But now the Hell Diamond's power has been shattered…."

Jibarial pauses and stares deeper into the flames.

"…well, there will always be powers that will want to control. New powers. Different powers. Perhaps Almas's destiny lies in Almas's hands. It will be his choice as to whether he is controlled again. A lot will depend on his choices from here on. Where he goes, what he does, who he meets."

"But the Night Reivers," injects Titus. "He was obviously talking to them somehow, telling them where we were all the time. They might find him again and….and…"

Titus trails off, not really knowing how to finish his train of thought, or not wanting to.

"I do not think that Almas ever knowingly betrayed your location before he had fully grown in stature and power. That was merely the demonic forces controlling his mind communing with those that indwelled the Night Reivers. As for them, well, I believe that without their leader they have scattered," explains Jibarial, before adding: "For now."

"It's going to be hard…" begins Bina before Jibarial interrupts her.

"….hard to continue in this fight, knowing that your precious adopted boy is alone and scared out there in the world, without you to look out for him?

Yes, I know, Bina, I know. But try not to worry too much. We will not forget him and I know that Sanntu and other angel forces are trying to locate him, even as we speak. It is not the end. And in these coming days and weeks, my Sleepwalkers, you will continue to visit us here in Somnambula with Yanni as your Sentry. But not for anything more than to learn of this realm and of what you are capable of here. You were both thrown into the fray so abruptly and now it is time for you to be trained more thoroughly. The time will come for you to fight again, but, for now, Somnambula will be your classroom."

With that thought, the angel stands abruptly and beckons them both to his side. He puts his mighty arms around them both. Bina looks up into his face and holds his gaze. Jibarjal kisses her forehead and then quickly lets them both go.

"Just remember what Axyl said, my Sleepwalkers."

"Fight on," Titus recalls.

"Fight on," repeats Bina cheerfully.

"Fight on," Jibarial agrees. "Now, go home."

Margot Preston looks out from her aisle seat on the top deck of the number 24 double-decker Routemaster bus and wonders if the lovely Jupiter flute was still in her favourite music shop window on Denmark Street.

She had seen the flute several weeks ago and pointed it out to her mother and father in the hope that they would consider it for her birthday in April. She wishes the condensation on the window were not so heavy so she could get a better look down Denmark Street as the bus stands in stationery London rush hour traffic.

It is a frosty English morning and Margot is snuggled into a thick, fluffy woollen scarf that obscures most of her face. Her fellow passengers on the packed bus read newspapers and paperbacks, stare into space, snooze or chat to their neighbouring travellers.

The bus lurches into sudden motion again, causing the man who had just stood up near to Margot to stumble forward and instinctively reach out to steady himself. His hand lands on Margot's shoulder and she looks up to see him smiling down at her.

"My apologies, Margot," says Sanntu kindly.

"You?"

"Me."

"The book man."

"Yes, the book man."

The bus picks up pace and Sanntu readjusts his stance, holding on to a ceiling strap.

"I am getting off at this stop," he informs her.

"Oh."

"I just wanted to say a final thank you for helping. What you did was very important, Margot. Very important to the story."

"The story in the book?"

"Yes, it is all worked out as it should."

"Is it a happy story?"

Sanntu ponders Margot's question carefully.

"It is a *good* story. But it is not all happy. They are not always the same thing. And although this one is over, there are many more to come and there have been many, many before it."

Sanntu gives a conspiratorial smile, lowers his head towards Margot and whispers.

"And, you never know, but I think you might just get a mention."

"In the book?" says Margot, confused.

"In the book."

"But it was already written. I handed it in at the museum. How could....."

Another smile from Sanntu, bigger this time.

"Got to go, Margot. Keep practising the flute, I think you will be a very fine flautist one day. Now, this is my stop. I have a few errands and then I have to go and meet a very special person in…"

Sanntu thinks for a moment or two, as if trying to work out exactly where he has his meeting.

"…ah, a library!" he announces with the joy of someone discovering a valuable coin down the back of a sofa.

The bus stops sharply and Sanntu continues along its aisle, giving a final wave without turning around.

Margot watches him disappear down the curved stairs.

"Goodbye," she breathes through her scarf before drawing a smiley face on the window.

And that, my cherished reader, is nearly the end of the events of the *Sixty-Fourth Book of Dreams*, but yet it is only the beginning for you, if, indeed, you understand it and acquiesce to its implied challenge. You have a choice.

All that you have read in these pages will have bewildered, shocked, terrified and worried you. You now have knowledge of things most humans will never realise in all their lifetime. Your head is filled with unearthly wisdom and even if you choose to ignore it, you can never forget it. You can never unknow it. It will stay with you forever. But if you choose to make it part of your destiny then that is a grave and solemn thing indeed. You will be required to be courageous like you have never been and resourceful in ways you yet cannot imagine. Your life, as it is, will cease to be and you will become something else entirely.

And with that, dear human, we will finish and you will close *The Sixty Fourth Book of Dreams*.

EPILOGUE:

Having read every word, Aleck did what he was told and closed *The Sixty-Fourth Book of Dreams*, rested both hands on its cover and then both he and Professor Venetia Pipkin sat in silence. For the first time in the entire day, Aleck heard the ticking of the Professor's wall clock.

"I need to get out of here," Aleck announced plainly and quietly after nearly a minute.

"Let's go," agreed the Professor as if it was the best idea she had ever heard.

Within ten minutes, the book was locked away in the British Museum archives and Aleck and the Professor were standing outside in the dark winter evening on Great Russell Street, gratefully breathing in the chill air after their day spent in the confines of the subterranean office.

Taxis and double-decker buses swished by on the lightly rain-soaked main road, and people finishing work after a long day scurried with their umbrellas and their collars up. It looked like any other London evening, with normal folk rushing back home to be with loved ones and friends, thinking about dinner, dog-walking and whatever was on Netflix. But to the ex-soldier and the academic, nothing was normal and nothing ever would be again. The curtain that had masked the facade had been violently torn down, and they were the only ones that seemed to know it.

"I think you know what you must do, Aleck."

Aleck nodded thoughtfully.

"There are a *few* things I must do, Venetia."

"Yes?"

"Firstly, and possibly, most importantly...."

"Yes?"

"I need a drink."

"I know the very place. Follow me."

Professor Pipkin patted Aleck firmly on the arm and headed towards Great Russell Street.

"And what are the other things?" she shouted over her shoulder to Aleck as he ran to catch up with her.

"I need a library. A decent library. Is there one around here?"

The Professor stopped suddenly and turned around to face Aleck, delivering a stern look.

"Er, yes, I think here in London we can manage to find you a library. There's a little one up on Euston Road that I know of. It's called the *British Library*. Sadly, it's only the second largest library in the world, but I suppose it will have to do."

Aleck enjoyed the sarcasm, smiling back at the Professor.

"Will they have books on sailing?"

"They probably have a whole floor on sailing. Why?"

"Well, looks like I might have to brush up on my skills."

The penny dropped for her.

"Oh yes, I see. And what after that?"

Aleck took a deep breath.

"An airline ticket. An airline ticket to Venice."

The Professor opened her eyes wide and tilted her head with that exaggerated pose that parents adopt when gently telling off a mischievous toddler.

"*Two* airline tickets, Aleck."

"What?"

"If you think you're going alone, you can think again. I've just been given a glimpse into heaven itself, Aleck. I've spent my life searching the world for rare antiquities, translating mysterious manuscripts and documenting valuable finds, but I can never go back to that now that I've heard the most important story of this or any age. Whether you like it or not, I am part of that story, too. Going to Venice on your own? Not likely. I'm jolly well coming with, Aleck. Oh, and none of that economy class nonsense, we're going first class. On me. Now then, first thing's first," she concludes, jabbing an index finger decisively into the night air.

"Let's get that drink!"

About the Author

Damian Scott has been a serious writer ever since Miss Hill said "not bad" to his essay on 'What You Did At The Weekend' in his second year at Bramhall High School. Well, kind of. He ended up as a copywriter working in numerous UK ad agencies as well as being a part-time musician – singer and guitarist with blink-and-you-missed-them nineties band Boat Thief. He now lives, writes and strums from his English Lake District home. Damian is married to renowned artist Julie Ann Scott and has two amazing daughters – Ella and Libby. Rise of the Sleepwalkers is his long-gestating first full novel and the beginning of his Somnambula Instalments series. He likes to think that Miss Hill would be proud.

Follow Damian on **Twitter** using **@Damian_Scott**
And like the Somnambula page on **Facebook**
Or visit the official book website: **www.somnambula.co.uk**

Acknowledgements:

My eternal thanks go to my wife Jools, for enabling me to fly; to my old mucker Richard Simpson for the invaluable advice and guidance throughout the whole writing and publishing process; to Alisa de Borde for initial help with the first draft (especially with those pesky commas!); to Jean for essential proof reading; to Miss Hill for that first spark. And, most importantly, to God - for life, gifts, inspiration, blessings and grace.

Printed in Great Britain
by Amazon